ISLAND
TRILOGY

P9-BJU-870

ISLAND TRILOGY

SPECIAL EDITION

GORDON KORMAN

SCHOLASTIC INC.

New York Toronto London Auckland Sydney
Mexico City New Delhi Hong Kong Buenos Aires

Shipwreck, ISBN 0-439-16456-7, Copyright © 2001 by Gordon Korman.

Survival, ISBN 0-439-16457-5, Copyright © 2001 by Gordon Korman.

Escape, ISBN 0-439-16452-4, Copyright © 2001 by Gordon Korman.

All rights reserved. Published by Scholastic Inc.
SCHOLASTIC and associated logos are trademarks
and/or registered trademarks of Scholastic Inc.

12 11 10 9 8 7 6 5 4 3 2 1   5 6 7 8 9/0

Printed in the U.S.A.   40

ISBN 0-681-15634-1

First compilation printing, January 2005

Contents

ISLAND

For Wayne Turner
Without your help, I would have
been lost at sea.

And special thanks to Chris Shields
and "Skipper" Bob Abrams for helping
me find my sea legs.

PROLOGUE
Saturday, July 15, 2010 hours

For a heart-stopping moment, the bow of the *Phoenix* pointed straight up at the boiling black clouds of the storm. Then the wave broke in a cascade of spray, and the schooner was headed down, plummeting into the trough. Shakily, she righted herself and began the long climb up the next thirty-footer.

A streak of forked lightning silhouetted her against white water. She was two-masted, small for a schooner — her deck wasn't much longer than the tallest of the waves. Her sails were down and secured, and she moved under engine power, steered gamely into the oncoming seas.

Suddenly — a flash of white. The mainsail began to rise. It was unthinkable!

No vessel could survive such a storm-carrying sail.

Pandemonium. Angry shouts from the deck. A desperate run for the halyard.

And then the brutal power of the storm filled the half-open sail with violent wind. The ship spun around and heeled over, its twin masts dipping dangerously close to the punishing swells. The

SHIPWRECK

next wave took the *Phoenix* broadside. A torrent washed over the deck.

There might have been a scream when the body hit the water. But the howling of the gale was all that could be heard. . . .

CHAPTER ONE
Sunday, July 9, 2140 hours

Luke Haggerty squeezed into the tiny bathroom and pulled the door shut behind him.

Not the bathroom, he reminded himself. The *head*. Luke knew he'd been sentenced to this boat for the next month. What he didn't know was that it was going to be a never-ending vocabulary lesson. Not walls — *bulkheads*. Not beds — *berths*. The kitchen was a *galley*; a room was a *cabin*. And who cared?

Sudden pounding on the door — was it still called a door?

"What are you doing in there?" growled the voice of Mr. Radford, the *Phoenix's* first mate. "Writing an opera? Let's go, Archie!"

Luke reached for his belt and bashed his elbow against the small sink. This bathroom — *head* — was a shoe box! "Ow!"

More pounding. "You okay, Archie?"

"My name is Luke."

Even as he said it, he knew it was a waste of breath. All the way from the Guam airport to the marina, Radford had leaned on the horn and cursed out Archie the truck driver, Archie the cop,

SHIPWRECK

4

Archie the pedestrian, Archie the cyclist, and even Archie the priest.

By pressing himself into the corner and resting his left hip against the sink, Luke managed to finish up in the head. He hesitated. The flusher was some kind of pump. Instructions were scribbled on a plastic-coated card tacked to the wall — *bulkhead*: OPEN VALVE, PUMP THREE TIMES, CLOSE VALVE, PUMP THREE TIMES, DUCK.

Duck? Why duck?

Wham! He smacked his head on the low doorway on the way out.

"Watch your head," grunted the mate, not at all better late than never. "Did you remember to close the valve?"

Luke nodded. "What's the big deal?"

"The head flushes with seawater. Last thing you want to do on a boat is let the sea on board. That's a one-way ticket to the bottom."

Luke felt queasy. Ever since he'd learned he was coming here, his uneasy dreams had been a catalog of all the ways to die at sea — hurricanes, tidal waves, giant sharks, and collisions with supertankers, just to name a few. Now he had to add toilets to his list of things to worry about.

"Okay," he sighed. "Where's my cabin?"

Radford brayed a laugh. "You're standing in it, Archie."

"But this is just the — uh — " His voice trailed off. He had been about to say, "The hallway outside the bathroom." But in the dim light, he could make out four narrow bunk beds — bunk berths? — two on either end, and two mini-dressers — all built right into the bulkhead.

"These are your quarters."

"Quarters?" repeated Luke. "As in a quarter of a room?"

"This ain't a luxury liner." Mr. Radford shrugged. "Archie, meet Archie. Lights out at 2200." He heaved himself up the companionway out onto the deck.

Luke cast his eyes around. A tousled head of sandy hair poked out from one of the upper bunks. "What time is it?" Sleepy eyes peered down over rounded, heavily freckled cheeks.

"2145," Luke replied. "I think that's a quarter to twenty-two."

The boy groaned and yawned at the same time. "My system is totally messed up. I was on planes for twenty-one hours to get here."

"Tell me about it," said Luke, beginning to fill a narrow drawer with the contents of his duffel bag. "Why Guam?"

"It's supposed to be just us and the ocean," replied the other boy. "No ports, no nothing. The brochure said we probably won't even see another boat for the whole month." He sounded mournful, like it was a death sentence.

Luke applied a hip-check to the overstuffed drawer. "Nobody showed me any brochure."

"Really?" The boy was surprised. "How'd you end up here?"

The horrible movie replayed itself in Luke's head as it had so many times before. The crack of the judge's gavel; that single word: *guilty;* his mother's tears. And later, in the judge's chambers: "I'm reluctant to sentence a thirteen-year-old to Williston, especially on a first offense. There's one other possibility. It's a program called CNC — Charting a New Course. . . ."

Luke cast his roommate a strange smile. "I'm a convicted felon." He held out his hand. "Luke Haggerty."

"Wow!" The boy's eyes widened. "I'm only here because I fight with my sister. I'm Will," he added, shaking hands. "Will Greenfield."

"Fight with your sister?" Luke raised an eyebrow. "So your parents had to put an ocean between you?"

"Nah, she's in the girls' cabin next door. I guarantee you'll hate her. I should have been an only child."

Luke laughed shortly. "I *am* an only child.

It doesn't help. If you don't have any brothers and sisters, your parents are on your case extra."

The lights flashed once and winked out. Except for the dim glow from the porthole, the cabin was in total darkness.

"Well, I guess I've decided to go to sleep," Luke said sarcastically. He established himself on the lower bed — bunk — *berth!* — on the opposite side of the room. Uncomfortably, he curled up in the coolest spot he could find.

For a few minutes, the only sound that could be heard was the creaking of the mooring lines and the soft lapping of water against the hull. Then —

"What felony?" Will asked.

Luke laughed without humor. "Not murder, if that's what you're worried about."

But even as he said it, the voice of the prosecutor was ringing in his ears: "Felony possession of a firearm."

"Come on," coaxed Will. "I told you why *I'm* here. What was it? Breaking and entering? Vandalism? I know — assault!"

"That'll be my *next* felony," yawned Luke, "if I ever get my hands on the kid who put that gun in my locker."

SHIPWRECK

CHAPTER TWO
Monday, July 10, 0820 hours

Captain James Cascadden had a rugged leathery face that looked like it had been rubbed against every coral reef in the seven seas. He was six-foot-five, so he had to duck through the tight hatches and companionways of the *Phoenix*. But the movement was so natural, almost graceful, that Luke had the impression that the man had been born and lived his entire sixty-plus years on boats like this one.

Captain Cascadden hated long speeches, except when he was the person giving them. "None of you came to me because you want to learn the ways of the sea." His voice was a deep bass with the rich tone of a bassoon. "Many of you are from troubled backgrounds, some including difficulties with the law." A flash of penetrating eyes. "Aboard this ship, all that means nothing. The slate is clean. I don't care about who you are now. All that matters is who you *will be* — a crew. My crew. And together we will serve this vessel. Join me, and we'll sail off to adventure."

"Like I've got a choice," Luke mumbled under his breath.

ISLAND

Mr. Radford was there to keep the audience in line. "Shut up, Archie! When the captain talks, only the captain is talking!"

The first "adventure" turned out to be swabbing the deck. Luke found himself mopping and fuming. Only three of the six crew members had arrived for the trip. How fair was it for half the people to do all the work?

He slaved alongside Will, listening to his bunk mate bicker with his sister, Lyssa.

"Why are you mopping *there*? I already did that part!"

"Yeah? That's why it needs doing again!"

Luke smiled in spite of himself. Will and Lyssa were such opposites of each other that it almost made sense that they didn't get along. He was husky; she was skinny. His face was round; hers was angular. His eyes seldom left the deck and the job at hand; she seemed bright and fascinated by everything that was going on around her. She watched the captain and Radford, and even Luke, with a friendly interest.

"I hear you're a felon," she said cheerfully.

Luke's face flamed red. The Greenfields may have hated each other, but they obviously didn't mind sharing a little gossip. "It's a long story," he muttered.

"We almost got a criminal record once,"

she went on, "but our lawyer got the charges dropped when we promised not to do it again."

"Hey!" Mr. Radford called from partway up the mast, where he was adjusting some rigging. "Less talk and more work, Archie! Same to you, Veronica!"

Well, that explained where the names came from. Mr. Radford was a reader of fine literature — comic books.

Luke turned back to where brother and sister were snapping at each other. This family was some piece of work. Real funny to joke about criminal records to a guy who had one that would never go away. Like you could get arrested for sibling squabbles, anyway. What kind of nut-job parents would send their kids halfway around the world just because they argue like every other brother and sister on the planet?

And then it happened. One second they were bickering. The next, Lyssa cocked back her mop and took a home-run swing at her brother's head, missing by half an inch. It was that fast. Luke blinked and almost missed it.

In a split second, Radford was out of the rigging and poised between them. "If you two want to kill each other, don't do it on my watch!"

And then they were back to their work as if nothing had happened.

Maniacs, thought Luke. *I'm surrounded by maniacs.*

The job of swabbing was short, if not sweet. For a sixty-foot boat, there was practically nowhere to stand on the *Phoenix.* The whole center of the vessel housed the system of sails and the masts, booms, lines, and rigging that supported it. The cockpit and main cabin top took up most of the aft space. The sleeping quarters dominated the forward part of the boat, with the galley and cargo hatch toward the middle — *amidships.* So all that was left to walk on was a thin path of deck ringing the schooner and a couple of very tight cut-throughs between the masts. Equipment was piled on every surface — poles, fenders, anchors, the *Phoenix's* twelve-foot dinghy, and what seemed like enough rope to stretch across any ocean. In a way, it was brilliant, Luke thought. There was room for everything — everything except people. Surely even Williston provided more space for its inmates. An only child who had never even shared a bedroom, he could almost feel the squeeze in his gut. The idea of living on this floating sardine can made him shudder.

In addition to being the first mate and the warden, Mr. Radford was also ship's cook. At lunch in the tiny galley, he proved that he could open a tin of baked beans as well as any of the great chefs of Europe.

While cooking was the mate's job, cleaning up and washing dishes turned out to be just another part of the adventure. The galley was ventilated only by a small smoke-head on the cabin top. It seemed twice as hot as the rest of the boat — as the rest of Guam, for that matter. Luke and Will did the work in sweaty silence. Talking just didn't seem to be worth the effort.

After lunch, Mr. Radford headed to the airport to meet a plane, and the three crew members were given a tour of the cockpit.

"Now, what's the most important instrument here?" asked Captain Cascadden.

"The wheel?" suggested Will.

"Of course not," snapped Lyssa testily. "How about the radio?"

"That's downstairs in the navigation room, *stupid!*" Will snapped.

"Not 'downstairs,' " the captain amended. "On shipboard we say 'below.' "

"How about the compass?" suggested Lyssa brightly. If her brother's constant attacks bothered her, she didn't show it. *Probably,* thought Luke, *because she didn't have a mop in her hand.*

"All those are important," the captain agreed. "But," his hand touched a small, ordinary-looking switch on the instrument panel, "this is more important than all of them. This is the blower switch. It turns on the fan that airs out the engine room. Never, ever start the engine of a boat without starting the blower first. Otherwise, fuel vapors that have built up there could explode when the engine ignites." He stared at them with burning black eyes. "If you forget everything else you learn here, remember this one thing."

That turned out to be a favorite line of Captain Cascadden's. Like when he told the group that a boat does not respond immediately to a turn of the wheel. "It's not like your bicycle that goes where you tell it when you tell it. An inexperienced helmsman will oversteer because he keeps on turning until he feels his ship change direction. If you forget everything else you learn here, remember this one thing."

He also said it about storing ropes and lines in a coiled position to keep them straight and ready to use, tying the sails down in a storm, and even cleaning up the sleeping quarters.

Captain Cascadden pointed ashore. "Oh, look, here's Mr. Radford, bringing us two more crew members. It's important to make the newcomers feel welcome."

"And if you forget everything else," Luke whispered to Will, "remember this one thing."

SHIPWRECK

Will covered up a snicker with some coughing.

The two new arrivals looked terrible, but a lot of that could have been the daylong flights. Charla Swann seemed to be about Luke's age. She was tall and rail-thin and moved like a cat. There was a no-nonsense look to her. Her hair was plain, her clothes were simple. Her appearance was engineered for efficiency rather than show. Ian Sikorsky was at least a couple of years younger. The slight boy with sad eyes was already embroiled in a battle with Radford over his luggage. The mate had removed a sleek laptop computer with wireless modem, and Ian seemed ready to try to swim home rather than part with it.

Soon the captain got himself in the middle of it. "Crewman, Charting a New Course is about casting off your old life for a new and better one."

"But what about the Internet?" the boy asked plaintively.

"We have our own Internet out here," Cascadden assured him. "It's called teamwork. A ship and her crew, coming together to form a web of comradeship and cooperation. What electronic gadget could give you that?"

Radford put it less poetically. "No computers, Archie. CNC rules. It goes home UPS — PDQ."

Ian looked so miserable that he barely raised his head as he walked up the gangway onto the deck.

"Hey, Ian," Luke said kindly, "when you see our room, you'll be happy it had to go. We need all the space we can get."

"Well, Mr. Radford," Captain Cascadden said cheerfully, "that's our whole load, then?"

"One more, skipper," the mate replied.

The captain frowned. "Now, how could that be? There aren't any more flights due in."

"This isn't your regular Archie," said Radford. "This kid's coming by private jet."

CHAPTER THREE
Monday, July 10, 1805 hours

As soon as the door of the Learjet opened, J.J. Lane's one-of-a-kind designer sunglasses fogged up with the oppressive blast of Guam humidity.

"Whoa! Aloha!" the fourteen-year-old chortled, handing the glasses over to his traveling companion, Dan Rapaport, for cleaning.

Rapaport was personal assistant to the world-famous movie star Jonathan Lane, J.J.'s father. Lately, though, it seemed like his new job was as the keeper of J.J., who had turned into a real Hollywood brat.

"Aloha is what they say in Hawaii," Rapaport told his charge. "I don't know what they say here."

J.J. shrugged. "Doesn't matter." He hopped down to the tarmac. "Where's my luggage?"

Rapaport permitted himself a secret smile as he handed over a small duffel bag.

"No, really," J.J. insisted. "There's half a dozen suitcases in the cargo hold."

Rapaport shook his head. "We left those when we stopped in Honolulu."

"On *purpose?*"

ISLAND

"CNC gave us a list, J.J., and it didn't say anything about hang gliders."

The movie star's son folded his arms across his chest. "I'm not going."

"Suit yourself," said Rapaport. "But you're not coming back with me. Have a nice month on Guam. And — oh, yeah — I canceled your credit cards."

J.J.'s reaction was equal parts shock and fury. "I'm calling Dad!" He pulled out his cell phone and dialed furiously. He listened for a moment, then threw the phone down to the pavement. "My service has been terminated."

"You're lucky. It's midnight in L.A. right now. I doubt your father would be thrilled to hear from you." Rapaport took a deep breath. "Listen, J.J., when you brought a case of champagne to the eighth-grade dance, I worked hard to keep it out of the papers. When you sold the video of your father's pool party to *Entertainment Tonight*, I covered for you. When you did all that upscale shoplifting on Rodeo Drive, it was me who arranged for your father to make that donation to the Policeman's Brotherhood Fund. But when you took your father's Harley and drove it through the plate-glass window of that art gallery — that's when it became time to get out of town for a while."

"Out of town means Santa Barbara — maybe even Tahoe. Not *Mars!*"

"You're a flake, J.J.," said Rapaport, "but you're not an idiot. Even you can see that these little happenings of yours are getting worse and worse. You're going to kill somebody one of these days — maybe even yourself."

The boy wrinkled his nose. "You're enjoying this, aren't you?"

A wide grin split Rapaport's face. "Oh, yeah." He noticed the CNC logo on the hat of the man striding across the tarmac toward them. "This must be Mr. Radford now." He turned to the sailor and held out his hand. "I'm Dan Rapaport from Jonathan Lane's office."

Radford brushed right past him and took the duffel bag from J.J. "Okay, Richie Rich. We sail in an hour."

Totally ignored, Rapaport withdrew his hand. For a brief instant, he looked like he wanted to rescue J.J. from his fate. Then he remembered the art gallery window and the Picasso with the tire treads on it. He got back in the Learjet and pulled the door shut behind him.

CHAPTER FOUR
Tuesday, July 11, 0730 hours

"*Heave!*" bellowed Mr. Radford, untying the lines and pitching them onto the *Phoenix*.

Luke, Charla, and Lyssa stood on the edge of the deck, poles in hand, pushing against the dock to move the schooner away from its mooring.

"Put some back into it!" howled the mate.

Luke strained until he felt his spine was about to snap. Water opened up between dock and boat. Radford jumped on board. He cupped his hands to his mouth.

"Clear!"

In the cockpit, Captain Cascadden engaged the engine. The *Phoenix* began to pick her way delicately out of the harbor.

Luke watched the multicolored sails of the other boats go by as the deck thrummed under his feet. Sure, he would have given his right arm to be almost anywhere else. But there was a certain majesty to gliding across the water — definitely a feeling you couldn't get in Williston Juvenile Detention Facility. He could see that his fellow crew members felt it too — all except one.

"Captain, my father is a powerful man in Hollywood," said J.J. smoothly. "I know he'd make it worth your while if you put me on a plane back to the States."

The captain's eyes never wavered from the course he was steering. "This *is* the States, crewman."

"You know — the *real* States. L.A."

"Coast Guard cutter off the starboard bow, three hundred yards!" warned Radford from his perch on the ratlines.

"Your father," said the captain, "paid good money for you to be on this trip. I saw the check, crewman."

"It's a misunderstanding," J.J. insisted. "He signed me up for the boat thing, just not *this* boat thing. I mean, no offense, but you've got four people sleeping in a closet! And the bathroom is a phone booth! I can't even — "

HONK!!

Will clamped himself onto a bulwark and held on until the earsplitting blast of the air horn died away. His racing heart slowed. What was he doing here? How had his life come to this — on the wrong side of the globe, setting sail on a wooden cracker box?

If I get out of this, he made a deal with the sky, *I swear I'll never cheat on another math test*.

The *Phoenix* didn't put on the brakes and turn

around. Instead, the schooner eased through the mouth of the harbor.

So he sweetened the pot. *I swear I'll floss from now on. Every night!*

Rough hands grabbed him by the collar. "Off your butt, Archie! This is a working ship!" Radford cupped his hands to his mouth. "Ready on the mainsail, Skipper!"

"Haul!" bellowed the captain.

Will and Charla began yanking away at the halyard, hand over hand. With a creak of the rigging, the mainsail began to rise.

Ahead of them, Luke and Ian were hauling up the foresail, their faces taut with concentration.

Closer to the bow, J.J. and Lyssa worked on the smaller staysail.

Didn't it figure? They gave Lyssa the easy sail. It had been like that from the beginning. She was always the sweet little baby, while Will was the older one who should know better. People loved Lyssa. The good looks in the family were all hers; he got stuck with freckles. She was a straight-A student; he struggled.

"I should have been an only child," he grunted through the strain of his effort.

Charla looked down at him like he was crazy — Lyssa's fault as usual.

When the wind caught the half-open mainsail,

its force pulled the halyard right out of Will's hand, delivering a painful rope burn. Charla held on, but with the sail taut, the line was difficult to budge. Will clamped himself on again, and both leaned into it with all their might. Up went the sail, flapping full.

"You'll earn your dinner tonight!" roared Radford. The mate had joined Luke and Ian. Soon the foresail was up.

Last came the jibs, two small sails extended from the head of the foremast to the bowsprit — the long thin spar that stretched forward from the bow.

The crew fell back, exhausted.

Will looked down at his hands, which were blistered and bleeding. You'd think they'd figure out a way to put up sails without taking off all your skin!

He caught sight of his sister. She was smiling! *Smiling!*

If this is over really fast, Will promised, *I swear I'll get in shape! I'll jog every day! I'll lift weights! I'll* —

"Don't get comfortable!" bawled Radford. "This is the mainsheet! It's not a sheet off your bed; it's a line. And these pulleys are called blocks. Watch what happens when I ease up on the mainsheet."

Expertly, the mate undid the knot and gave the rope some slack. He turned to Luke. "Hey, Archie — "

Luke turned. "Yeah?"

A gust of wind took the sail and swung it out over their heads at right angles to the boat.

Bang! The block swept around and smacked Luke full in the face, knocking him off his feet.

Radford laughed out loud. "I was going to warn you, but never mind."

When the foresail was aligned, Captain Cascadden cut power and let the schooner run with the wind. The crisp ocean breeze blew away the stifling Guam humidity in an instant.

"Now you're sailing!" rumbled the captain behind the wheel. "There's no feeling quite like it!"

Lyssa hopped up on the engine housing, threw her arms wide, and let her long hair whip in the wind. "Feel that breeze!"

"Where I come from," Charla told her, "a wind like this would knock you right off the fire escape!"

Will burned. Lyssa was making friends here like she did everywhere. By the time this trip was over, she was going to be voted Miss Congeniality on this tub. This would be like a vacation for her while he suffered.

It was so unfair. If it wasn't for Lyssa, they wouldn't even be on this dumb trip! Sure, he got in her face a lot. She deserved it. Besides, when they were fighting, it was always Lyssa who went ballistic.

Involuntarily, his mind jumped to the incident that his parents had come to call The Last Straw. The argument started out small — two Halloween parties, who would get dropped off first, something like that. No big deal.

He remembered Mom in the background, screaming for them to calm down. And then the marble rolling pin from Lyssa's chef's costume was hurtling toward his face. He heard, rather than felt, his nose break. The blood poured like somebody had busted a hydrant. He couldn't even recall fighting back. He must have, though. Because when he woke up in the hospital, Lyssa was in the next bed with a concussion. Both of them were so beaten up that the cops had to file a special report to rule out child abuse.

"Take my word for it," the officer assured the Greenfield parents. "If you don't do something about these two, they're going to kill each other."

And — just their luck! — the admitting nurse happened to have a third cousin whose juvenile delinquent son had been sent on a boat trip called Charting a New Course.

Tears stung Will's eyes as Guam became smaller and smaller. Oh, great! Now he was going to be ship's crybaby too!

He ran for the companionway to the main cabin, determined that no one should see him.

There he came face-to-face with Luke, who was holding a cold towel to his rapidly swelling eye.

"You're my witness!" Luke seethed. "You saw that lousy Rat-face! He did it on purpose!"

Will smiled, his first of the day. "Rat-face Radford. Why didn't I think of that? That's funny."

"No, it isn't," Luke raged. "It's the least funny thing on a very unfunny trip!"

With a sigh, Will followed him back on deck. It was some small comfort that he wasn't the only one who was miserable.

Lyssa was hanging around the captain, schmoozing him while he explained how the boat's motor worked.

Will snorted in disgust. One science fair project on the internal combustion engine and Lyssa thought she was Jeff Gordon's whole pit crew.

He looked back to the sky. *If I get out of this —*

But he wasn't getting out of anything. Guam was barely a speck on the horizon. The best he could hope for was a sign. Something — anything — that hinted all this might turn out okay.

26

An odd look came over Lyssa's face as she stood with the captain halfway down the engine hatch. With a strangled sound, she scrambled to the side, draped herself over the lifeline, and was thoroughly, violently sick.

CHAPTER FIVE
Wednesday, July 12, 1100 hours

Lyssa hit the water first, a cannonball that sent a splash all the way back to Captain Cascadden in the cockpit.

"It's *warm!*" she shrieked, amazed.

Will was next, climbing carefully down the boat's swim ladder. He submerged and bobbed like a cork. "It *is* warm! It's great!"

Luke jumped in and paddled around happily. It felt good to be cool and clean.

"Hey, Ian," called Will. "Come get your feet wet."

The younger boy averted his eyes. "I don't think so."

"Come on! You'll love it!" Lyssa promised.

But Ian had disappeared down the companionway to the sleeping quarters.

Luke shook his head. "Poor kid. He forgot to download his personality before they made him ship his computer home."

"I wonder why he got sent here," mused Lyssa.

"He probably wouldn't mind his own business, just like you," snickered Will.

SHIPWRECK

"Shut up."

Charla stood poised on the gunwale. She was perched only on the tips of her toes, but she didn't move a muscle, even with the gentle rocking of the boat. Gracefully, she sailed off the side in a perfect jackknife, hitting the water with barely a splash.

The other swimmers and even Captain Cascadden burst into cheers and applause.

Charla broke the surface, took a few smooth powerful strokes, then flipped effortlessly to float on her back. She had always been comfortable in the water, but it was more than that. Swimming somehow seemed to relieve her pressures and tensions, and she had quite a few.

"You're a fish!" cried Will.

She shrugged modestly. "I'm on the swim team at school."

"And the diving team?" asked Luke.

She nodded shyly.

"But you were talking about track and field before," put in Lyssa.

"Only the hundred meters and the hurdles," said Charla, embarrassed by the attention. "I like gymnastics better, anyway." She felt a twinge of uneasiness. Why was she talking so much? These people didn't need to know her private business.

"Man, what are you doing *here*?" exclaimed

Luke. "You're the perfect kid! What — your parents signed you up because you're too good? Maybe you can take rotten lessons from Ratface."

Charla's smile disappeared. "I'm not so good." In two textbook strokes, she was at the ladder and clambering back on board.

Luke was mystified. "What'd I say?"

"Don't worry, Luke," said Will. "You can accuse me of being good. I can take it."

Lyssa splashed him in the face. "There are a lot of words that describe you. *Good* isn't one of them."

Charla glared down at them from the gunwale. Rich kids always acted like they knew everything. What did they have to worry about, besides deciding which mall to shop at? The other athletes she knew — the ones whose dads weren't working three jobs — could enjoy their sports. It wasn't their *ticket.*

"It's your ticket out, Charla. . . . It's your ticket up. . . . Your ticket to college . . . Your ticket to a better life."

She heard those words twenty times a day from her father. "Pick one sport. You're spreading yourself too thin. It's your ticket to the Olympic team. Go, go, go."

I'm twelve, Dad. And isn't this supposed to be

SHIPWRECK

fun? I don't want a ticket. If I even hear the word again, I'm going to scream!

Maybe if she'd had the guts to say that, she might have avoided that fateful morning when she couldn't get out of bed because her arms and legs wouldn't move. Charla Swann, who could twist herself into a graceful pretzel on the uneven bars, could barely walk into the emergency room. And yet there was nothing physically wrong with her.

"Burnout. Classic burnout," the doctor had said.

And that had led to a *ticket* even her father hadn't anticipated — the one to Guam that included a berth on the *Phoenix* with a bunch of spoiled rich kids.

Well, okay, they weren't *really* rich. Just richer than her, which wasn't hard to be. Except for that hotshot from California. He was loaded. He had a pair of sunglasses that would probably sell for more than her dad's car.

Come to think of it, where *was* J.J.?

And then a voice yelled, "Aloha!"

A voice from *above*. There was J.J., high up in the mainsail rigging.

Captain Cascadden saw him too. "Crewman — get down from there *this instant*!"

J.J. waved. "Sorry, Captain! Can't hear you!"

"Mr. Radford!" roared the captain. "I need you on deck!"

The mate was asleep in his berth, after taking last night's watch. But the captain's strident voice brought him up the companionway in a matter of seconds. He took in the scene in an instant.

"Don't even think about it!" he barked furiously.

Too late. With a cry of *"Geronimo!"* J.J. grabbed onto a loose rope and swung himself off the mainmast, clear past the deck and out over the open sea. There he let go and dropped like a stone into the water.

It seemed like a long time — a breathless time — before J.J. surfaced again, howling in triumph. The celebration was short-lived.

Cursing with rage, Mr. Radford took a running leap off the side of the boat and hit the water swimming. His form was crude and untrained, but Charla had never seen anybody move that fast in water. He scooped J.J. up Red Cross style, towed him back to the swim ladder, and hauled him, still protesting, on board.

"You miserable little muckworm, do you know what mutiny is?"

J.J. blinked innocently. "Wasn't that a classic movie from way back when you were — you know — still old?"

SHIPWRECK

Now Radford was screaming. "Listen, Richie Rich! When we left Guam, we left the United States! In international waters, the captain is God! And I'm assistant God! When we say come down, down is where you come!"

He turned his fury on the three still in the water. "Okay, swimming's over! You've got your friend Richie Rich to thank for that!"

Charla watched in sympathy as Luke, Will, and Lyssa scrambled nervously up the swim ladder. Captain Cascadden was a nice man, she reflected, but he didn't seem to notice that his mate was more than just a gruff sailor. Mr. Radford didn't like people, especially kids. And his bullying seemed to increase with their distance from land.

She swallowed hard. They were going a lot farther than this. . . .

CHAPTER SIX
Thursday, July 13, 2235 hours

Luke had plenty of complaints about shipboard life, but he couldn't say there was nothing to do. In fact, he'd never been so busy. The sails alone were a full-time career. They constantly needed raising, lowering, trimming, letting in, letting out — somehow, the state they were in was never the right one.

When Luke and the others weren't fussing with the boat, they were fussing with the sea around it. Science stuff, mostly. Whale watching, plankton tows, identifying schools of fish. They did math with wave heights and water temperatures and indexed it to their location, which they got from the handheld global positioning satellite system.

It was all supposed to go in their logbooks, but Luke could never think of anything to write. He was sitting on deck, trying to describe a fish he'd seen ten hours ago, when a shadow fell across the flash-lit page.

Captain Cascadden was unfolding his six-foot-five frame out of the companionway. "Evening, crewman." He noticed the logbook in

SHIPWRECK

Luke's hand. "Ah, keeping a log is one of the great pleasures of life at sea. As the years go by, you'll read this over many times."

Right. Like he wanted to relive this lousy trip any more than he wanted to remember the arrest and trial leading up to it. But he bit his tongue and said nothing. Captain Cascadden could be annoying with his long, boring speeches about the joys of the sea. But he was a nice guy at heart. You definitely had to respect him. Not like Rat-face.

"Here's something that would make a fascinating entry," the captain rambled on, pointing to the sky. "Notice the bright halo around the moon. According to legend, that tells of a coming storm. Count the stars inside the ring — one, two. That means the storm is two days away."

"Really?" Luke was amazed. "And that works?"

The captain chuckled. "It's just an old salt's tale. But a hundred years ago, it was considered science." He made a great show of lighting a corncob pipe. "Today we get constant weather updates by fax."

"So there's no storm," said Luke.

"We're fine," the captain assured him. "Rougher seas tomorrow, though. No swimming."

Luke said good night and slipped down the companionway to the boys' cabin.

"Bad news, Evel Knievel," he said to J.J. "No swimming tomorrow. You'll have to find another way to kill yourself."

"Bug off," yawned the actor's son. He rolled over in his bunk and banged on the bulkhead. "Hey, ladies, which one of you wants to come over and give me a nice foot massage?" There was a scrambling sound on deck above them, followed by the shuffling of shoes on the companionway.

The furious face of Mr. Radford soon appeared. "Hey, Richie Rich. The girls' cabin is on the starboard side. Behind this bulkhead is where I sleep. And if I get any more invitations like that, you're going over the side with an anchor in your pants."

"Way to go," Luke muttered in a low voice as the mate stormed away. "Rat-face isn't the friendliest guy in the world as it is. Thanks for putting him in an even worse mood. We really need the grief."

"It's not smart," added Will in a softer tone. "When he's mad at you, he's mad at all of us."

"Thanks for the life lessons," said J.J. sarcastically. "Don't you know who I am? My father is Jonathan Lane!"

SHIPWRECK

"And I'm Bugs Bunny's kid," snorted Luke. "Notice the family resemblance?"

"I *am!*" J.J. insisted. He pulled his sunglasses out of his shirt pocket. "Paul Smith, the fashion designer, gave these to my dad in England last year. They're custom-made. There's not another pair exactly like them in the world!"

Luke examined the sleek silver shades. On one earpiece was engraved: JONATHAN LANE, THE TOAST OF LONDON — P.S.

Will was impressed. "Your dad's an amazing actor."

It all came together in Luke's mind — rich father, fancy lawyers. If Luke had had that . . .

"This is just great!" he exclaimed. "You're allowed to be a maniac because you know your big-shot daddy has the power to get you out of anything!"

Furious, J.J. leaped out of his bunk and leaned into Luke's face. "Well, I'm stuck here with you! So obviously there are a few things he can't get me out of, right?"

They stood seething, toe-to-toe.

"Hey, come on — " began Will. But a brawl seemed unavoidable.

And then a muffled sob broke through the tension. All three turned to follow the sound.

Ian Sikorsky rocked back and forth on his

bunk. His knees pulled into his chest, he was crying as if he had just met the end of the world.

"Hey," said Luke in a voice that was none too steady. "Don't do that. Nothing's worth it."

"Yeah," echoed J.J., speaking as much to Luke as to Ian.

Ian nodded and sniffled, struggling to get himself under control.

It was Will who couldn't leave well enough alone. "Ian, what did a nice kid like you do to get yourself a seat on this Windjammer cruise?"

"I — I watched TV," quavered the younger boy, and the tears started up again. This time there was no stopping them until sleep claimed him.

SHIPWRECK

CHAPTER SEVEN
Friday, July 14, 0610 hours

Slam!

Four orange life jackets came sailing down to the deck of the crew quarters.

Will came awake with a start. He sat up and was nearly tossed from his berth by the rolling of the cabin.

"Personal floatation devices!" barked Mr. Radford. "Get dressed and get in them!"

Will's heart was in his throat. "Is the boat sinking?"

"They're called waves!" snarled the mate. "Maybe you've heard of them. Now hurry up!"

The four boys got themselves ready in a tangle of elbows and knees. On deck, they found Lyssa on her hands and knees at the gunwale, throwing up over the side.

It was the one sight that could have brought a smile to Will's gray face. "Mom and Dad always tell us: Find what you do best and do your best with it. You're turning into a real whiz at barfing, Lyss."

Lyssa was too weak to fire off a retort.

"Good morning!" bellowed the captain from

the cockpit. "I think today might test your sea legs a little. We're seeing eight-foot waves with swells in the ten-foot range. And the wind's going to pick up later in the day. So let's be extra careful on deck. Now I want all of you to go and eat a hearty breakfast. You'll need your strength. That's all."

The six crew members crept gingerly aft and climbed down the companionway to the tiny galley, which was just off the main cabin. There the powerful odor of sizzling butter practically knocked them over.

"Scrambled eggs!" crowed Mr. Radford. "Nice and greasy! They'll slide all the way down!"

In a flash, Lyssa was back up on deck, gulping air.

Luke opened the latch and folded the table down from the bulkhead. The crew gathered around it.

"That Rat-face is some piece of work," he muttered. "Three days of dry toast, but now that we've hit heavy seas, he decides to get creative in the kitchen!"

It was a rough day on the inexperienced crew. The wind was whipping around the rigging, and the deck pitched to and fro. They struggled through the fine chilling spray off the whitecaps, their shoes slipping on the slick deck. By 1100 hours, Will was beside his sister at the rail, giving up his scrambled eggs to the Pacific.

"It's days like this," yowled Mr. Radford, "that made me become a sailor!"

The *Phoenix* tacked, sailing close-hauled at an angle, first to port, then to starboard.

"It's called beating to windward," the captain explained. "We can get where we're going in a zigzag without ever having to sail into the wind."

The constant changes in direction meant a lot of work on the sails. Their hands were raw and bleeding by the time Mr. Radford called lunch.

The meal was another rough-weather master-piece — liver and onions with canned succotash. The mate took great delight in watching the faces turn green. Ian and J.J. barely touched their food, but Luke refused to give Radford the satisfaction of hearing him say uncle. He sat across the table from the cook, glaring into his eyes, and match-ing him mouthful for mouthful.

"Ready for seconds?" challenged the mate.

"Bring it on," replied Luke, tight-lipped.

The wind got stronger. Captain Cascadden ordered the sails trimmed and took down the two jibs on the bowsprit. By this time, the swells were reaching twelve feet.

"It's like a roller coaster!" moaned Will, hugging the mainsheet as if he were trying to enmesh himself in the ropes and pulleys.

If I get through this day, he vowed, *I swear I'll give up smoking if I ever start!*

"I love the sea!" roared Mr. Radford, shaking off a faceful of spray like a sheepdog after a bath. "We'll make sailors of you lot yet!"

"I'm a landlubber," J.J. groaned defensively. "And the more time I spend on this boat, the more I lub the land."

Luke had never seen the mate this happy. Rat-face was so nasty that it took everybody's combined misery to put him in a good mood.

"Hey, Archie," he called to Luke. "You don't look so hot. You'll feel a lot better if you let that seasickness out."

Luke grimaced. His stomach was doing serious backflips. That would put the crowning touch on Rat-face's day.

He set his jaw. It was never going to happen. Grim with determination, he staggered forward, stumbled down the companionway, and squeezed himself into the tiny head. He couldn't even get down on his knees — there wasn't enough room. He just bent over the bowl and surrendered to his overwhelming nausea.

Then he flushed away all traces, rinsed out his mouth, and washed his face.

SHIPWRECK

Back on deck, the captain was addressing the assembled crew. "There's no break from these rough seas yet. We're going to have to strike the sails and heave to under power."

"I heaved already," said J.J. feelingly.

"Shut up, Richie Rich!" snapped Radford. " 'Heave to' means turning into the wind. If you listen, you might hear what you don't hear because you're not listening!"

"Captain," said Will in a timid voice, "how scared should we be? I mean — are we in trouble here?"

The captain threw back his head and laughed heartily. "Steady on, my boy, this is an ordinary day at the office for the *Phoenix*. She's been in seas twice this size and come through with flying colors. She's a fine ship, seaworthy in every way."

So down came the sails.

No one felt like eating. But the captain ordered toast and ginger ale for all hands. The swells were reaching fifteen feet. Standing near the bow, it looked as if the sea were opening up to swallow the *Phoenix*. The troughs between waves were so low that, for a second, there was dead calm down there — no wind, no spray. It was the eeriest part. Luke actually found himself yearning for the blustery chaos atop the crests.

Ian was the first to decide to ride out the rough seas strapped into his bunk. He disappeared down the companionway. A moment later there was a bloodcurdling scream.

"We're sinking! *We're sinking!*"

Mr. Radford ran over to the companionway. "Take it easy, Archie. We're not sinking." He looked down and saw the boy standing up to his ankles in water. "Holy — Skipper, we've got water in the crew cabin!"

Captain Cascadden turned on the bilge pump and grabbed the person closest to him. "Crewman, take the wheel!"

Will stared at him in shock and horror. "But I don't know how to drive!"

"We're in the open Pacific," the captain assured him. "You're not going to hit anything. Just hold her steady. I'll be right back."

Will stood there with an iron grip on the wheel. The captain hurried below.

"A leak?" he asked his mate.

"Negative."

Lyssa jumped down the companionway to the girls' quarters. "No water in here, Captain!" she called.

Captain Cascadden opened the door to the head. Eight inches of water poured out into the cabin. The toilet bowl was full and overflowing.

Seawater surged out of the flusher pump with each wave that hit the boat.

The captain reached down and twisted the lever on the pump. "False alarm, Mr. Radford. Somebody forgot to close the valve."

"I'll kill him!" threatened the mate.

"You'll do no such thing," chuckled the captain. "In fact, I don't even want to know who it was. Get a pump and bail out this cabin."

A bell went off in Luke's mind. He pictured himself sick as a dog but determined that Rat-face would never find out about his Technicolor yawn. He'd put so much energy into cleaning up the evidence that he'd forgotten to shut the valve.

Guiltily, he volunteered for the worst job in the pumping operation. His pants rolled up to his knees, he stood in the head, holding the sucking tube and trying not to fall in the toilet as the deck tossed under his feet.

Mr. Radford ranted through the whole business. "How many times do I have to tell you to close *that valve*? Does anybody have half a brain on this ship?"

It was torture, Luke thought. But it was better than having to confess that all this was his fault.

CHAPTER EIGHT
Saturday, July 15, 0650 hours

J.J. Lane was dreaming about bikinis. The pool deck was packed with them.

"You must be an actress," he said to a yellow one with stars on it.

The girl reached out to him and . . .

Smack!

Will Greenfield's arm came down off the upper bunk, and the open hand slapped J.J. full in the face.

The actor's son sat bolt upright, visions of swimsuits popping like soap bubbles before his bleary eyes. Bright sunshine shone down the companionway. He checked his Rolex watch, a birthday gift from Madonna. 6:53.

Huh? Radford usually had them up by six. He heard the deep rumble of the captain's voice above them.

"Let them sleep, Mr. Radford. They were pretty sick yesterday and they need their rest. You and I can get these sails up."

Radford laughed. "Sure can, Skipper. And we'll have an easier time of it than they do."

J.J. heard the captain chuckle. Then he heard

another sound — a power hum, and the scrape and squeak of a mechanical winch in operation.

Frowning, he crept up the companionway and peered out on deck. The captain and mate were both in the cockpit. And the mainsail was rising — *all by itself!*

He let himself drop to the deck of the cabin. "Unbelievable!"

The other three boys stirred.

"More trouble?" Will asked fearfully.

J.J. was so angry he could barely speak. "The captain and Radford — they're raising sails!"

Luke climbed down from his bunk. "Just so long as we don't have to do it."

"They're raising sails *automatically!*" J.J. exclaimed. "There's a gizmo in the cockpit that does it like a garage door opener!"

Ian spoke up. "You mean all that halyard work — ?"

"For nothing," confirmed the actor's son. "They could have done it with the touch of a button — like they're doing *this minute!*"

"Those jerks," Luke muttered. "I'll bet Rat-face is laughing inside every time we rip up our hands hauling those ropes."

"It's probably CNC's policy — you know, learning teamwork by doing everything the old-fashioned way," Will put in.

"By suffering," Luke added.

"We can't let them get away with this," J.J. said, tight-lipped.

"What can we do about it?" asked Ian. "They're in charge, and we're not. We have to do what they say."

"We can fight back," J.J. insisted.

Luke glared at him. "I don't like CNC, but it's better than jail — and that's where I go if I don't complete this trip! Don't even *think* about messing it up for me."

Will struggled into his life jacket and pulled the straps tight around his back. That was the fourth time. Six more to go, Radford's orders. Yesterday, Will had spent the entire day with the device on backward, and the punishment was to put it on and take it off ten times in a row.

"Not like that!" From behind, iron hands seized the ties and yanked them to strangulation level. "It's supposed to be snug!"

"Hey, that hurts!"

"Perfect," Radford confirmed. "If it's comfortable, it's on wrong. Ten more times, Archie."

Will smoldered as the mate strode away. It was humiliating! Why wouldn't Radford let him do this in the privacy of the crew cabin? He had to be out here in front of everybody — even

SHIPWRECK

Lyssa. She wasn't saying anything, but he could feel her scorn.

She stood behind the wheel of the *Phoenix*, piloting the schooner through the waves. Captain Cascadden was at her side, beaming his approval.

Wouldn't you know it! Out of the six of them, his sister was turning into the star sailing pupil — while he was the sweat-hog in the back row, too stupid to figure out how to put on a life jacket.

Look at her, chatting with the captain like they're old friends. A bitter taunt began to form in his mind, something like: *Hey, Lyss, make sure you don't slip in any of that barf from yesterday!* But he didn't dare say it with Cascadden right there.

Besides, Lyssa wasn't letting the seasickness bother her at all. Lyssa, who had more reason to hate this trip than anybody, actually seemed to be liking it!

I should have been an only child.

The captain resumed his stance at the wheel, while Lyssa began examining various gauges and dials on the control console.

Yeah, right, thought Will. *Like she knows what she's looking at.*

He watched as his sister's features contracted into a frown. "Captain, I forget. What does it mean again when the barometer is falling so fast you can see it moving?"

The captain scanned the glassy sky to the west. The line of black clouds was as solid as a wall stretching clear across the horizon.

CHAPTER NINE
Saturday, July 15, 1750 hours

The news from the weather fax was all bad.

A tropical storm near the equator had suddenly turned their way. It was set to collide with a large mass of cooler air dipping down from the north.

Will was making deals even before the captain explained their situation. *If the storm misses us, I'll keep my room so clean you could eat off the floor!*

"So I'm afraid we've got a bit of a rough ride ahead of us tonight," the captain told them grimly.

"You mean last time *wasn't* a rough ride?" Charla said in dismay.

"My dear," the captain replied evenly, "last time was a lap around the duck pond compared with what the next few hours might bring us. But the *Phoenix* is a fine ship. We'll make it through if we keep our heads."

The first order of business was to take down the sails.

"I can't believe they're making us do this by hand!" complained J.J. as he and Luke hauled on

ISLAND

the main halyard. "There's a storm coming, and we're doing work when we don't have to!"

"Hey!" Luke said sharply. "This is no time to get on the captain's nerves."

"But it's such a *snow job!*" He belted out the last two words so they would reach the mate on the ratlines. Radford glared down at them.

They heard the engine come to life. The *Phoenix* would face this gale under power.

The weather roared up quickly. At dusk, the rain started pelting down on them. The wind came with the dark — a blustery blow that had the crew hanging onto bulwarks and rigging as they made their way around the deck. Mr. Radford handed out life jackets and safety harnesses.

"Always keep your belt locked onto something that's attached to the boat," he ordered sternly. "When you move from place to place, hang on with two hands. Don't be embarrassed to crawl. Got it?"

The waves grew, slowly but steadily. At first, they weren't any bigger than the seas that had turned the *Phoenix* into a roller coaster ride a day before. But Luke could see they were more dangerous. Yesterday the swells had been like mountains, forcing the schooner to climb and descend, climb and descend from peak to peak. These were more like a series of oncoming cliffs,

SHIPWRECK

vertical walls of water. A ship can't climb a cliff. Instead, wave after wave broke over the bow, sending a constant knee-deep flood surging across the deck.

Ian's feet were swept out from under him — and down he went. Luke caught him and yanked him upright.

Luke wasn't sure whether or not to be alarmed. The storm was howling worse every minute, but the captain and mate were working calmly and efficiently in the battering wind and rain.

"This is bad, right?" he shouted to Mr. Radford. "Shouldn't we go below?"

"Don't panic, Archie!" ordered the mate. "Let's batten everything down first."

"No!" J.J. protested "We don't have to get blown around like this!"

Radford shot him a fierce look. "You gonna ask your famous daddy to pay off the storm and make it go away?"

"We can outrun it!" J.J. argued. "We've got more wind than we know what to do with! Just put up the sails and fly!"

Radford shook his head in disgust and rushed away.

J.J. threw up his arms. "What'd I say?"

He got a faceful of spray for his answer.

Great patches of foam blew in dense streaks. At one point, Luke looked over the gunwale and saw nothing but white water — not a speck of blue or green. Every minute or so, the *Phoenix* was lifted bodily and then flung contemptuously aside by a thirty-foot wave.

The deck lurched violently. Unlike yesterday's up and down, the tumbling of the sea was heavy and shocklike. Even athletic Charla couldn't keep her balance. She sat down on the cabin top and tried to slide along on her behind. Will crawled across the deck on all fours, unable to trust his own feet. A rush of sea washed over him, leaving him flopping and sputtering.

Lyssa was clamped onto the ratlines, her face green. "I'm gonna lose it!" she warned.

"That's so typical!" howled her brother, spitting salt water. "All day long you're Sinbad the Sailor, and now you can't hang on to your lunch!"

Radford turned to the cockpit. "We're secure, Skipper!"

Harnessed to the wheel stand, Captain Cascadden was barely visible through the rain, foam, and spray. Out of the chaos came his order. "All hands below!"

"You don't have to ask *me* twice!" exclaimed Will, sprint-crawling for the companionway to the main cabin.

Lyssa was hot on his heels, followed by Charla, high-stepping to keep her balance. Next came Luke, dragging Ian by the arm. At the last second, a huge wave broke over the bow, jolting the stern upward and pitching the two boys down the companionway.

Radford hooted with laughter. "You guys should join the circus — the flying Archie brothers!" His brow clouded as he did a head count. "Where's Richie Rich?"

Luke froze as J.J.'s words came back to him: *Just put up the sails and fly!* "That maniac," he muttered, clamboring up the companionway again.

"Hey!" barked the mate. "Get back here, Archie!"

At that moment, J.J. was clamped around the wrapped mainsail, hanging on with one hand and untying lines with the other.

When the furled sail was free, he stood up. Instantly, he was thrown to the deck. His father had once gotten him a bit part in a movie — an earthquake scene. There had been thirty special effects guys underneath them, pitching the floor every which way. It was *nothing* compared with the *Phoenix* right now! They had to get out of here! They could beat this storm no matter what Radford said! All they needed was some sail. . . .

Crouching low, he dashed astern through the rain and spray, steadying himself with an arm on the cabin top. He peered around the corner and set his eyes on the instrument panel behind the wheel. Six, maybe seven feet away. He'd be seen, but by then it would be too late — *if* he could keep from falling flat on his face!

Counting silently — one, two, *three!* — he launched himself past the captain and reached for the mechanism that raised the mainsail.

Luke hit him at hip height, diving like a linebacker. The two of them fell hard to the slick deck.

"What the — ?" The captain spun around to face them. "What are you doing here, crewmen? Get yourselves below!"

"You lunatic!" Luke rasped at J.J. "You'll get us all killed!"

"I know what I'm doing!" J.J. insisted frantically. He lunged for the panel, but Luke grabbed him once more.

"Archie!" Radford struggled onto the scene. The beam of his flashlight captured Luke and J.J. locked in a wrestling match.

"Break it up!" ordered Cascadden. He unhooked his safety harness and stepped between the two combatants, separating them with a heave of his powerful arms.

The schooner lurched suddenly, and J.J. was tossed off his feet. The deck wash had him, was about to sweep him away. In a single motion, Captain Cascadden clamped his right hand onto J.J.'s wrist and reached back with the left, groping for something, anything, to hold on to. His fingers closed on the side of the instrument panel and gripped hard. His palm pressed against a small button.

The roar of the waves covered the mechanical *clunk* as the mainsail began to rise automatically.

Radford ran over, and he and the captain set J.J. back up on his feet.

"*Captain!*" Luke spotted the white canvas flapping wildly as it rose from its boom. "The *sail!*"

Captain and mate turned just as the fifty-knot wind filled the half-open mainsail with an overpowering force.

It was as if the whole world suddenly tilted ninety degrees. The sixty-foot boat was blown all the way over on its side, its masts barely out of the water. Radford grabbed the mainsheet, which now extended over his head like monkey bars. The captain hung on to J.J. and the instrument panel.

The next thing Luke knew, he was moving, falling parallel to the deck. Only the gunwale — eighteen inches of wood — stood between him and a violent ocean.

Wham! He bounced off like a Ping-Pong ball, snatching wildly for the lifeline. He felt the wire in his hands and held on, his feet dragging in the water.

"Archie!" Radford called. "Lock your harness on the lifeline!"

"I can't!" he tried to answer, but a torrent of sea and spray found his throat. He came up choking.

Waves crashed over the twin masts. The automatic halyard winch ground to a halt.

The captain secured J.J.'s safety belt around the wheel stand. Then he hit the button to lower the mainsail.

Nothing happened.

"No power to the winch!" howled Radford. "I'll have to lower it manually!"

Like Tarzan moving from vine to vine, the mate grabbed the halyard and swung over. He hung there, trying to use his full weight to pull the sail down. "Too much blow, skipper!" he called. "I can't budge it!"

"Take the helm, crewman!" the captain ordered J.J. He heaved himself up on the side of the cabin top to make his way over to the mate.

Clinging to the wire at the starboard gunwale, Luke was the first to see the great wave. It was enormous — a forty-footer — curling over the high side of the *Phoenix* like a giant hand about to crush the small ship.

He shouted, "Captain — !"

And then the monster broke. To Luke it seemed like Niagara Falls raging down the upturned deck toward him.

Crack!

The mainmast snapped like a toothpick under the weight of the thundering sea. An avalanche of rope and canvas pelted down. As if in slow motion, the broken peak of the mast toppled over, striking Captain Cascadden across the shoulders.

Fierce lightning backlit a terrifying scene. Luke watched in horror as the captain was pitched from the deck into the foaming ocean.

"Man overboard!" he tried to shout.

But the force of the wave drove the gunwale of the *Phoenix* — and Luke with it — deep beneath the rampaging sea.

CHAPTER TEN
Saturday, July 15, 2015 hours

Underwater.

It was a strangely quiet and peaceful place. Luke was in a trance, experiencing a few seconds in a slow, almost lazy time warp of crystal-clear thought. He was going to drown — he was sure of that. The *Phoenix* was sinking, taking everybody with it. Even if he could make it back to the surface, then what? A lone swimmer — even one with a life jacket — had no chance against thirty-foot waves.

It was almost funny. Luke Haggerty had avoided Williston. Instead he had chosen — a *death sentence*.

The gunwale sprang back out of the sea as the *Phoenix* righted herself with heart-stopping suddenness. Luke lost his grip on the lifeline and sailed through the rain and spray. Flying again . . .

The pitching deck swung up to meet him. There was a painful thud, and he saw stars. He looked around. He was right in front of the cockpit. There, a terrified J.J. clung to the wheel, wrapped in rigging and torn canvas.

"The captain — !" Luke gasped, choking and spitting.

J.J. was sobbing out of control. "I'm sorry! I'm sorry! I'm sorry! — "

"*Did you find the captain?!*"

J.J. shook his head. "He told me to hang on to the wheel!"

"You picked a heck of a time to start following orders!"

Mr. Radford waited for a break in the wave action to roll like a landing parachutist to the starboard deck. He clamped his harness onto a bulwark and began hurling life preservers into the water.

"Skipper! *Skipper!*" He panned the waves with his flashlight.

"The mast hit him!" Luke shouted, tethering his belt to the base of the instrument panel. "He could be unconscious!"

The mate leaped for the cockpit, shoving J.J. aside with a football straight-arm that left the boy swinging like a pendulum in his harness. Radford grabbed the throttle and thrust it forward. "We're circling back!"

With a cough and a sputter, the engine died. Cursing, the mate tried to restart it. It turned over but wouldn't catch. Then it stopped turning over. "Check the engine room, Archie!"

"We can't unhook our belts!" Luke protested.

"Right below you!"

Luke knelt down and threw open the hatch. There was the engine, half submerged in three feet of water. He turned to the mate, but his mouth couldn't form words. Fear had frozen his jaw.

"Well?" Radford prompted angrily.

J.J. supplied the answer in the form of a question. "If we're flooded here, does that mean the whole boat's flooded?"

Charla's upper body emerged from the main cabin. "We've got water down here!" she cried.

"How much?" called the mate.

"A couple of feet at least!"

"Son of a — " The mate switched on the electric bilge pump. It was as dead as the engine.

"Get on the manual pumps!" he roared.

"What about the captain?" Luke insisted.

"We're looking for him!"

J.J. pointed frantically astern. "But he's back there somewhere!"

"We can't get back there without engine power!" Radford snarled. "*He* has to find *us*! Get all hands on deck to man the pumps!"

Luke saw Captain Cascadden in every wave, heard a call for help in every gust of wind. His eyes searched the backwash of each breaker that

SHIPWRECK

rocked the deck, half-expecting the ocean to return the old sailor to his ship.

J.J. never stopped yelling, "Captain! Captain!" He got no answer.

The feeling of hope on the schooner was so strong that Luke could almost reach out and touch it, could taste it in the salt spray. But it was only a feeling, trumped by the reality: pumping — hard work, simple, repeating, exhausting. No one dared unhook the safety harness for fear of being pitched overboard as the *Phoenix* was brutalized by the killer storm.

It was hours and it felt like years before the wind began to subside. The rain kept coming, but it weakened — a soaking shower rather than a driving attack. The terrible lightning ceased. Finally, the waves rounded off.

When Mr. Radford ordered them all to bed, nobody asked about the captain.

They already knew.

CHAPTER ELEVEN
Sunday, July 16, 0825 hours

Luke awoke with blond hair in his face. He tried to sit up and couldn't budge an inch.

"Man overboard . . . man overboard . . ." murmured a voice beside him, very close.

J.J.

Luke started to complain and then remembered. The captain . . .

He shut his eyes tightly and shook his head, but the awful image wouldn't go away — the six-foot-five Cascadden, disappearing into the foam.

When Radford had finally ordered them to bed, the lower bunks were underwater. They were sharing the uppers, packed like sardines, two to a berth, strapped in with lee canvases.

Luke leaned over to unfasten the hook, elbowing J.J. awake in the process.

"I had a nightmare," J.J. mumbled.

"No, you didn't," Luke told him soberly.

Will peered out from the bunk he shared with Ian. "Is it just me, or is the water getting higher?"

J.J. jumped down with a splash. "Feel that? Calm. And look." He pointed outside. "Sun's back."

SHIPWRECK

The four sloshed out of bed and climbed up the companionway. On deck, crusted sea salt crunched under their feet. In the light of day, the *Phoenix* was a floating plate of spaghetti — rope and rigging lay tangled everywhere. The main-mast looked like giant hands had snapped it in two. Equipment, most of it smashed, was deposited in clumps all over the deck. The radio antenna was gone, and the bowsprit was cracked and off-center. The ship's dinghy, which was usually stowed upside down in the rigging, was now pointed straight up, as if it were a rocket about to be launched at the moon.

Ian summed up everybody's feelings when he said, "Wow."

Lyssa and Charla worked one of the pumps, trying to clear the water out of the engine room. Mr. Radford manned the other, which was draining the main cabin and galley.

All activity ceased when they saw the boys on deck.

J.J. spoke first. "Shouldn't we still try looking for the captain?"

Radford stood up. If looks could kill, J.J. would have been fried to a crisp. "To look for the captain, you don't use a boat; you use a submarine."

"Hey!" Luke said angrily. "You're talking about a real guy who died. It's not a joke."

"No, it's not," the mate agreed unpleasantly. "Someday I want to sit down with you and your friend Richie Rich and find out why you needed to play WWF in a full gale. You damn near got us all killed. And you *did* get one of us killed."

Dan Rapaport's words at the Guam airport echoed in J.J.'s ears: *You're going to kill somebody one of these days. . . .*

"Well, don't blame me!" Luke exclaimed hotly. "I was trying to keep this maniac from raising the sails just to show you he knew how!"

"Not true," said J.J. in a hollow tone. "I thought I could help — "

"Next time," snarled Radford, "help somebody else."

Lyssa stepped forward. "Let's forget about who did what and concentrate on how we're going to get out of this."

Calmly, the mate went over their situation. According to the GPS, they were four hundred eighty miles east-northeast of Guam. Nearest landfall: Guam. No SOS had been sent, and the radio was out. Even if the radio could be fixed, the call couldn't travel much more than fifteen or twenty miles without an antenna. Their only chance of being spotted depended on the schooner's Emergency Position Indicating Radiobeacon — EPIRB. This was unlikely to reach other ships but might be detected by passing airplanes.

"How many air routes fly over this part of the Pacific?" asked Luke.

"None," Radford replied.

The engine was dead and full of seawater, which pretty much guaranteed that it would never work again. The mainsail was gone, and the staysail and jibs couldn't be used because of the damage to the bowsprit. That left just the foresail. It was fine — if they could ever get past the thousands of pounds of tangled ropes and fallen rigging.

The drinking-water tanks were okay. But there was no electricity and no refrigeration. The food stores and medical supplies were at least partly damaged by salt water.

Worst of all, the *Phoenix* wasn't expected in for three weeks. That meant no one was looking for them.

"Are we going to *die*?" asked Will in a small voice.

"I won't lie to you," said Radford. "We're in big, big trouble. To get through this we're going to have to work twenty-hour days, ration our supplies, and — " he glared at Luke and J.J. " — no more crazy stunts! We've lost a man already, and we're all going to have to live with that — *if* we live."

* * *

According to the mate, there were three main jobs that needed to be done to ensure their survival.

1. Pumping. "Pump like your life depends on it . . . because it does."

2. Clearing the foresail. "If we go anywhere, that's how we'll get there."

3. Lightening the ship. "If we can't eat it, wear it, or sail it, we pitch it."

That included luggage, books, all pots, pans, and dishes except the bare minimum, and the waterlogged mattresses off the lower bunks. The drawers from the built-in dressers went over the side next, along with any cartons of spoiled food from the galley.

"Are you sure we should be doing this?" Charla asked nervously. She watched a load of instant mashed potatoes swell up like a swamp creature before sinking out of sight. "It can't be good for the environment to just throw garbage in the ocean."

"Are you kidding?" Lyssa managed to manufacture a smile as she pumped. "These fish never had it so good. They're probably going to ask us for gravy."

Mr. Radford clung to the mainmast, chopping at the splintered wood with an ax. Will and Ian worked at the tangle of rigging with hacksaws. It took until noon, but all hands paused to watch the top of the mast and hundreds of pounds of ropes and shredded canvas slide over the side and disappear under the waves. It brought up a halfhearted cheer. Even Mr. Radford added a grunt of approval.

Lunch was the *Phoenix*'s entire store of frozen hot dogs, which were thawing out since there was no electricity for the freezer.

Charla made a face. "Any vegetables?"

The mate pulled out a huge tub of chocolate ice cream and tossed it to her.

"I can't eat this!" she exclaimed.

"Wait a few hours," grunted Radford. "You can drink it."

She bit her lip. Without the captain around, that terrible man was becoming meaner and more obnoxious. She felt instantly guilty. Was that all the captain meant to her — an authority figure to keep Radford in line? How selfish was that?

While the crew was eating, the mate let himself over the side and down the swim ladder to check the waterline on the hull. When he came back, his face was gray.

"Not enough!" he panted. "We've got to dump more gear!"

"There's nothing left to dump," J.J. protested.

Radford looked at him sourly. "Don't tempt me, Richie Rich."

They removed the boom of the mainsail and slid it into the water. The galley's refrigerator and the backup generator — both ruined — were next.

Then the mate's attention fell on the *Phoenix*'s three anchors. One by one, they were cut loose and dropped into the sea.

Luke was worried. "What if we need one of those to — you know — anchor?"

"If we get that close to land, Archie," Radford promised, "I'll jump in and hold the boat personally."

"Hey, what's the big idea?" demanded J.J. from the open cargo hatch. He stepped onto the deck, dragging a large bright yellow suitcase. "I had to leave my Jet Ski in Hawaii! But someone's allowed to bring the world's biggest piece of luggage on board!" He fiddled with the catch. "Whose is this?"

Radford's eyes bulged. "*No!*"

Pow!

With a hiss of compressed gas, the "suitcase" burst open, shooting out to ten times its original size. J.J. was knocked back into the flooded cargo hold, where he landed with a mammoth splash. The thing kept on growing, unfolding at the corners like a flower. By the time J.J.'s head poked out of the hold, an eight-foot rubber life raft sat on deck, complete with sun canopy, seating for ten, signal flares, first aid kit, and provisions.

The roar that came from Radford was barely human. "Why is it always you, Richie Rich?"

J.J. was soaked and sulky. "You should have told me there was a boat in there."

"The label said CONTENTS: ONE LIFEBOAT. What did you want? A singing telegram?"

"We'll just fold it up again," J.J. said defensively. "What's the big deal?"

"The big deal is you *can't* fold it up again!" the mate howled. "It has to go back to the factory to be recharged!"

"Well, that's stupid."

"Yes, it is! And it's even stupider to waste our precious space tying this thing down so it doesn't blow out to sea with the next puff of breeze!"

Will spent the day cringing as he waited for the mate's furious criticism to fall on him. Everyone was getting yelled at — even little Miss Perfect, Lyssa. When she delivered the news that their EPIRB had conked out, Radford hollered at her like she had personally smashed it with a hammer. Maybe Captain Cascadden had thought Lyssa could do no wrong. But Radford was an equal-opportunity offender.

It was tough to be captain's pet when the captain wasn't around anymore.

Instantly, Will felt terrible for his thoughts. A man was dead and gone, and he was almost celebrating the fact that it made things harder for Lyssa.

If, by some miracle, the captain turns out to be okay, I'll take out the garbage; I'll give to charity if I ever get any money; I'll be a better person, I swear!

The problem with the EPIRB turned out to be a fixable one. J.J.'s inflatable lifeboat had its own beacon, which was moved to the navigation room and switched on.

"You're welcome," J.J. gloated. "Opening that raft seems like a pretty smart move now, huh?"

It was the kind of comment that would have guaranteed a screaming broadside from the old Radford. But the mate gave no sign that he'd even heard. Something had changed about him — almost as if there had been an audible click.

Later, when Radford went over the side to recheck the waterline of the boat, Luke was waiting for him at the swim ladder. "How are we doing? Do we need to get rid of more stuff?"

Radford grunted and wouldn't answer.

At four o'clock, when he went to assess the water in the hull, Lyssa went with him to hold the flashlight.

"It looks worse than ever," she said in concern. "Are you sure all that pumping is doing any good?"

The mate remained sullen and silent.

"I liked him better when he was yelling at us," was Will's opinion. "You know where you stand with a guy who hates you. But one who ignores you — that's scary."

"I miss the captain," Ian said simply.

Long faces nodded all around.

At dinner, the mate wouldn't even eat with them. He took a tin of cold beans and sat atop the main cabin, staring into the sunset and shoveling with a plastic spoon.

It was a moonless night — impossible to tell the *Phoenix* from the vast ocean around her. Luke couldn't see his own sneakers without a flashlight, and the crew walked carefully despite the calm waters.

It had taken all day, but the foresail had finally emerged from the mountain of tangled ropes and rigging.

"I think it's ready," Luke called to Mr. Radford.

The mate was still atop the main cabin — flat

on his back now, staring up at the stars.

"We're ready to raise the foresail," Luke repeated, louder this time.

No answer.

Ian tried his luck. "Excuse me," he ventured. "Uh — Mr. Rat-face?"

A collective gasp went up on deck. J.J. stopped pumping and laughed out loud.

The mate sat up suddenly. "What? What did you call me?"

"Mr. — " Ian caught a desperate look from Luke and realized his mistake. The younger boy went pale.

"Foresail's ready," Luke put in quickly. "Want us to raise it?"

Radford jumped down from the cabin top. Even in the pitch-black, they could see his burning eyes glaring at them. But when he finally spoke, his tone was light and easygoing.

"Tomorrow's another day," he said. "Why don't you kids get some sleep? I'll look after things up here."

"What about pumping?" asked Lyssa.

"You can't save your life if you kill yourself doing it," the mate told her. He paused. "You did a lot of good work today — in a tough situation. I'm — " His face twisted. "I'm proud of you."

Will held it in until the four boys were splash-

SHIPWRECK

ing around the cabin. "Mr. Rat-face!" he guffawed at Ian. "Man, I was expecting him to go berserk and throw you overboard!"

"I thought it was his name," Ian said honestly.

"Nobody's name is Rat-face!" Luke exclaimed, hoisting himself onto the upper berth and drying his wet feet with a towel. "Not even in TV land!"

Ian flushed. "You know how sometimes you hear a word, but you don't think about what it really means? It's just *sounds* to you."

Luke patted him on the shoulder. "We forgive you, kid. He needed to hear it, anyway."

"Well, he didn't get mad," the younger boy added. "In fact, I thought he was pretty nice about it."

"Yeah, right," snickered J.J. "Radford — nice. That's a good one."

CHAPTER TWELVE
Monday, July 17, 0645 hours

"Will! Wake up!"

Will rolled over and cast a baleful eye at his sister. "Beat it, Lyss. You're not supposed to be in here."

"Come on!" She dragged him out of the narrow bunk. His elbow smacked Ian in the back of the head as he splashed to the deck. The water was now well over his knees, halfway to his waist.

"Ow!" The younger boy sat up. "What's going on?"

"Yeah!" stormed Will. "This better be good, Lyssa!"

"Radford's gone."

"Gone?" scoffed J.J. "Where could he go? Out for a stroll?"

"He just — disappeared," she said. "Maybe he fell off the boat."

"I couldn't get that lucky," grumbled Luke. "Besides, Rat-face is a career sailor. He'd never go overboard, not in calm seas like this."

Up on deck they found Charla waiting for them.

SHIPWRECK

"Notice anything missing?" she asked.

"You mean besides one psychopath?" J.J. retorted.

She pointed to the rigging around the foresail. There hung the inflatable lifeboat, exactly where they had stowed it the day before. But the *Phoenix*'s twelve-foot wooden dinghy was gone. "He must have sailed off in the middle of the night. Took the GPS too. And most of our food."

"He *left* us?" Ian was wide-eyed. "All alone?"

"Impossible," Will insisted. "Nobody's that rotten. Not even Radford."

"It doesn't make sense," said Luke. "Why would he set out in a wooden bathtub? Surely it's better to stay on a sixty-foot boat."

"It's not exactly in mint condition," Lyssa put in. "The mast's busted, the bowsprit's useless — "

"Not to mention the cabins are full of water — " added Charla.

It took a few seconds for the truth to seep down.

"We're sinking!" cried Will. "That's why Radford split! Water's coming in faster than we can pump it out! And he knew!"

Shocked silence followed. All six waited for someone to speak out, to say, "Of course not!

That's not what's happening at all. *Here's* the real story — "

But the facts were undeniable. They had pumped all day to lower the water level, and in the morning it was high again — higher even. The schooner was leaking — *sinking* — and they were on their own.

Heart pounding, Luke thought back to the moment yesterday when the mate had gone from his usual loudmouthed, bullying self to quiet, sullen, and withdrawn. In that instant, Rat-face must have made up his mind to desert them. He might as well have signed their death warrants. What chance did six inexperienced kids have on a sinking boat?

The unfairness of it suddenly seemed so weighty that it threatened to crush him. He was only here because he'd trusted a false friend with his locker combination. Never in Luke's wildest nightmares had he imagined it would cost him his life.

"That scumball," he said finally.

"Oh, *no*," breathed Lyssa.

Charla sat down on the deck, her head in her hands.

"It's all my fault!" moaned Ian. "I messed up his name. I got him mad at us!"

SHIPWRECK

"Hey!" Luke grabbed him by the shoulder. "You don't leave people to die because somebody made fun of you. God, to do something like this, you've got to be *evil!*"

"So what do we do now?" asked Will in a daze. "We just *sink*, and that's it?"

"That's what Radford must think," Luke said seriously. "If we make it to some port and tell the story of how he deserted us, he's in big trouble. In his mind, we're already fish food."

"He's right," gasped Will, fighting back tears.

"How do *you* know?" Lyssa snapped angrily.

"He's a sailor!" he yelled. "He knows a sinking boat when he sees one, idiot!"

"Not now," commanded Luke. "We have to think. There must be something we can do."

"We can pump," Charla ventured.

"Radford knew that," Lyssa pointed out, "and he still split."

"But it'll buy us time," Luke argued. "Every gallon we pump out must mean a few more minutes before we sink. Now, what else have we got?"

"The foresail," said Ian. "We never raised it, but it's ready."

"And the engine," Lyssa added thoughtfully. "I could be wrong, but it's just wet."

"Wet?" cried her brother. "It's underwater!"

"We pump out the engine room, take the motor apart, dry it out" — her eyes gleamed " — maybe I can put it back together again."

"This isn't your science fair project!" Will exploded. "It's real life!"

"Well, have you got a better idea?" she shot back.

J.J. shook his head. "Could I just say something?" One by one, he looked them in the eye. "No offense, but I've never seen such a bunch of total saps in my life!"

"Oh, no offense taken," Luke said unkindly.

"Seriously," J.J. persisted. "I mean, don't you think all this is a little too convenient?"

Luke looked daggers at him. "No, I think it's pretty *inconvenient* that Rat-face left us for dead in the middle of the Pacific Ocean. And when the boat sinks, that'll be even less convenient!"

"The boat's not sinking," scoffed J.J. "And Radford didn't leave us either."

Will was confused. "Then where is he?"

The actor's son shrugged. "On another boat just out of sight, watching us through binoculars. And you know who's with him? The captain."

"You're sick!" stormed Luke. "The captain's dead. I saw him go over the side, and so did you!"

J.J. chuckled. "The special effects guys who

work on my dad's movies — they can make anything seem like anything. The captain's 'death,' the sinking boat, Radford's disappearance — they faked all that."

"But why?" Charla asked in a small voice.

"To see how we'll react under pressure," J.J. explained. "That's CNC's whole gig! Cooperation. Teamwork. They're probably watching us right now, making notes on what we say and do. I'll bet they've got hidden cameras and microphones all over this boat."

"You know what?" said Luke. "You're crazy."

"I'm the only sane one here," J.J. replied coolly.

"I've got news for you," Luke told him. "You're not the center of the universe. Nobody's watching you through hidden cameras. If this boat sinks, you're going to drown along with the rest of us, because the ocean doesn't care who your daddy is!"

"That's your opinion," J.J. said smugly. "If you guys want to break your backs on those pumps, then be my guest. I'm on vacation. If anybody needs me, I'll be working on my tan."

And before their shocked eyes, J.J. Lane spread a towel across the cabin top, flaked out on it, and surrendered his body to the sun's rays.

CHAPTER THIRTEEN
Monday, July 17, 1440 hours

It was fairly easy to raise the foresail and get the *Phoenix* moving again. But as to whether or not it was in the right direction — that was anybody's guess. Radford had given their last position as east-northeast of Guam. Even though they had drifted a lot since that reading, they were following the compass west-southwest. It seemed the only course.

"I don't know," Luke said uneasily. "We're probably wasting our time. We could be getting even more lost than before."

"In a crisis," lectured Ian, "it's always best to keep busy to prevent the onset of panic."

Luke stared at the boy who spoke so seldom that they often had to remind themselves he was aboard. "Since when did you become ship's counselor?"

Ian flushed. "I saw it on a documentary once."

Luke sighed. "Ian, did anyone ever tell you that you watch too much TV?"

"My parents." Ian nodded sadly. "Right before they put me on this trip."

SHIPWRECK

Luke sent Ian below to the navigation room to see if he could find any maps — *charts*, the captain had always called them. In open ocean there were no landmarks. But it might be helpful to know the course the *Phoenix* had been following before disaster struck.

He watched the younger boy's careful footsteps. The schooner's deck now sloped dangerously down toward the bow. This was because both pumps were working in the engine room near the stern. For the time being, anyway, they were letting the forward compartments fill up with water. It was a big risk, no question about it. If the *Phoenix* got too far out of balance, Luke reflected, it could take a diagonal dive just like the *Titanic*.

But tough times called for tough choices. They needed the engine, and Lyssa couldn't fix it if the thing was underwater.

Luke looked up, squinting in the sunlight. He could barely make out Charla perched atop the foremast. She was scanning the horizon for signs of other ships, ready to fire off distress flares if she spotted anything. The job had fallen to her mostly because she was the only one with the guts to climb up the ratlines — her and J.J. But Luke doubted J.J., the daredevil, would be interested unless there was a reasonable chance of killing himself. And besides, the actor's son was boycotting the effort to be rescued, still convinced that their current peril was all part of CNC's plan.

Lyssa had already started taking apart the motor, even though the engine room was still under two feet of water. She was working by snorkel mask. Every few minutes she would surface like a submarine, and another wet part would hit the drying towel with a dull clink.

Will's official job was pumper, but he doubled as a nervous nag. "You remember where that piece goes, right?" he kibitzed down the open engine hatch. "You'll know how to put it back together?"

"No," she said sarcastically. "I'm busting it up just to get you killed."

Will couldn't decide what made him more uneasy — their current danger, or the fact that Lyssa was emerging as the big hero.

Ian came running up the companionway, waving a thick folder with the CNC logo on the cover.

"You found the maps?" Luke asked.

Ian shook his head. "Files."

"Files?" Luke repeated.

"On us."

Luke gave Ian the wheel and fished through his own folder. Now that he thought about it, of course Charting a New Course would need information on its charges. Still, it was eerie to see his whole life between the covers — almost like the FBI had been keeping tabs on him. But this stuff must have come from his parents. There were school pictures and report cards; medical records — it said he'd been allergic to milk as a baby. Was that true? No one had ever mentioned anything to him.

All the court documents were in there, along with the arrest report and his suspension papers from school. And — what was this?

Luke recognized his mother's handwriting on the letter:

> . . . Luke is a good boy, but lately he's been running with a tough crowd, including a boy named Reese, who has had trouble with the law before. We want to believe him when he says that the gun wasn't his, but we don't want to be naive either — not where Luke's future is concerned. We can't take the chance that this Reese has gotten him involved with a gang. We think it might be a good idea to get him away from here for a while. Therefore, we're accepting the court's proposal to send him to you. . . .

Luke put the letter down, blinking hard. "They *said* they believed me."

By this time, all pumping work had stopped for the crew members to dig into their files. Lyssa emerged from the engine room and Charla abandoned her lookout post to join them. Even J.J. interrupted his tanning to flip quickly through his folder.

He was unimpressed. "Big deal. So I'm a flake. What else is new?" He peered over Ian's shoulder. "Couch potato. No friends. What a surprise."

"Lay off," Luke warned.

But J.J. had already moved on to Will and Lyssa. "Whoa, what are you guys, hit men? There isn't this much violence in the James Bond movies!"

Will flushed. "I don't know how it happens. One minute we're just arguing — "

Lyssa cut him off. "Shut up, Will! We don't have to explain anything. Mind your own business, rich boy."

J.J. shrugged. "I don't see any of you guys in the poorhouse. CNC doesn't come cheap, you know."

"You find the money," Luke put in grimly, "when your two choices are either here or jail."

"Or you borrow it," Charla added bitterly. "Not all of us live in Beverly Hills."

"Yeah, what's *your* story?" asked J.J., snatching the folder from her hands.

She reacted like a wildcat. "Give that back!"

J.J. held the file up out of her reach and kept on reading over his head.

Charla leaped like a basketball player, grabbed the papers from his hand, and fixed him with a withering glare. "Moron," she muttered.

He looked bewildered. "What'd I do?"

"That's private!" she raged.

"You know what it says? That you're world-class at, like, fifteen sports. What a deep, dark secret! My own father sends me halfway around the world just so he won't have to look at me, but you don't want anyone to find out you're a star!"

"You didn't get to the part where it says what a head case I am," she mumbled.

"We're all head cases," J.J. told her. "This is a trip for head cases. That's why we're here."

Lyssa pushed her snorkel mask back down over her face. "Well, this was fun — " She stepped into the engine hatch.

J.J. regarded the pile of folders. "What are we going to do with these?"

Luke glared at him. "You really want to hear my suggestion?"

J.J. picked up the files and walked to the gunwale. With the exaggerated windup of a major league pitcher, he flung them into the sea.

"How's the environment now?" he asked Charla.

"It'll live," she replied, tight-lipped.

"Well, let's get back to work," said J.J.

Luke raised an eyebrow. "Look who's admitting that we might be in trouble."

"I'm bored, that's all," J.J. insisted. "Gotta have something to do till the cavalry arrives. Which pump is mine?"

CHAPTER FOURTEEN
Monday, July 17, 1640 hours

As the day wore on, Luke watched the bow of the *Phoenix* sink lower and lower into the sea. At least a dozen times he was tempted to send the pumpers forward to try to even out the schooner's balance.

No. If they had a chance, it was with the motor. They had to pump out the engine room first.

It was an agonizing decision. If they took a nosedive to the bottom, it would be all his fault.

Even in a glassy calm, sleepy waves broke over the gunwale. The water puddled for only a moment before rolling down a deck that was sloped like a parking ramp. If another storm blew through, the *Phoenix* wouldn't last five minutes.

In the crew cabins, even the upper bunks were swamped now. Where the crew members were supposed to sleep was anybody's guess. Probably they just wouldn't sleep anymore. Luke thought back to the night before, crammed next to J.J. in the narrow berth. That misery might go down as his final night of sleep ever. The thought coaxed a nervous chuckle from him, but beneath

ISLAND

the surface lingered a feeling so awful he didn't dare dwell on it.

By five o'clock the entire engine was spread across two beach towels in the stern.

Will surveyed the scene with a frown. "I hope you can look at this stuff and see a motor, because all I see is a huge pile of junk."

Lyssa looked preoccupied. "I've got it straight in my mind. Don't bug me."

It took another hour to get the last few inches of thick murky slime off the floor of the engine room. Then Lyssa eased herself down the hatch to start the long task of reassembly. The pumpers rushed forward to work on the crew cabins and the fo'c'sle — the area belowdecks directly under the bow. They were exhausted, but there was no time for a break. As Luke put it, their next break could be spent on the ocean floor.

The sun was setting when Will stepped into the cockpit and joined Luke at the wheel. He checked their direction — still west-southwest. "How do we know that's right?" he asked uneasily. "Maybe the compass is broken like everything else on this tub."

Luke shrugged. "You can't be off-course when you don't know where you're going in the first place." He regarded the foresail. "Wind's picking up. We should probably let out the sheet a little."

Will groaned. "If you're turning into a real sailor, I'm going to have to start treating you like Radford."

Luke shot Will a look. "Don't mention that name, not even as a joke."

Will shook his head. "How could anybody do what he did? I mean, we're talking about *dying* here! Are we so worthless to him?"

Luke looked at him sharply. "We're not worthless; Rat-face is worthless. If there's any justice in this world, he'll get his."

"Unless — " Will frowned. "You don't think J.J. could be right? That all this is part of the CNC thing?"

"It's pretty crazy," said Luke. "They'd have to trash their own boat, wash the captain into the sea on purpose. Anything's possible, I guess. I'd love to believe that the captain's okay."

"Me too," Will agreed fervently. "That's probably what's in J.J.'s head. He feels responsible."

"He *is* responsible," Luke said flatly. "He was born with a dream life. He gets whatever he wants whenever he wants it. And he's still the biggest screwup I've ever met."

Lyssa heaved herself through the engine room

hatch, dusting ineffectually at the caked muck on her knees.

Will looked at his sister anxiously but couldn't read her expression. "Tell me it's good news."

"It's back together," she replied. "That's all I know for sure."

"The captain said never to start the engine without the blower," Luke reminded her.

"The blower's electric," Lyssa explained. "If we run it before the engine's on, we could drain the battery charge — "

"English, Lyss," Will interrupted impatiently.

"We'll have to improvise." She picked up the grease-spattered beach towels that had been used to dry off the engine parts and tossed one to Luke and one to Will. "When I give the word, you guys stand over the hatch and fan like crazy."

Luke was amazed. "And that's safe?"

"She knows this stuff," Will said fervently. "She got an A on that science project."

Lyssa replaced Luke at the wheel and waited for the two boys to establish themselves above the hatch. "Okay — now!"

Like palace guards fanning the sultan, Luke and Will began waving their towels up and down, ventilating the engine room. Lyssa hit the starter button. The motor turned over, choked once, and died.

Will cursed and threw his towel to the deck.

"Don't stop!" she ordered briskly.

They resumed fanning and she tried again. This time the engine *put-putted* itself to life.

"All right, Lyss!" shouted Will.

His sister looked at him sharply but found no sarcasm in his praise.

Cheering and applause came from the pumpers above the crew cabins. Charla flashed them thumbs-up from her spot atop the foremast.

"Okay," exclaimed Luke, "put 'er in gear!"

Lyssa pushed forward on the throttle. The motor coughed and sputtered out.

"Aw, man!" moaned Will.

So the whole process began again. Luke and Will fanned while Lyssa tried to nurse the starter along.

"It's not easy, you know!" Will protested as the motor roared to life only to die with a wheeze and a hiccup of machinery. "It's murder on your shoulders!"

"You're such a crab," Lyssa sneered.

Luke rolled his eyes. What was with these two? They were on a sinking boat; this could be their last conversation. Why did it have to be fighting words?

As they continued to work and bicker, Luke noticed in alarm that the roar of the motor was becoming less and less frequent. After a few more minutes, the engine wouldn't even turn over.

Will was worried too. "Aw, Lyss, I knew you'd bust it!"

"Probably just flooded the carburetor," said Lyssa, grabbing the toolbox. "I can smell the gas." Once again, she lowered herself into the engine hatch.

"What's the problem?" Charla called.

Luke could only shrug. "You should come down. It's getting dark."

"Give me another half hour," came the reply. "I can still see a little."

After a few minutes, Lyssa emerged, reeking of fuel. "I think I've got it this time." She climbed into the cockpit and reached for the starter.

Luke and Will resumed fanning.

"My arm's falling off!" Will complained. He only let go for a second to rest his aching shoulder. But at that moment, a gust of wind snatched the greasy terry cloth from his other hand. The towel spread open like a full sail and floated slowly down over the engine hatch.

"Hey, wait — " Will began.

But Lyssa's oil-stained finger was already pressing the button.

SHIPWRECK

The spark from the starter ignited the trapped fumes in the engine room. It made a *phoom*, like the lighting of a propane barbecue, only a lot louder. This was followed by a split-second pause as the fire shot up the fuel lines to the *Phoenix's* ninety-gallon gas tanks.

"Get down!" howled Lyssa, hurling herself to the deck of the cockpit.

A mammoth explosion rocked the schooner, and for a moment, dusk was bright as day. Suddenly, the main cabin and galley were gone, replaced by a pillar of flame. The force of the blast threw Luke, Will, and Lyssa out over the transom, clear into the sea. Luke tasted salt water for a moment and then resurfaced into a burning hailstorm. Bits of cabin, deck, and galley — all on fire — pelted down on him, forcing him to dive. The blazing cookstove of the *Phoenix* hit the waves right where he had been a split second before.

On the foredeck, the shock wave knocked J.J. and Ian off their feet. When they recovered, they found themselves facing a wall of fire that engulfed two-thirds of the boat.

"The extinguisher!" cried Ian, reaching down the companionway and yanking the small tank from its mounting on the bulkhead. He pulled the pin and sprayed foam at the blaze. J.J. picked up a bucket and began bailing water from the cabins and sloshing it into the firestorm. The heat was unbearable, and they stumbled on the ruined deck, which was a tangle of twisted planks and splinters.

"It's no use!" bawled J.J. "We might as well be throwing Dixie cups of Kool-Aid!"

The blast had knocked Charla out of her post atop the foremast, landing her upside down in the ratlines. It took every ounce of her gymnastics training to right herself again. Through the waves of heat and smoke that billowed over her, she spotted J.J. and Ian. But when she looked aft, she saw only the boiling orange of the blaze.

"Where are the others?" she called down.

"In the stern!" shouted Ian.

"There *is* no stern! It's all fire back there!"

With a terrible creaking sound, the flaming stump of the mainmast toppled over in a shower of sparks. It crushed the cabin top, cutting the younger boy off from J.J.

"*Ian!*" J.J. cried.

Ian jumped back, stumbling on an upended deck board. The extinguisher dropped from his hands, rolled into the fire, and exploded in a *whoosh* of compressed gas.

The blazing mainmast ignited the foresail. J.J. sloshed water onto the smoldering sail, but flames quickly licked up the canvas, forcing Charla back atop the mast. The fire soon spread to the sheets and rigging.

"Ian, can you hear me?" called J.J.

"Get out of there!" came Ian's voice from the inferno.

J.J. spun around. "To where?!"

There were only two choices: Either stay on the burning boat or take his chances in the vast, inhospitable, and terrifying sea.

CHAPTER FIFTEEN
Monday, July 17, 1825 hours

Luke paddled like a four-year-old at his first swimming test. Just keeping his upper lip above water seemed almost impossible. This was crazy! He had a bronze badge from the Red Cross — why was he so helpless?

Panic and shock, he thought. And fear. He was trembling all over.

Stay close to the boat. That was the first rule for a man overboard. But a widening pool of burning gasoline was spreading around the *Phoenix*, making it look like the waves themselves were on fire. Luke found himself drifting farther and farther from the ship. If he got separated from the others, only the fish would find him.

"Luke!" It was a faint call from the gloom.

Will. The voice seemed to be coming from miles away, although Luke was sure Will couldn't be very far. "Will, are you okay?" he shouted.

No answer.

Luke looked around, fighting hysteria. The sun was down. Detail disappeared against the incandescent orange of the fire. He saw nothing. Except —

SHIPWRECK

There it was. A flash of color a few yards away. He made for it, splashing wildly.

In the pool at the Y, it would have been a ten-second swim. But *now*, but *here* — a distance marathon.

"Will!" Luke's voice was breathless, unsteady. Nothing.

And then his flailing arm smacked right into it — a six-foot piece of the *Phoenix*'s cabin top, floating in the water. The corner glowed like hot coals. Luke used his weight to submerge the smoldering portion. With a puff of steam, the fire was out. He hauled himself on top and lay back, gasping.

"Ow!" His head banged against something hard. He rolled over to find himself staring at a steel-gray smoke-head vent. This was the galley ceiling! It must have been broken off and thrown free when the explosion launched the stove overboard. That's why it was still in one piece when most of the deck and cabin had been blown to toothpicks.

"Will!" he called again with growing urgency.

The *Phoenix* was completely engulfed in flames now. As he watched, a large charred section of stern broke off and disappeared below the waves. The rest of the schooner resettled herself, rocking to and fro into a new balance. Could there be anybody alive on there? Surely he wasn't the only one left?

"Will!" he bellowed. "Lyssa! Ian! Charla!" A pause. "J.J.!" He'd even be happy to see J.J. at this point.

"Luke!"

It was Will. No question about it this time. Careful not to lose his balance on the cabin top, Luke rose to his knees. It was almost completely dark now.

Then he saw it — a flailing arm. He stood up — did he dare stand up? There, twenty yards away, someone — Will? — was rolling in and out of the waves, clinging desperately to a mangled deck plank.

Luke flung himself back on his stomach and began to paddle. He looked up. Will wasn't an inch closer. Here in the open ocean, the wave action canceled out whatever progress he could manage. To save Will, he would have to swim for it.

Swim for it? Was he nuts? He was weak — could hardly force his arms into a dog paddle. A few minutes ago, he'd barely made it to the cabin top ten feet away. This was five times that distance — at least! And the same again coming back, dragging Will, who might be hurt or

SHIPWRECK

burned. It was insanity. He'd drown the both of them.

"I can't hang on much longer!" Will called.

The decision was made. A slim chance was better than no chance at all. Luke threw himself off the cabin top and hit the water. He drove each stroke deep into the waves, fighting the sea and his own exhaustion. His eyes stung from salt, but he forced himself to keep them open. *Can't lose him. Can't lose him.* He tried to call Will's name and came up choking on seawater.

Alone! Where was Will? Oh, no! He'd lost Will and — a frantic look backward — he could no longer see the floating cabin top!

He'd given up his raft — his one chance at survival — for nothing.

And then a wave broke, and Luke saw him, still clinging to the piece of deck —

"Will?" Luke blurted.

The boy's face was completely blackened with soot.

Will blinked in amazement. "Luke?" In that instant, Luke realized he must look the same.

He struggled to focus his racing mind on what was important. "Can you swim?"

"I — I'm not sure." Will seemed aimless and confused. "I found a piece of wood — "

"Hang on to it," Luke commanded. "It'll help us float."

Grabbing Will Red Cross style — oh, how he wished he'd paid better attention in that lifesaving class! — Luke started back in the direction of the cabin top. *We'll find it*, he told himself. If they didn't, they would both drown. Sidestroke — shuttle-kick. Will's deadweight threatened to drag him down.

"There's a cabin top floating up ahead," Luke managed to say between tortured breaths. His paddling arm throbbed with pain. "Can you see it?"

"Too dark," replied Will. He sounded sleepy.

"*Try!*" Luke demanded, wasting precious strength shaking his friend. "It's around here somewhere! It has to be!"

"There's nothing," insisted Will, a little more alertly.

Agony pulsed from every muscle in Luke's body, from his cramped feet to the aching knuckles that were locked on to Will's shoulder. It would be so easy to give up right now. There would be no disgrace in that. Who could have expected him to make it this far? The call to quit radiated from the very core of his being. *Just let go*, it seemed to say, *and surrender to the waves* . . .

SHIPWRECK

"Wait a minute," came Will's voice. "What's that?"

Luke kicked like he had never kicked before, as if he had reached down and opened a hidden supply of emergency energy. He screamed as he swam — from pain and rage but mostly from sheer effort.

Whump! His head knocked against something.

"This is it!" he exclaimed. "Will, we found it!"

Luke pushed Will, plank and all, onto the cabin top. Then he scrambled on himself and collapsed, choking and gasping.

"The others? Lyssa?" asked Will.

Luke could only shake his head.

"*Nobody?*"

They turned to face the *Phoenix*. It was a floating bonfire. White-hot flames covered every inch of the schooner except the very peak of the foremast. The bow, which had hung so low, was now pointed up like a cannon as water flooded into the ruined stern.

"They abandoned ship," said Will. "They *must* have!"

Using the deck plank as an oar, Luke paddled alongside the doomed ship, looking for a path through the burning gasoline that coated the sea.

"Hey!" came a voice. "Over here!"

"Where?" chorused Luke and Will. It was pitch-dark now. The fire was the only light on the moonless night.

Suddenly, Luke saw a faint glimmer of canvas struggling through the waves. And attached to it —

"Ian!" Luke cried. "Drop that sail!"

"We need it!" Ian insisted, panting along.

"For *what?*"

Luke and Will almost capsized hauling Ian onto their raft. The younger boy was ready to sink to the bottom of the ocean rather than let go of a large piece of half-charred foresail and a yellow rubber rain hat. Quickly, Luke rolled to the far end of the cabin top to restore balance. The raft wobbled dangerously for a moment and stabilized.

"Where are the others?" rasped Luke.

Ian shrugged helplessly. "I was with J.J., but we got separated."

"What about my sister?" demanded Will.

"I thought she was with you."

"She *was!*" Will was frantic. "But she disappeared in the explosion!"

"And Charla?" asked Luke.

"Charla's — I mean she *was* — " Ian's eyes fell on the flaming hulk of the *Phoenix*. "Oh, God!"

SHIPWRECK

With an audible groan, the burning schooner seemed to give up the fight before their very eyes. Slowly — agonizingly slowly — the ship slid into the sea, following the angle of its raised bow. A split second before it disappeared beneath the waves, a dark shape plunged off the tip of the foremast.

It was a desperation dive, yet it was *perfect*. A graceful arc, and then the slim figure slipped into the ocean with barely a splash. It could have only been one person.

"Charla!" they chorused.

Pointing straight up to the sky, the flaming bowsprit of the *Phoenix* sank out of sight. CNC's schooner was no more. There was a mournful hiss as the ocean extinguished the blazing wreck. Suddenly, all light was gone, save for the few patches of burning gasoline.

Luke picked up the plank and began paddling toward the spot where the girl had entered the water. "Charla!"

"I hope she knows to splash around and make noise," Ian said. "Style counts for nothing when you're being rescued."

They made their way through the gloom, bellowing her name.

"Over here!" She was plowing through the waves in a textbook freestyle.

Luke had to smile. "Maybe we can tie her to the raft and she'll tow us home."

The light mood didn't last long. As they heaved Charla on board, the cabin top overbalanced, flipping them all into the water. Several more tries gave the same result.

"It's too much weight!" Ian shouted, treading water. "This thing won't hold more than three of us!"

"What are we supposed to do?" asked Charla, her voice shrill with panic. "Go eeny-meeny, and the loser drowns?"

"Nobody's going to drown!" panted Luke. "You three climb on; I'll hang off the side!"

Charla was aghast. "Are you crazy? You're shark bait!"

"We'll switch every few hours," Luke decided. "It's only going to get more crowded when we find the others." He cupped his hands to his mouth. "Lyssa! J.J.!"

But his calls went unanswered. And when the last of the gasoline had burned itself out, the cabin top bobbed and rolled in a silent world of limitless black.

CHAPTER SIXTEEN
Tuesday, July 18, 0700 hours

Morning found the makeshift raft still adrift in the middle of nowhere. Luke, Will, and Ian slept the sleep of the exhausted side by side on the tight cabin top. Only Charla, who hung in the water, was awake. She scanned the dawn-gray waves, hoping against hope for some sign of Lyssa and J.J.

Nothing. Less than nothing. No debris from the *Phoenix* — not even a toothpick.

She checked Ian's *National Geographic Explorer* watch — a cheap mail-order thing, but hey, it was the only one that still worked.

Gently, she shook Will's arm. "Will, wake up."

"Lyssa?" murmured Will.

"No, it's me. Your turn for shark-bait position."

"It's the middle of the night," he complained.

"It's seven A.M. Two hours, same as always."

"No fair," grumbled Will, sliding himself over the side.

The switch had to be made carefully to avoid flipping over, but after the long night, they were getting better at it. Charla squeezed herself gingerly on board. Before she lay down, she got her

ISLAND

first real look at the cabin top. It was the galley roof, all right, just like Luke had said. The name of the *Phoenix* had been painted there. Now all that remained were three letters: NIX.

A rueful laugh escaped her lips.

Luke opened a bleary eye. "What?"

She pointed. "We're the *S.S. Nix.*"

"It figures," he groaned. "Come on, get some sleep."

But as the tropical sun rose higher and higher in the cloudless sky, sleep became difficult and finally impossible. On board the *Phoenix*, the sails had provided comfortable shade. Now the blazing heat was almost unbearable.

That's when Ian explained why he had risked his life to save a charred piece of the foresail. "It's sun protection," he explained. "We dip it in the water and then pull it over us. See?"

Luke had to admit it was a lot cooler under the dripping canvas. He repositioned the scrap of sail so that it covered Charla, who was once again in the shark-bait spot.

"What's the hat for?" asked Will.

"To collect rain," replied Ian. "It's rubber, so it won't leak. We can't drink the ocean water because of the salt. We need freshwater."

Charla was amazed. "How did you think of all this in the middle of a burning boat?"

Ian shrugged. "I once saw this show on ship-wrecks on the Discovery Channel. The big difference between who survived and who didn't was thirst and sunburn."

"Geez, that's smart," commented Will. "I sure hope Lyssa thought of that when she — I mean, *if* . . ." His voice trailed off.

"Did anybody see her last night?" asked Luke.

"No, not Lyssa," Charla said slowly. "I remember J.J. trapped on the foredeck. But once the sail caught fire, I lost him in the smoke."

"I was with him for a few seconds," Ian added. "Then the mast came down and we got split up. But he was definitely okay. I heard him calling for me."

"Did you see him after that?" asked Luke.

Ian shook his head. "But I don't think he went down with the ship. I mean, the heat was unbelievable. The fire was spreading — there was nowhere to stand. Sooner or later, he would have had to jump."

Charla looked alarmed. "Then why didn't we see him in the water? Or at least hear him? And what about Lyssa?"

There was a sober silence, broken only by the *slap, slap* of the water lapping at the wooden platform.

Then Will spoke. "Aw, Lyss, I knew you'd bust it."

Luke gazed at him in concern. "Will? You okay?"

"That's the last thing I said to her," he replied quietly. "She rebuilt the engine on guts alone, and that was the thanks she got from me."

Nobody could offer a single word of comfort.

Will looked out over the miles of empty sea. *I should have been an only child.* How many times had he said it? How many more had he thought it? And now . . .

If Lyssa's okay, he vowed, *I'll —*

Automatically, his mind sorted through the dozens of promises he might offer up. Suddenly, they all seemed so meaningless — a collection of tacky New Year's resolutions.

He finally settled on the one he feared he might not get the chance to make good on:

If Lyssa's okay, I'll never be mean to her again.

CHAPTER SEVENTEEN
Wednesday, July 19, 0030 hours

Night was the worst. The darkness closed in like an endless canopy of absolute blackness. With no moon, Luke couldn't even see Charla a few inches away.

"Ian, what time is it?" came Will's voice from the void.

"It's twelve-thirty," Luke said irritably. "We just checked two minutes ago."

"I don't really care about the time. I just want to see the light." He was talking about the tiny light on Ian's watch. "Every time I fall asleep, I dream that I've gone blind. I need to see something."

"Try looking at the stars," suggested Ian from the water beside the raft.

"I can't sleep on my back."

Luke was growing impatient. "You might have noticed this isn't the Hilton. Make do."

As Will struggled to roll over, he kneed Charla in the thigh. Reacting in shock, she elbowed Luke in the ribs. And as he jackknifed in pain, the edge of the raft dipped, dunking Ian underwater. The tiniest move had a ripple effect through the whole

ISLAND

group. It was that close and uncomfortable.

Sputtering, Ian checked his watch. "Twelve-thirty-three," he reported.

"Do it again. I missed it," said Will.

Although the temperature never dropped below seventy degrees, the night felt almost bone-chilling after the burning heat of the day. Taking turns in shark-bait position kept the castaways soaked to the skin, and the six-hour shifts out of the water did little to dry them off. The seas had picked up, and even the smallest waves washed over the cabin top.

They had tried again to find an arrangement where all four of them could sit on the raft at the same time. But after repeated dunkings and one real scare — the raft had almost bobbed away — they had decided that three riders and one shark bait was the only way to go.

Secretly, Luke didn't mind his shifts in the water, especially at night. While the air cooled down, the ocean stayed warm. It also provided protection from the wind. In fact, the only problem with shark-bait position was exactly what the name implied: sharks. Dangling there, you were a sitting duck for any sea creature that wanted to take a bite.

They had seen fins cutting the surface around the raft, but Ian insisted they were dolphins. "A shark fin is larger and more triangular, with a small slot near the bottom."

The kid was an endless fountain of information that nobody wanted to hear. "*Carcharadon carcharias*, the great white shark, could destroy this raft in a single bite. A really big specimen can swallow a person whole."

"Let me guess," said Will. "They did sharks on *National Geographic Explorer*."

"Don't knock it," mumbled Luke. "Those guys make one heck of a watch."

"I'm more afraid of the tiger shark," Ian went on seriously. "They're pack hunters and they can go into what's called a 'feeding frenzy — ' "

"Enough," interrupted Charla, who was in shark-bait position at the time. "I don't want to hear another word about it until *you're* hanging down here like a worm on a hook."

With the heat of the second day came thirst — thirst beyond anything they had experienced before in their lives. It was a familiar feeling at first — like the desire to hit the water fountain after a long boring class on a steamy June afternoon. But then it transformed into something deeper and stronger. There was no water fountain; there never would be. Throats burned. Lips cracked and bled.

Charla held the empty rubber hat. "Did that show about shipwrecks mention what to do if it doesn't rain?" she asked Ian.

"It'll rain," the boy promised.

The other three noticed, though, that this was one statement with no backup research from television.

There was hunger too — they hadn't eaten for a full forty-eight hours. The hunger mingled with the thirst to produce a never-ending dull ache that gripped each survivor from head to toe. It was a pain that radiated lack — lack of water, lack of food, lack of sleep, lack of comfort.

As the afternoon progressed, a few clouds appeared overhead. The castaways cheered them on as if the Super Bowl were being played out in the sky above them. A cool wind picked up, creating a chop on top of the water.

"All right, rain!" croaked Will. "Let's see what you've got!"

"We should trap water in the sail and drink it as it runs over the sides," Ian lectured. "Get as much as you can while it's still raining, because the hat won't hold a lot."

Luke had his hands out, palms up, waiting for the downpour.

It didn't come. Or, at least, not to them. They could see it raining a quarter-mile ahead of them, but they didn't get a single drop. There was genuine agony on the cabin top when the overcast thinned out and the sun broke through once again.

"No fair!" Will moaned, addressing the clouds. "Come back! Come back! Where's our rain?"

That night, Luke hung over the side, drifting in and out of an uneasy world of half-dreams. You never really slept in shark-bait position for fear of slipping off the raft and being lost forever. Suddenly, he heard a strange gurgling noise. It sounded like — drinking?

Will had edged his way forward and was now lying with his head over the side, swallowing greedily.

Aghast, Luke grabbed him by the collar and pulled his face out of the water. "Don't do that, Will! It's suicide!"

It was so dark that all Luke could see were Will's eyes. They seemed dazed, glassy, and feverish. "It's water, man! Who cares if there's salt in it?"

Luke shook him angrily. "That salt dehydrates you worse than going thirsty. You might have just cut a whole day off the time you can hold out! Maybe more!"

"No, it's okay!" Will insisted urgently. "Listen,

I figured out why we never found Lyssa and J.J. — they've been rescued already!"

"It doesn't make sense, Will," Luke argued. "How could rescuers spot them and miss us?"

"J.J. was right all along!" Will explained. "The captain and Radford are watching us! The others were in trouble, so they moved in and saved them. They haven't saved us yet because we're doing okay."

"Okay?" Luke repeated. "You call this okay? We're starving — *dying* of thirst! One of us has to hang in the water or we all drown. *Think!* A shark could bite me in two this minute, and the rescue boat would get here in time to save three and a half people. There *is* no bigger trouble than what we're in right now. If there were rescuers out there, they'd be rescuing us!"

Will looked at him pityingly. "Take it easy, Luke. Everything's under control. Don't panic."

Luke stared back at him in growing horror. The kid was totally serious. There was only one explanation for this: Hunger, thirst, grief, and fear were causing Will Greenfield to lose his grip on reality.

How long would it be before the same thing happened to the rest of them?

CHAPTER EIGHTEEN
Thursday, July 20, 1645 hours

When it finally rained, everybody was unprepared. Luke and Charla both pulled the sail canvas in opposite directions, spilling most of the water onto the raft, where it rolled off into the sea. Will had the shakes and the dry heaves from drinking salt water. He tried to stand up and catch the drops in his cupped hands but succeeded only in tumbling off the cabin top headfirst into the ocean. By the time they managed to haul him back on board, the tropical cloudburst was over. The rain hat held about an inch and a half of water. It was enough for two mouthfuls each.

The water was warm and tasted a little salty — the rain hat, along with the raft and everything on it, was crusted with sea salt. But it was freshwater — their first in three days.

"Every little bit helps," muttered Luke in disgust. "What a joke! It's better to have nothing than a thimbleful."

"This was just enough to remind us how much we need and we're not getting," Charla agreed mournfully.

Will's stomach was in such bad shape that he

ISLAND

couldn't even keep his share down. He took one gulp and spit up over the side.

The other three looked on in agony. To them, nothing could be sadder than the thought of wasted water.

Boredom became as much of a problem as hunger and thirst. Minutes rolled into hours, which rolled into days with a dreary gray sameness. The overwhelming dullness canceled out every other emotion — even, at last, fear. It teamed up with the body's weakness to sink Luke into an almost sleepy fog.

A couple of days before, his every thought had been of rescue. Now it seldom crossed his mind. He didn't expect to be rescued; sometimes he was so numb that he couldn't have cared less whether he was rescued or not. There were moments when the Coast Guard could have rear-ended the cabin top and he probably wouldn't even have noticed.

He could tell he wasn't the only one. By the next day, Will had virtually stopped talking. He lay on his side under the damp sail, his parched lips slightly apart, drifting in and out of a light doze. If anyone spoke to him, he only answered about half the time. More often than not, his replies made no sense at all.

When Ian informed Will that it was his turn for shark-bait position, he was told, "You know, Lyssa came in second in chess club, but she lost to Seth Birnbaum in the final."

By unspoken agreement, Luke, Ian, and Charla stopped asking Will to take his turn dangling in the ocean. One thing was obvious: If they spent much more time lost at sea, Will was not going to survive.

From the start, Charla had stubbornly insisted on exercising, doing aquatics, and taking short swims during her shark-bait time. Now she hung off the edge of the raft, gazing at the horizon with vacant eyes and never making an unnecessary move.

Of the four of them, only Ian seemed to have the energy to talk. He filled the endless hours with a tedious monologue of every single detail he knew about the ocean. And he knew plenty.

"Hey, Ian," mumbled Luke listlessly. "Don't you think it's time to close up the Encyclopedia Boronica and give us all a break?"

The boy flushed redder than his harsh sun- and wind-burn. "I talk too much," he said sadly. "I'm boring."

"I was just kidding." Luke was instantly sorry. "If it wasn't for you and the Discovery Channel, we'd be dead already. Talk all you like."

"I shouldn't," Ian conceded. "When you talk, the moisture inside your mouth evaporates, and you get dehydrated faster."

"Man," sighed Luke, "I'd give anything for a Gameboy. Or even a lousy deck of cards."

"I'd settle for a piece of string," Charla put in. "I used to know how to do Cat's Cradle."

"A lot of people don't know that blue whales are bigger than sperm whales." Ian took up his lecture. "They said on TV once that a blue whale's tongue weighs as much as an elephant."

"Ian — " Luke groaned.

"Seriously," the boy continued earnestly. "Look at that one over there. It must be thirty yards long."

Luke sat up in sudden surprise. "What one over where?"

"The whale," Ian insisted. "He's spouting water twenty feet high."

Luke stared. Before them the Pacific Ocean stretched, blue-gray and unbroken, to the horizon. There was no whale. He exchanged a worried glance with Charla and turned back to the younger boy.

"In that show about shipwrecks," he asked carefully, "what were the warning signs? I mean, how do you know when you're not going to make it?"

"Slow, lazy behavior," Ian replied. "Too much sleeping. Followed by hallucinations — people see things that aren't really there." He pointed. "Look — he's spouting again."

CHAPTER NINETEEN
Sunday, July 23, 1320 hours

Sun.

Luke was aware of its harsh glare even through closed eyes. He could feel the pain of sunburn on his face and arms.

But no. This wasn't right. There was supposed to be protection. Something white. A large sheet — a sail? Where was his corner?

He spoke to the others. *Cover me up, here. I'm getting fried.* Funny — why couldn't he hear his own voice? *Come on, guys.* This time he held his hand to his mouth. His lips weren't moving either. His brain was talking, but it didn't seem to be connected to his tongue.

He had been in shark-bait position for two — three — how many days now? He would have loved to stretch out and sleep.

Hey, Charla, he tried to say. *Your turn.*

Was she ignoring him? No, his mouth was still not working. He couldn't expect people to read his mind — especially not unconscious people. And they were. All three of them.

Will had been first, even before their second rainstorm. They'd forced water down his throat,

SHIPWRECK

but it hadn't revived him. And anyway, Ian and Charla had gone down the very next day. Poor Ian. None of them deserved this, but the little kid was the most innocent of them all, guilty of nothing more than watching too much TV. Now here he lay, with a bird perched on his head.

A bird?

No, that couldn't be right. Luke's eyes were playing tricks on him again. There were no birds out here in the open ocean. They had to stay within flying range of land.

He'd been having a lot of hallucinations. Like a couple of hours ago — days ago? — when he'd had a very clear memory of Reese stashing that gun in his locker. Crazy! How could he remember what he hadn't seen? Of course, he *knew* it had been Reese, even though the jerk denied it. So Luke's hazy mind had put together what must have happened and constructed a fake memory out of it.

It was not very different from Ian's whale — the beginning of the end.

It was a terrible end, Luke decided, because your last thought is the one where you realize you're losing your mind.

What was this? His body wriggled with revulsion as a long slimy shape attacked and wrapped itself around his neck. He let go of the raft and tore at it, ripping it to pieces. An eel? The tentacle of a giant squid? Through the fog of his confusion, he struggled to focus on what was in his hands.

Seaweed. Another hallucination. There was no seaweed in the open ocean either.

Splashing wildly, he managed to regain his grip on the raft. He had no idea why he was struggling so hard to preserve his doomed life a few extra minutes. What was the point? They were all dead, courtesy of Rat-face.

Rat-face — what a waste of a thought when there weren't many thoughts left.

Luke forced the mate's picture out of his brain. But its replacement image was too painful — a fleeting glimpse of his parents, who would mourn him. He closed his eyes tightly, but they were still there.

Make this stop! he tried to exclaim.

And when he opened his eyes again, he saw the fin.

Another hallucination?

Maybe, but this one struck him right in the ribs.

Shark! He tried to sound the warning, but the technical difficulties between his brain and his mouth still existed.

The raft bobbed away from the fin. Luke held

SHIPWRECK

his breath. The long shape in the water followed.

Another bump! Luke braced himself for the ripping, tearing bite that was to come next. But when he looked down, he saw the bottle-nosed snout of a dolphin.

This time it nudged the raft, and Luke was pulled along. He remembered somewhere in Ian's rambling lecture stories of dolphins pushing drowning sailors to safety. Surely this was the final hallucination, the last desperate brain impulses of a dying mind. He was amazed at how vivid it was — the white water roaring around him, the pounding of surf, the sudden thump of his dangling feet onto shallow sandy bottom.

Instinct took over — instinct and a frantic desire to die on dry land. Luke pushed the raft with every ounce of strength that remained in his exhausted body — kept on pushing, even when the cabin top dug into the beach and would move no more.

CHAPTER TWENTY
Sunday, July 23, 1555 hours

It was a drenching rain, a downpour, a deluge. As Luke slept, he dreamed that hundreds of tiny jackhammers were working on his face. The water quickly puddled up in his eye sockets and in the hollows on both sides of his nose. The trickle found his lips.

Water. Real water. Drinking water.

He sat bolt upright and stared around him in confusion. Palm trees. Jungle. A sandy beach.

He leaped up too fast, toppling over and landing in the surf. As he lay there in the shallows, an amazing sight met his eyes. The cabin top was jammed into the heavy sand just above the tide line. Will, Charla, and Ian lay upon it, still unconscious. Between Ian and Charla sat the rain hat, propped up by their bodies and full to overflowing with freshwater.

Luke crawled through the surf, bent over the raft, and stuck his head into the hat, drinking greedily. Nothing had ever tasted better. He could have happily remained there, draining the hat dry. It took a gigantic effort to pull himself away.

SHIPWRECK

Carefully, like he was handling nitro, he picked up the hat and held it to Will's cracked lips.

Luke watched the precious water roll down Will's chin. Finally, a tiny amount managed to find its way into his mouth. It dribbled down the back of his throat; he choked suddenly. Poor Will still couldn't keep anything down.

He moved on to Charla. He propped her up on the sand and began by wetting her lips with water from his finger. The girl opened her eyes and her mouth at the same time.

"Where — ?"

"Drink," Luke interrupted.

And she did, gulping so deeply that she ended up choking too, although not a drop was wasted.

The two attended to Ian. The younger boy smacked his lips at the first taste. Then he swallowed and kept on swallowing. He sat up, grabbed the hat, and chug-a-lugged.

In the spot where he had been lying, the raft still said NIX.

"Save some for Will," ordered Luke.

Charla looked worried, still disoriented. "I don't know," she said nervously. "Will's really messed up. He hasn't moved in days."

Luke spilled water on Will's upturned face and forced some past the parched lips. The boy choked again, but this time the water stayed down. Luke dropped to his knees and gently slapped Will's cheeks. "Come on, Will. Join the party."

No response.

All three hunkered down and tried everything they could think of to rouse their friend. No amount of shaking, pinching, chafing, and massaging had any effect.

"He's definitely alive," concluded Ian, "but there's no telling when he'll snap out of it. It could be five minutes from now; it could be never." He flushed at Luke's angry look and explained, "I saw it on the Learning Channel."

Charla looked around. "What *is* this place?"

"Who cares?" Luke replied. "It *isn't* the raft. It's land, and that's all that matters."

"It must be an island," mused Ian. "There's no way we could have drifted far enough to reach continental land. This is a miracle! To hit an island in this part of the Pacific is as unlikely as two bullets striking each other head-on. We lucked out."

"Luck had nothing to do with it," said Luke. "It was that dolphin."

SHIPWRECK

They stared at him. "Dolphin?" repeated Charla.

"You must have seen it," Luke insisted. "It pushed us in to the island. Just like you told us, Ian. Dolphins try to help people. This one saved our lives."

"You must have been hallucinating," Ian said kindly. "There wasn't any dolphin. A big wind blew us here. Don't you remember? One minute we were drifting, and the next we were being carried along by a hot wind. It felt sort of like the dryer in a car wash."

"You're both crazy!" exclaimed Charla. "Nothing brought us here. We swam in. We lined up along the raft and kicked like crazy. When I close my eyes, I can still see us doing it."

They stared at one another, bewildered, as the rain beat down.

Ian seemed to choose his words very carefully. "I think maybe we're *all* right — inside our minds."

By that time, the rubber hat was full again. Charla drank some more and passed it around.

Luke raised it like a champagne glass. "To *us*, man! I can't believe we made it!" His face fell suddenly. "And to those who didn't make it."

It was a painful thought, one that packed the wallop of a sledgehammer. But the castaways had more pressing problems — the need for food, the need for shelter, the need to help their unconscious friend. So they set aside their grieving and made plans to explore the island that had risen from the sea to save their lives.

ISLAND

For Socrates and Krista Panageas

PROLOGUE

On the beach of the small coral island with no name sat all that was left of the schooner *Phoenix*. It was a tiny wooden raft, six feet long and not quite four feet wide, and had once been the roof over the proud ship's galley. Now it was scorched by fire, battered by weather, and encrusted with sand and sea salt. Barely visible through the battle scars were three letters: N-I-X. The rest of the *Phoenix*'s name, along with the ship herself, lay at the bottom of the deepest part of the Pacific Ocean.

On this piece of flotsam, four young people had braved seven days and nights at the mercy of the sea. Their captain was gone, drowned. The mate had deserted them, leaving them to die. Two of their companions were lost without a trace. Close to death from hunger, thirst, and the blazing sun, the four survivors had ridden the wind and waves. Three of them were in a desperate condition, the fourth deeply unconscious when they washed ashore on this rugged cay, six thousand miles west of Los Angeles, eleven hun-

SURVIVAL

dred miles south of Tokyo, and nine hundred miles east of Hong Kong.

It was a tiny dot in the vast ocean, a dot that appeared on no maps, overlooked no shipping lanes, and was observed by no passing aircraft — an island with no name.

CHAPTER ONE
Day 1, 4:45 P.M.

They had survived forty-foot waves, an explosion and fire at sea, and a week adrift on a tiny raft. But now Luke Haggerty, Charla Swann, and Ian Sikorsky faced their greatest challenge so far:

A coconut.

It had fallen off a tall palm, missing Luke's ear by inches. To three people who had put nothing but rainwater in their stomachs for seven long days, it represented what they needed most: food.

Charla, the city kid, turned it over in her hands. "Where's the opener on this thing?"

"What do you expect?" Luke shot back. "A pull tab?"

It was a joke, but it underscored the tension and fear in the group. Will Greenfield, the fourth survivor, lay unconscious and unmoving on a beach not far away. He needed medical attention. Probably they all did. But they were far from any doctor or hospital, stranded on a — on a what? It had to be an island. But how big an island? And where? It was anybody's guess.

SURVIVAL

Be grateful, Luke reminded himself. *You're alive.*

But he was not grateful. Captain Cascadden wasn't alive. Lyssa Greenfield and J.J. Lane weren't alive. Luke felt their absence in his every breath, an overwhelming sadness that weighed on him as heavily as exhaustion and dehydration.

What was so special about Luke that he deserved to live when others had perished? Why was he still here?

Good luck?

Or maybe the luck wasn't so good after all. The hunger felt more powerful than death. Forget hunger pangs. Luke hadn't felt those in days. Instead, there was a grinding hollow emptiness where his stomach should have been. The sensation was so intense that it seemed to go outside the limits of his skin. With it came a nervous trembling weakness that was only going to get worse.

And here was this coconut . . .

"You have to break it," explained Luke, banging it on the damp ground. "You have to get through that tough skin." He snatched up a rock and began bashing it against the greenish shell. "It takes patience!" He picked it up and hurled it at a tree. "Open, you miserable, rotten — "

It bounced off with a thwack and hit the ground, unbroken.

Ian spoke up. "I once saw a documentary about native tribes who could crack coconuts with their bare hands."

"Did you bother to find out how they did it?" Luke asked irritably.

Ian shook his head. "That was in Part Two. They showed it the night I left for this trip."

The three exchanged a stricken look. It was hard to believe that, barely two weeks ago, they had been safe at home, packing for Charting a New Course, a monthlong boat excursion meant to help troubled youth.

Charla sounded slightly hysterical. "It's like starving to death at Thanksgiving dinner!" she cried. She picked up the fallen coconut, spun around, and hurled it like a discus into the jungle.

Crack!

"It broke!" exclaimed Ian. "I heard it!"

They rushed into the dense trees, but their coconut was nowhere to be seen. Vines and underbrush snatched at their legs.

Luke grabbed a branch and began hacking away at the tangle. The coconut! The food! It had to be down here somewhere! He began to flail wildly, like a crazed golfer in knee-deep rough.

He roared in anger; it was stupid, he knew — a waste of valuable energy when there was so little left. But his frustration mixed with his hunger, and he didn't care, couldn't help himself. . . .

"Luke!" Charla grabbed him from behind. "Stop it! It's only a coconut."

"Guys!" came Ian's excited voice. "Over here!"

They followed his call to a small grove of leafy tropical trees and shrubs. There the younger boy was gathering an armload of strange green fruits that had fallen to the ground.

Charla wrinkled her nose. "What stinks?"

"These are durians," Ian explained breathlessly. "They have a strong odor, but they're food." He broke one open against a tree trunk and handed half to Luke. The powerful smell tripled.

Luke stared at it. "You're kidding, right?" The thick skin was covered in spikes. It looked more like a deadly weapon than a fruit.

Charla accepted a piece, handling it as if it might explode. "But — how do we know it isn't poison?"

Ian plucked out a gigantic seed and began to eat the grayish mush around it. "There was this documentary on TV — " he began, mouth full.

Luke and Charla locked eyes. They had

learned from experience that Ian was never wrong about something he'd seen on television. His stockpile of knowledge had saved their lives more than once on the raft.

They fell on the offering like starving sharks. It wasn't good, Luke reflected. It wasn't even acceptable. But in his voracious hunger, he barely noticed, gorging himself on fruit the consistency of gritty pudding, but with an odd garlicky flavor. Back home, he wouldn't have given this stuff table room. But here he ate greedily, even crunching the rock-hard seeds because Ian said they needed the protein.

The feast soon turned into a frenzy. After no food for so long, once they started eating, they couldn't stop themselves. The three stumbled around the grove in a fever of appetite, tripping and falling over the dozens of discarded rinds even as they rushed to break open new fruit. The rough spikes scratched their knees and shins, yet none of them felt the sting. Nothing mattered, nothing but the breathless race to get on the outside of as much nourishment as humanly possible.

As he stuffed himself, at long last Luke could feel his stomach again, back where it belonged and comfortably full. The sensation came along with something unexpected — sudden, overpowering sleepiness. All at once, his eyelids were so heavy that he couldn't keep them from closing.

Drowsy panic. Had they poisoned themselves?

The others must have experienced it too. Just before he lost consciousness, he heard Charla say, "God, what did we eat? I can't stay awake!"

Seconds later, the three of them lay motionless, the remnants of their feast still scattered around them.

CHAPTER TWO
Day 1, 10:50 P.M.

Locker inspection.

It flashed before Luke's eyes in a series of still pictures: The assistant principal flipping through his untidy collection of books and sneakers. A pause to wave those sweaty gym shorts to everybody in the hall — the guy was a real comedian. And then . . .

A small hard shape in his wadded-up backpack; stubby fingers drawing it out — a thirty-two-caliber pistol.

"It's not mine, Mr. Sazio!"

Even now, lying unconscious in the jungle of a deserted island nine thousand miles away, Luke protested his innocence.

"Somebody framed me!"

And just like it had happened in real time, he was not believed.

The rush began: the trial, the choice — six months in Williston Juvenile Detention Facility, or a program called CNC — Charting a New Course. Four weeks of sailing aboard the *Phoenix*, a majestic schooner. There he would

SURVIVAL

learn discipline, cooperation, and respect for law and order.

The images changed. He could hear the tremendous explosion, feel the hot wind of the blast on his face, see the approaching wall of fire. . . .

Something snuffled, and it wasn't an explosion. Luke awoke with a start. It was so dark that, for an instant, he thought he was back on the raft. A sliver of moon provided the only light.

Then he saw the creature. It was just a few inches away, staring back at him with glowing red eyes.

Luke gasped in shock and revulsion. Instinct told him to back up. But flat on the ground, he had nowhere to go.

The beast retreated a couple of steps, snorting and puffing. It was four feet long, seemingly all head and bull neck, with a body that tapered to short legs and a tail. On either side of the flat snout curled small gleaming white tusks that gave the animal the appearance of sporting a well-groomed mustache.

A boar! Luke thought. A wild boar! And he was lying here helpless. . . .

All in one motion, he rolled away and scrambled to his knees. The boar was startled and thundered into the jungle, its massive head pumping up and down like a piston as it ran.

Luke squinted around the clearing, making out the shapes of his two companions, still lying there asleep. At least, he *hoped* they were asleep. He stood up and felt a paralyzing cramp grip his stomach.

He doubled over and tried not to panic. "If it were poison, you'd be dead already," he told himself out loud.

They had eaten some very weird stuff — too much, too fast after a week of no food at all. That had to be a shock to the system, and Luke's stomach was letting him know it.

An itch on his cheek took his attention from his digestion. He reached up and scratched. Bumps. At least a dozen. Bug bites, all over his face. His eyelid was starting to swell. There were welts on his arms too, and the bare part of his legs below his ragged shorts. On his head, even, beneath his thick brown hair! While he'd been sleeping, he had provided a banquet for the local island insects. He could hear the buzzing in his ears. He flailed his arms, but the sound didn't go away.

Charla stirred and immediately curled into a ball. "Oh, my stomach! What was in that fruit? Cyanide?"

"I think we just overdid it," Luke groaned.

SURVIVAL

She was unconvinced. "Are you sure? I'm breaking out in a rash. I itch all over!"

"Bugs!" Luke exclaimed, slapping and swatting. All at once, a thought came to him that made him forget insects and stomach cramps. "Will!" he exclaimed in horror.

Ian sat bolt upright. "He's awake?"

"We just left him there on the beach!"

"Well," began Charla, working hard to sound calm, "it's not like he can go anywhere — "

"I saw a wild boar tonight," Luke said breathlessly. "It didn't hurt me, but Will can't defend himself. We've got to get back there!"

They ran through the dense brush, stumbling with heavy legs over the spaghetti of vines. Luke tried to will his feet to step higher, but he couldn't seem to summon the energy.

"Hold it! Hold it!" Charla grabbed him by the arm and stopped him. "Do you remember how to find the beach? I don't."

The three looked around, struggling to sharpen senses that were dulled by fatigue and discomfort. In the darkness, all directions seemed equally possible.

"I can't see it," Luke said finally. "I can barely see you guys."

"Be quiet," ordered Ian. "Now, what do you hear?"

"I hear mosquitoes, and lots of them!" moaned Charla. "Let's get out of here!"

"Listen to the silence," Ian insisted.

This time Luke fought the impulse to run from the insects that were devouring him. Instead, he forced himself to open his ears and mind. There was the buzzing, sure. Against a backdrop of nothing, it seemed as loud as a squadron of planes. But slowly, he became aware of other, quieter sounds — the scurrying of small nocturnal birds and animals; the rustle of the wind in palm fronds; and, over it all, a distant, rhythmic pounding.

His brain was working in slow motion, so there was a delayed reaction. "The surf!" he exclaimed finally.

Ian pointed. "This way!"

A few minutes later, they broke out of the trees. Running had served to clear their heads a little. Luke offered up a high five that Charla took a weak slap at. The celebration was short-lived.

An indentation in the soft sand showed the spot where Will had been lying.

Their friend was nowhere to be seen.

CHAPTER THREE
Day 1, 10:35 P.M.

When Will Greenfield finally regained consciousness, it was sudden, with a start. One moment he was in a faraway, dreamless place, and
the next he was sitting up, awake, alert. Wired,
even.

"Where am I?" His voice was hoarse,
scratchy. Man, he was thirsty! Hungry too. And
what a headache!

It was pitch-dark, but he could feel the sand
beneath him and hear the ocean.

What was going on? Had he fallen asleep at
the beach?

He tried to think, but he couldn't focus on anything past the pounding of his head and the relentless gnawing in his stomach. His brain was in
a fog. He could almost see it — waves of silvery
gray mist.

But mist shouldn't be visible in the blackness. . . .

Think! he ordered himself.

The last thing he remembered, he had been
on the plane bound for Guam and Charting a
New Course. His sister, Lyssa, got the extra pea-

ISLAND

nuts and — big surprise — refused to share.

Peanuts. He sure could use some peanuts now. . . .

Forget the peanuts! Think!

Guam. This must be Guam! But what happened to Charting a New Course? And where was Lyssa?

His freckled features formed a nervous frown. His parents had sent him and his sister halfway around the world for CNC. The trip was supposed to teach them to get along. It was a huge deal to Mom and Dad — big money too. If he missed it, they'd never forgive him. Lyssa was already their little darling. That would only get worse if everybody was mad at him.

He felt white-hot rage. Lyssa did this! She set him up so he would miss the trip. Only — why couldn't he remember her doing it? Why couldn't he remember how he got here at all?

He stood up — muscles very stiff. How long had he been sleeping? Wait a minute — these weren't the clothes he'd been wearing on the plane! He was clad only in shorts and a T-shirt, both absolutely ruined.

Oh, Lyssa was going to pay for this one. . . .

He began to explore the beach — slowly; his feet were unsteady. He felt as if he might overbalance and fall flat on his face at any moment.

SURVIVAL

There was just enough light for him to make out the ocean on one side and a jungle of palm trees on the other. What he couldn't make out was anything else — no people, no buildings, nothing. Guam wasn't exactly New York City, but it was a place with towns, an airport, a marina where the *Phoenix*, CNC's boat, was supposed to be parked.

Not parked, he reminded himself. *Moored*.

He stopped in his tracks. How would he know something like that? He was totally clueless when it came to sailing.

"*Will?*" came a voice from the distance.

Lyssa?

No, the voice was male.

"Will, where are you?"

Now *that* one was definitely a girl.

"Lyssa?" He broke into a sprint. "Lyss, I don't know what kind of a joke you think this is — "

He pulled up short. Two boys and a girl were running across the beach, staring at him as if he'd just come back from the dead. Lyssa was nowhere to be seen.

"Who are you?" demanded Will. "Where's my sister?"

They froze, eyes widening.

The first boy — the leader? — took a cautious step forward.

"Will, it's me. Luke. And Charla and Ian."

Will squinted at the strangers. Should he know these people? They seemed to know him. "Listen, I think I'm lost. I'm looking for a boat called the *Phoenix*. Know it?"

The three exchanged an uneasy glance.

"The *Phoenix* sank, Will," said Luke. "We were all on it."

"What are you talking about?" Will stormed. "I've never been on a boat in my life! Where's Lyssa?"

"She didn't make it," Charla said gently. "The four of us managed to get on the raft, but we never found Lyssa or J.J."

"I don't know any J.J.! I don't know you! Where's my sister?"

"Will, think!" urged Luke. "You have to remember! We were all together on the CNC trip. There was a storm and then an explosion. We're lucky to be alive!"

"Listen," Will said impatiently, "you've got the wrong guy. My boat trip hasn't started yet. I don't know anything about any shipwreck!"

Charla tried reason. "Please, Will. Try to remember! We were shipwrecked together. How else could we get to this island?"

"You mean Guam?" Will was exasperated. "I *flew* here! With my sister!"

SURVIVAL

"This isn't Guam," Luke said soberly. "We don't know where we are."

"That's *your* problem!" He looked past them into the gloom. "Lyssa! *Lyssa!*"

"It must be amnesia," Ian said in a low voice.

"You're crazy!" exclaimed Will.

"No, really," Charla pleaded. "You were so sick on the raft! You were unconscious for days — "

"That's a lie! What have you done with my sister?"

Luke stepped forward and put a comforting hand on Will's shoulder.

Wild with panic, Will shook him off and staggered back.

"Will, don't!" Charla cried. "We can help you!"

Like a hunted animal, Will stared from face to face. They were lying, all three of them. They were trying to trick him into — what?

He had no way of knowing. He was lost — so lost. But whatever was going on, these three were mixed up in it somehow. He was in trouble, and who knew what had happened to Lyssa!

Animal instinct took over. With an inarticulate cry, he wheeled on the sand and sprinted down the beach.

He stole a quick glance over his shoulder.

They were gaining on him! The girl ran like a cheetah. "Leave me alone!" he yelled. Desperately he made a right turn and disappeared into the jungle. Charla was hot on his heels.

"No!" cried Ian. "If we get lost in there, we won't even find one another!"

Charla stopped just inside the trees. "We can't just leave him!"

"We can't help him if we're worse off than he is," Luke argued. "We've got to stay cool."

"But — " She began to cry. "It starts bad and just gets worse and worse! Losing the captain was terrible enough. I keep seeing it in my sleep. Then Lyssa and J.J. And now Will — "

"We haven't lost him," soothed Luke. "Maybe the bugs will drive him out of there. They did it to us."

"And maybe they won't!" she sobbed. "He could trip and break a leg. He could fall unconscious again. There are wild boars out there!"

"They're not hunters," Ian put in. "The Discovery Channel did a show on them once. They can be nasty, but they won't hunt a fellow animal for food."

Charla was bitter. "Will's not an animal; he's our friend."

"In the jungle, we're all animals," Ian said seriously. "We have to hunt and forage to survive."

Luke eased himself down on the soft sand. "A wild pig means only one thing to me," he said, rubbing his stomach. "Bacon."

Charla sat beside him. "We can't even open a coconut. You expect to track a boar, kill it, skin it, and cook it? We don't even have a fire."

"That should be job one," Ian said positively. "A big bonfire would signal ships and planes that we're here. Then we could get Will to a doctor."

Charla looked out into the great blackness of the sea. "Do you *really* think we have a chance of being rescued from this place?"

Luke considered the problem. "The whole CNC thing is about isolation. They start you in Guam, which is nowhere, and they take you out to nowhere squared. And this" — he gazed around the beach — "this has to be even farther than that."

"But they'll definitely look for us," Ian argued. "I mean, they send in half the army when some balloonist or mountain climber gets lost. They'll search for us when we don't show up back in Guam."

"Searching and finding are two different things," Luke pointed out. "In case you haven't noticed, it's a really big ocean with thousands of islands that look exactly like this one. Who knows how long it could take to track us down?"

"Months," Charla predicted mournfully. "Years. Never, maybe."

Her words seemed to hang there for a long time, underscored by the steady pounding of the ocean.

It was Ian who finally broke the gloomy silence. "It's not impossible, you know. There are thousands of stories of survival in places like this."

"Maybe so," Luke said grimly. "But I'll bet there were even more that didn't get told because the people were never rescued. Remember, the Discovery Channel can't interview you when you've vanished off the face of the earth."

CHAPTER FOUR
Day 2, 11:55 A.M.

A single ray of tropical sunlight caught the left half of Ian Sikorsky's glasses. Carefully, the boy angled the lens to reflect the intensified beam onto the pile of leaves on the sand in front of him.

There was a breathless silence. Then —

"It's not burning," Charla observed, worried.

"The leaves are still a little damp." Ian's eyes never wavered from the tiny dot of light concentrated on the brush.

"No, they aren't," she said. "We've been drying them out on the beach for three hours."

"You've seen how it rains here. They're wet." A tiny but clear note of exasperation — Ian had little patience for people who disputed what was obvious.

There was an almost inaudible sizzle, and a tiny curl of smoke rose from the pile. And then — a newborn flame.

Charla let out a sigh of relief and realized she'd been holding her breath.

Luke was hard at work using vines to tie together a framework of branches for a lean-to shelter. He ran over to help Charla and Ian arrange kindling in a pyramid around the pile of burning leaves. Soon the fire was going strong. Larger and thicker pieces were added and the flames grew.

"How big does it have to be?" asked Charla.

"Big enough to be spotted from a distance at night," replied Ian.

"It'll be harder to see during the day," Luke pointed out.

"True," agreed Ian. "But if we notice a plane or boat, we can pile on wet leaves. That'll make a lot of smoke."

Wood gathering was a problem. Since they had no cutting tools, their fire had to be fueled by fallen branches and other deadwood. Stumps and thick logs were rare. Thinner twigs were plentiful, but they burned quickly. That meant a huge amount of wood had to be stockpiled to keep the fire going.

The three castaways made dozens of trips into the jungle that afternoon, returning with armload after armload of wood. It was backbreaking work. The sun was searingly hot, and the crushing humidity weighed them down as if they were wearing hundred-pound packs on their backs.

Luke was amazed they were able to do it all. Just yesterday, they had washed up on this island, more dead than alive. It showed what a long drink of water and some solid food could do.

In that area, things were improving. Just down the beach, a single spike of coral stuck out of the sand. Charla gave it its name: the can opener. Coconuts, tough, round, and stubborn, broke like eggs when smashed against it. That morning, she had shown why she was one of the country's top young athletes. She had shinnied up a thirty-foot palm tree as easily as she strolled the beach. From there, she sent a dozen coconuts plummeting to her friends on the ground. After durians, coconut meat seemed as delicious and substantial as a twelve-course meal. The sweet milk tasted better than any triple-chocolate shake Luke could remember.

They had also discovered banana trees. Finger bananas, Charla called them, because they were small — about as long as an index finger. They were light and sweet and plentiful. It was starting to look like starvation would be the least of their worries.

But that was only because they had a lot of worries, Luke reminded himself. Will . . .

He shook his head to clear it. Will was probably okay. They had to look after their own survival first. Then they could search for Will.

By midafternoon, the shelter was complete.

The three were as proud as if they had just built a skyscraper. It definitely wasn't beautiful, but it was a very functional structure. The framework of branches and vines was propped and tied against two trees at the edge of the jungle. Into it, they had tightly woven palm fronds to create an angled roof.

"It won't keep out the rain," Luke had said to Ian, who was the lean-to's designer.

"We'll put pieces of tree bark on top," Ian decided. "If you pile them thick enough, it's perfect for waterproofing."

Luke grinned at the boy. Ian had been sent on this trip because his parents were worried that he had no friends and spent all his time watching TV and surfing the Internet. But now, those hundreds of hours in front of the Learning Channel and *National Geographic Explorer* were starting to pay off. Without Ian's know-how, Luke reflected, they would all probably be dead.

Luke and Charla took the raft that had carried them to the island and propped it against one open end of their new home. The opposite side, which was going to serve as the entrance, they draped with a large, slightly charred piece of sail from the *Phoenix*. This had been saved by Ian from the burning boat and used as sun protection on the raft.

That left just the back end — the space between the two trees. There, Luke and Charla placed another framework of branches, with palm fronds basket-woven through the twigs.

"It's not exactly the Hilton," Luke said with a shrug, "but it'll keep us dry. The sand should be comfortable for sleeping."

They had been working nonstop since the sunrise had awoken them ten hours earlier. Now the castaways allowed themselves a thirty-second period of relaxation.

They were exhausted from their labors, and still weary from their ordeal on the raft, but when their eyes locked, there was perfect understanding and agreement among the three.

"Let's go get him," said Ian as they headed into the woods to search for Will.

CHAPTER FIVE
Day 2, 4:40 P.M.

At that moment, the three might not have recognized Will even if they'd found him. In a single night, their friend had changed. His face had been bruised by branches and scratched by the sharp edges of palm fronds during his frantic escape in the pitch-black. He couldn't believe how thick the foliage was here. At one point he had stumbled into a stand of ferns so dense that he'd been thrown back as if the plants themselves had pushed him away.

What was left of his body after that went to the mosquitoes — clouds of them, coming in waves like the Air Force on a bombing run. He'd tried slapping them away at first. But there were far too many — and too much of his skin left uncovered. Eventually, hundreds of bite-bumps grew together into a horrible shell of puffy red mottled skin. His face felt expanded, deformed. His eyelids were swollen partway shut. The discomfort was unbelievable — far more than itch. His entire body crawled with a churning irritation that scratching only made worse.

Sleep? — Hah! Who could sleep in a state

SURVIVAL

like that? Curled into a miserable ball on the ground, roots digging into his side, ants parading over him, mosquitoes . . .

Ugh, mosquitoes.

He had broken down during the night, screaming, *"How could you do this to me?!"* At that moment, he didn't care who heard him or even what happened to him. It was all so useless! He didn't even know who he was yelling at.

His parents? They had sent their son and daughter halfway around the world for a boat trip, but this couldn't have been their fault. Lyssa? She was rotten, sure, but not rotten enough to do *this.* Probably she was a victim just like he was.

Those kids? Luke, Charla, and that little guy — Ian?

Will peered out from behind a leafy fern and watched them disappear into the jungle, calling for him.

How did they know his name?

They had to be in on it somehow. They talked about Charting a New Course. And Lyssa . . .

Of course they could have gotten Lyssa's name from him. If only he could think straight!

It must be the mosquitoes. . . .

He stepped out onto the beach. A tiny droplet of blood hit the sand, and he quickly buried it with his tattered sneaker. He didn't want them to know he was watching them. He'd woken up with a leech clamped onto his cheek. It didn't hurt much — he barely noticed it, in fact, over all that itch. But the bite wouldn't stop bleeding.

The *creatures* they had here in Guam! Leeches, bugs, lizards, some kind of hairy wild pigs.

Frowning, he squinted at the crude shelter and the bonfire roaring beside it. If those kids were in on this, why were they living like cave people?

The shipwreck story, of course. Their whole lie was that the *Phoenix* had sunk, and they were marooned here. So they had to act like castaways. Only — why bother playing the game in the first place? Will was alone, stranded, defenseless. What threat did he pose to them?

His head pounded as he struggled to reason it out. Even though it was daylight, he still saw everything through the same silver-gray mist. But there wasn't a cloud in the sky! Maybe it was sun glare acting on eyes that were little more than slits.

A fresh blast of fear stiffened his body. They were after him! It was the only explanation. They needed him for something, and they couldn't leave until they had him.

Well, they won't get me!

SURVIVAL

He took a few steps back toward the jungle and froze.

This campsite was primitive, but it had fire, which was a lot more than he could say for his own sleeping arrangements. Although this was a hot climate, last night had been damp and chilly.

He rummaged through the woodpile and came up with a sturdy twig, which he held to the flame. In a moment he was wielding a torch. Tonight he would have his own fire.

His swollen eyes fell on the cabin top propped against the side of the shelter. He read the letters: N-I-X.

N-i-x . . . *Phoenix?*

He had a sudden fleeting vision of a tall ship. A schooner — two masts, her white sails gleaming in the sun as she glided through the harbor.

No, impossible. He mustn't let himself be duped.

He examined the sheet covering the entrance to the structure. It was canvas, with brown charring around one edge.

His fevered mind traveled back to Luke's words from the night before: *There was a storm and then an explosion. . . .*

An explosion.

"No," he said aloud. "You're trying to trick me. . . ."

He was about to bolt, to run for the trees, when he saw it. Just inside the shelter — two big bunches of finger bananas.

Food.

He set his torch down in the fire and attacked the meal with a ferocity that alarmed him. It was over in minutes, and he was still hungry, almost as if eating had unleashed his full appetite. And now dozens of peels lay on the sand, evidence of his presence there. He could get rid of them, but that wouldn't explain what happened to all those bananas. . . .

He stood up, mind racing. He couldn't let those kids know he was spying on them. He retrieved his torch and held it to the shelter. The dry twigs and bark went up like a tinderbox.

There, that should destroy the evidence. Except for footprints. And Will's looked no different than the hundreds made by those three kids. No way would they be able to tell they'd had a visitor. They'd have to blame the fire on the wind.

By the time he'd reached the trees, the entire lean-to was engulfed in flames.

SURVIVAL

CHAPTER SIX
Day 3, 9:05 A.M.

Stupid, thought Charla.
Stupid, stupid, stupid!

She dropped her armload of twigs for their new shelter. *Stupid to put the old one so close to the fire.* "What a waste of time," she complained.

Luke appeared, hauling a thin log that would be one of the main posts. "We're marooned on a deserted island," he reminded her. "Time is the one thing we've got lots of."

"Big joke," she muttered.

He awarded her an encouraging slap on the shoulder. "We were dumb. We'll know better next time. We won't put the lean-to where the wind can blow the fire into it."

She winced at the memory. By the time they'd returned from looking for Will, there had been nothing left but a pile of ash. Only their raft had been spared — the second blaze the cabin top had survived, although it was badly burned. The half name, NIX, was barely visible under the brown scorching.

ISLAND

"Come on," said Luke. "We need more vines."

In the jungle, they found Ian snapping branches off a large tree that had fallen over. "Jackpot," he called. "I'll bet there are enough sticks to fill in the whole roof and front."

Soon a huge pile of twigs sat on the soft ground beside them. Charla gathered up as many as she could carry and started back for the beach.

Suddenly, a long thin shape dropped from a treetop. It landed on Charla's shoulders and quickly wrapped itself around her neck.

Ian made the identification. *"Snake!"*

Charla tried to wrench it away, but the harder she pulled, the tighter the long body coiled around her.

"Yeow!" Needlelike teeth sunk into the skin just above her wrist.

Ian picked up a rock and smacked the snake on its squarish head. Dazed, it loosened its grip, and Luke managed to yank it off Charla.

"Get rid of it!" she commanded.

Luke threw. The snake was whirled away in a whiplike motion. It hit the ground and recovered with lightning quickness, lifting itself nearly vertical.

"Look at that muscle control," breathed Ian. "It's balanced on no more than a few inches of its tail."

"You know about these things?" Luke panted.

Ian threw his rock, missing the snake by inches. In a flash, it darted up a palm trunk and disappeared. "It's a brown tree snake," he explained. "We have to be more careful. There are zillions of them on Pacific islands like this."

"Never mind that," snapped Charla, holding her bleeding wrist. "Is it poisonous?"

The younger boy shook his head. "But you don't want the bite to get infected. You should soak it in salt water in the ocean."

"Good idea," agreed Luke. He turned to Charla. "Take a swim. We'll carry this stuff to the beach."

With long, powerful strokes, Charla cut through the waves. Her wounded wrist stung a little from the salt, but she was fine. Better than fine. She was amazed at how quickly her training had asserted itself. She could almost see the Olympic-sized pool at the Y. Breaststroke, butterfly, backstroke, freestyle — how many lengths had she done in that thing? A thousand? Ten thousand? At least. All of them timed by her father and his ever-present stopwatch.

She tried to judge her present pace, deducting time for wave motion and current. A breaker caught her in the face and brought her back to reality. Was she crazy? What did it matter if this swim took three seconds or three hours? She was shipwrecked in a primitive wilderness. She might never again see civilization, much less any swim team. Only a fanatic would continue training *now*.

Abruptly, she stopped swimming and stood on the sandy bottom. She was a fanatic when it came to training. That was how she'd gotten herself booked on the *Phoenix* in the first place.

On shore she could see Luke and Ian hauling armloads of wood out of the jungle. She felt a twinge of guilt. She should be helping instead of practicing for an event that was never going to take place. The sooner they were finished, the sooner they could continue their search for poor Will.

Bright flashes of silver caught her eye, and she looked down into the waist-deep water. A school of footlong fish darted all around her. She experienced a moment of fear — were they piranhas?

She relaxed. Whatever they were, they seemed just curious, investigating a novel shape in their ocean.

SURVIVAL

The next thought to flash through her mind was: food. Her years of training had made a healthy eater of her. She'd always said that she could survive happily on nothing but fruit. But after only a couple of days, if she saw another banana or coconut, she was going to scream.

Could she catch a fish with her bare hands? Were these things even edible? Ian would probably know, but by the time she could ask him, the school would be long gone.

It was a cruel reality out here in nature, yet in a way it was very fair. No judges to appeal to, no instant replay. You make a mistake and your boat sinks, or your shelter burns down. If she was going to do this, she had to do it *now*, without thinking.

A lightning thrust. She stabbed at the water and came up with a wriggling silver body.

Thunderstruck and delighted by her catch, she uttered a piercing shriek and began wading ashore, juggling the fish. Startled by her scream, Luke and Ian raced across the sand to her side.

"What's the matter?" barked Luke.

"Lunch!" she crowed. "I caught lunch!"

"It's a small bonito," put in Ian. They looked blank so he added, "Very edible."

Lunch thrashed wildly.

"But it's not dead!" Luke protested.

"Well, make it dead!" she insisted.

Obediently, Luke reached out and slapped the fish over the head with his open hand. The bonito went on struggling.

"Here!" Ian held out a short stick, part of their construction material.

Luke grabbed it and took a swing just as Charla, shocked, pulled back her hands.

Whap!

"Ow!"

Lunch dropped to the wet sand. Before they could react, the bonito flipped its way into an oncoming wave and disappeared into the surf.

"You were supposed to hit the fish, not me!" Charla snapped.

"You moved!" Luke accused.

They stared at each other for a moment and then burst out laughing. Relieved, Ian joined in. As their merriment died down, they heard another sound. Not the usual island noises — insects and birds and the lapping of the waves. This was mechanical — the drone of motor and propellers.

Ian was the first to look up. *"A plane!"*

It appeared as a dot in the sky that grew bigger and better defined. It was a twin-engine seaplane. And there was no doubt about it — it was heading for their little island.

SURVIVAL

"They must have seen our fire!" cried Charla, excitement vibrating her thin frame.

Ian frowned. "You know, the chances that we were spotted within a day because of a small bonfire are a million to one. I don't understand how it could have happened."

Luke slapped him on the back. "It happened because we got lucky for a change!" he said, choking back tears of emotion. "We've got to find Will! Now we can get him to a doctor."

They ran along the shore, waving their arms and cheering.

The plane roared right over their heads and started across the island, its pontoons barely clearing the tops of the trees.

"Hey, where are they going?" cried Charla.

The aircraft disappeared over the jungle. The castaways waited for it to circle back for them, but it never did. Instead, they heard the engine power cut back, indicating descent. A few minutes later, the noise of the motor disappeared altogether.

Luke was dumbfounded. "Why would they land all the way over there?"

"They didn't see us," breathed Charla, devastated.

Ian thought it over. "Maybe they're not here

for us. Maybe there's a village or outpost on the other side of the island."

"It's still good news," Luke decided. "We just have to get over there and ask them to give us a ride somewhere. Even if there's no room for us, at least we can get them to send help."

"What if we can't find them?" asked Charla.

Luke started out along the beach. "That plane landed in the water. If we follow the shore, we'll hit it sooner or later. Let's not waste any time."

Charla hurried after him.

"Wait," called Ian. He picked up the stick and wrote WE'RE ALIVE in the hard flat sand by the water's edge.

"Just in case they come looking for us while we're gone," he explained, rushing to catch up with the others.

What started out as a walk along the beach soon got a lot harder. Just around the bend from their campsite, the sandy shoreline ended, giving way to coral outcroppings and steep cliffs. In places, the rocks were so jagged and unclimbable that the three were forced to venture inland to make it over the rough spots.

"Keep your eyes on the water," Luke ordered when they had to veer through a dense grove of trees. "We don't want to walk right by that plane."

"How far do you think we've come?" asked Charla, swatting mosquitoes.

Ian looked thoughtful. "It's hard to say. We make great time on the beach, but when we have to start climbing, we're doing more up and down than forward. Three — maybe four miles."

It was like an obstacle course. Much of the coastline was a series of coves shaped like giant bites out of the shore. These had to be followed around, or sometimes waded through. High rocks bound the inlets, so the castaways were constantly climbing. As they rose with the terrain, their hopes rose with them — only to be dashed when they reached the top. For there lay another identical cove. The view was breathtaking, spectacular. But they had rescue on their minds. Any view that didn't include the plane was a bitter disappointment.

"I hope they haven't left already," said Charla. "We've been at this for three hours."

"We would have heard the engine," Luke panted, starting down into another inlet.

The next rise was a steep one, becoming a sheer cliff near the top. Luckily, there was a grove of leafy saplings on the crest. Luke was able to hoist Charla high enough to get an arm around one of the narrow trunks. With her gymnastics training, she pulled herself to the top. Then, locking her ankles around the base of the tree, she hung herself downward. This allowed the others to use her as a human ladder. They climbed up her athletic body to the flat area at the summit.

"Look!" breathed Ian, pointing.

It was the seaplane — not in the next cove, but in the one after that. It bobbed gently in a shallow lagoon formed by the curve of the coastline and a high jetty of dead coral. Four men waded in the waist-deep water, unloading crates from the cargo hold.

For nine days, the castaways had seen no living soul other than one another. Now — rescuers. With a plane.

Luke's heart was pounding in his ears so loudly that he could barely hear his own voice. "Hey! Over here! Over *here!*"

Charla and Ian began jumping and bellowing.

The four men continued ferrying their cargo. No one looked up.

"We're too far away!" Ian exclaimed, his throat hoarse from shouting.

Charla was in a full panic. "Let's get over there!" She started down the steep slope to the next cove so fast that the others, following her, tripped, fell, and rolled all the way to the beach.

They sprinted along the shore, running the anchor leg of a long race. Down at sea level, they could no longer see the plane and its four occupants. But Luke kept a vivid picture of them in his mind. It gave his feet wings as he started up the incline, right behind Charla. This was it. Beyond this rise lay rescue.

The slope was rocky, but shorter and much less steep than the last one. Charla leaped expertly from foothold to foothold. Luke was hot on her heels. His hands and knees bled from the sharp coral formations, but he didn't care. Nothing mattered — nothing except reaching those men.

He could see the top now, just a few feet away. Charla was already reaching for it . . .

Bang!

The shot echoed six times before Luke stopped counting. His arm snaked out, grabbed Charla by the back of her shirt, and pulled her down beside him. At the same instant, he used his other arm to halt Ian in his tracks.

"What's the matter with you?" Charla shrilled. "We're almost there!"

"That was a gunshot!" Luke hissed.

"No, it wasn't!" she argued. "Maybe the plane backfired or something!"

"Maybe," Luke said doubtfully. "But we've got to find out, one way or the other, before we let them know we're here."

Carefully this time, they crept up to the top and peered over the peak.

There was the seaplane. But now there were only three men wading in the lagoon. And one of them, a tall cadaverous figure with bright red hair, was holding a small snub-nosed revolver.

"Where's the other guy?" Charla whispered urgently.

Then they saw him — floating facedown in the clear water of the lagoon. He wasn't moving.

They ducked back from the top of the hill. Silently, they put together the sights and sounds of the last few minutes and realized that they equaled death.

Charla looked from face to face. "What? You're not saying we're not going down there?"

"We just witnessed a murder!" Luke insisted. "And those guys did it! I don't think they're going to be really psyched to see us!"

"I won't testify against them," Charla promised. "I know that sounds selfish, but we're talking about our lives! *Will's* life!"

"That's exactly why we can't go!" Luke argued. "Look — these are bad people. I don't know what they're doing, or what's in those boxes. But if those guys'll kill one person, they'll have no problem killing us!"

Charla began to shiver. "I'm sorry!" she quavered. "But this is so unfair! There are rescuers right here and we can't even go to them! We'll never see another plane. Never."

"It's unbelievable," agreed Ian, his voice hollow with shock and disappointment. "It would be better if nobody had come at all."

Luke nodded grimly. He turned their dilemma over in his mind every which way, but it always came out the same: They would have to conceal themselves from these men; that was definite. But if he, Charla, and Ian were hiding, how could they ever hope to attract rescuers in a passing plane or boat?

It was the only safe path. But would following it condemn them to a lifetime marooned on this terrible island?

CHAPTER SEVEN
Day 4, 6:20 A.M.

Will Greenfield's "camp" was less than half a mile from his fellow castaways', in a small clearing in some dense jungle. It wasn't much of a clearing, but then again, it wasn't much of a camp. A small fire was the only comfort. Will slept on the cool ground, wedged between tree trunks. A hump created by exposed roots provided his pillow.

Not exactly a four-poster bed, Will reflected, but he didn't seem to need much sleep anymore. Crazy but true — his bug bites and the on-and-off rain kept him awake; his fear and racing mind kept him alert. He lay down because, in the pitch-dark, there was nowhere he could go without getting lost. Even then, he only dozed off here and there. Mostly, he squinted at the fallen log that stretched over him, suspended a few inches above his chest. In the dim firelight, he could see thousands of ants scurrying across the rotting deadwood. A metropolis of them! They made him even more restless. They all seemed so *busy*. Watching them marching to and fro filled him with an urgent desire to *do* something.

SURVIVAL

The fire helped. Last night he had spent hours using a jagged rock to sharpen straight sticks into arrows. At least it had felt like hours; there was no way to judge time when the sun was down. And at very first predawn light, he was off through the jungle in search of a piece of wood he could use as a bow.

A bow and arrow. Even now, it seemed nuts. Like he'd ever have the guts to shoot at someone!

The idea sobered him up. Those kids were dangerous. He still wasn't sure how, but they'd gotten him separated from his sister, lost on Guam. They were keeping him from the *Phoenix*, which might have left without him. His life could be in danger; Lyssa's too. They were after him, and he was outnumbered, three to one. He needed some kind of weapon to defend himself.

He began testing twigs for their flexibility. The first snapped in his hands, and he dropped it with a yelp of shock. He was a wimp, that was for sure. He'd never even been in a fistfight, except with Lyssa. That was another story. He and Lyssa could really mix it up. No joke. They'd even put each other in the hospital once, which was why they'd been sent on Charting a New Course.

Even though Lyssa was a first-class pain in the butt, he would have given anything to see her face right now. Lyssa was smart. She'd be able to figure out what was going on. Every time he tried to think it through, the mist came back, and with it the terrible headaches.

Aw, Lyss, you're never here when I need you!

He found a supple green branch that was gnarled into a C-shape. Perfect.

He began experimenting with vines. Most broke at the slightest tension. Those that held up were too stiff. At last he found one with both strength and springiness. Carefully, he plucked off the leaves and knotted the ends to his bow.

Now to test it.

He positioned an arrow against the vine and drew it back. Even though no one was watching, he felt himself reddening. Who did he think he was, Robin Hood? He could almost hear Lyssa taunting him:

If you shoot anything besides yourself with that . . .

Before he could finish her sentence, there was a violent rustling, and out of the underbrush burst a dark blur.

Will froze in terror. It was one of those wild pigs! No, bigger than that — a boar! It had to be. The thing was a beast, with black fur and a swinelike appearance. It ran at full speed, no holds barred. Will was sent flying as the animal charged at him. Dark blood appeared on the calf of his leg where a sharp tusk had brushed by.

By the time he could scramble back up, the animal was bearing down on him again. Luckily, the boar was as disorganized as it was ferocious. It thundered every which way, turning constantly. Yet each charge was made with the utmost purpose. Gasping and snorting with rage, it wheeled for another assault.

A tree! Will thought desperately. *Climb a tree!*

In a panic, he looked around. Plenty of trees, but all the close ones were palms — long, smooth trunks, difficult to climb. His eyes fell on the bow, which lay on the ground right where he'd dropped it to make his escape. Where was the arrow?

Then he saw it, partly hidden by a fern. It stuck straight up, its point buried in the soft earth.

In an instant, his mind ran through all the reasons this was a bad idea: *You'll never make it in time. You haven't tested it yet. You'll put your eye out. Look at those tusks. . . .*

He dove just as the boar sprang forward. He picked up the bow and rolled, flailing an arm for the arrow. When he felt the stick in his palm, he yanked it out of the ground, sat up, aimed, and let fly.

The arrow shot from its bow at a wild angle, just as the attacking animal leaped. It caught the boar in the side of the snout, right behind its flat nose. Direct hit!

Wham! Will crumpled back to the ground as the animal's full weight slammed into him. It was on top of him. He could see it, feel it, smell it. He waited for the ripping force of the tusks to tear into him.

And suddenly, the black fur that filled his field of vision was gone. The wounded boar reared up like a frightened horse, squealing in pain. Then it turned tail and disappeared into the jungle once more.

Will lay flat, the bow across his stomach, waiting for the beating of his heart to return to normal. When his brain finally unfroze from terror mode, it was to admit a single thought:

I need more arrows. Lots more.

SURVIVAL

CHAPTER EIGHT
Day 4, 6:55 A.M.

Ian Sikorsky crawled out of the rebuilt shelter, scratching at ant bites and squinting through the brilliant morning at the lean-to's roof.

Rain had come on and off all last night. Huge clammy droplets had fallen like bombs from the shelter's ceiling. The three castaways had barely slept a wink. According to the documentary he'd seen, tree bark was supposed to be waterproof. It was a lesson he'd been learning over and over again since the sinking of the *Phoenix*: Real life wasn't the same as TV.

He sighed miserably. If he'd come to that conclusion a month ago, Mom and Dad probably never would have sent him on Charting a New Course in the first place.

The thought of his parents, so far away, choked him up a little. Odd, the things he missed the most. The labeled diagram of the solar system that hung on his wall — he couldn't remember the names of two of Saturn's moons. His goldfish, Dot and Com. Even his mother's pot roast, which was practically lethal, and the sound of his father practicing his trombone . . .

ISLAND

He forced himself to concentrate on the problem at hand. Did the roof need more bark? Different bark? Bigger pieces laid out in a new pattern? Mud for mortar, maybe?

Luke would know. He always knew what to do. It wasn't that he had so much information — he just knew exactly how to use the information he had. Ian could memorize the encyclopedia and still not be able to come to the courageous decisions that Luke made every day.

If there was one good thing to come out of this horrible situation, it was getting to know a great guy like Luke Haggerty.

The rain began again. At least the Discovery Channel had been right about that. The tropics were wet in the summer.

Look on the bright side, he told himself. Rain meant drinking water.

The castaways still hadn't found a freshwater stream or spring on the island. There probably wasn't one — they were rare on small cays like this. That meant they would have to survive on what fell out of the sky.

He walked over to the spot on the beach where they had stuck twenty-eight coconut shells in the sand to serve as rain-catchers. Along with them was a yellow rubber rain hat, which Ian had rescued from the burning *Phoenix*. Full marks to TV for that. The hat had been their only source of water on the raft.

"Aw — "

Each shell held maybe a couple of inches of water — less in the hat, which was wider. It was another example of how TV and reality were two different things. Yes, setting out receptacles would gather rain. But not *much* rain. The storms here were heavy but quick. For a good supply of water they'd need a lot more shells — or Noah's flood. With a sad shrug, he picked up the rain hat and drained it. Then he downed three coconut shells in rapid succession. It wasn't enough — not nearly enough. But this was all they had, and he wouldn't dream of drinking more than his share.

When he finished, he was even thirstier than before. It was a different kind of thirst than they had experienced during those awful days on the raft. That had been a burning, paralyzing feeling of parched desperation — you knew that if you didn't drink, you'd be dead very soon. Here there was always *some* water — a pint when they needed a quart; a quart when they needed a gallon. Enough to save their lives, but not to satisfy their constant craving. This was a kind of thirst that could go on for weeks, months, maybe even years. It wouldn't kill them, but it was sure to do something even scarier. It would wear them down and drive them mad.

Angrily, Ian took one of the empty shells and hurled it with all his might. It hit the sand and rolled, disappearing over the shelf where the beach angled down toward the water.

The guilty feeling came immediately. Who was he to throw away one of their precious rain-catchers? He ran over to retrieve it.

And froze.

His heart pounded like a drum solo in his chest. The effort to keep from passing out claimed every ounce of strength he had.

A body lay limp and motionless in the sand. Its lifeless outstretched arms framed a single word from his sign partially erased by the tide: ALIVE. Another bad joke in the long cruel comedy routine that had delivered them all here.

He couldn't bring himself to move any closer. If this was J.J. or Lyssa —

No, it was a grown man. The captain . . . ?

"Luke! *Luke!*"

The sound of his own voice, thin and high-pitched, terrified him. It must have terrified the others too, because they came running. All three fixed their eyes on the huddled shape and moved slowly toward it as though wading through molasses.

SURVIVAL

It was Luke who mustered the courage to reach down and roll the body over. Pasty gray skin and wild staring eyes. The face looked unreal, like a wax figure.

A collective moaning sigh escaped them. This was not the body of Captain Cascadden.

"It's the guy," gasped Luke. "The fourth man from the plane." He pointed to a neat bullet hole, dead center in the victim's forehead. "We were right. They killed him."

"But that happened all the way on the other side of the island," Charla said weakly. "What's he doing here?"

"The current must swing around this way," Ian decided.

He couldn't take his eyes from the fatal wound. Whatever blood had been there had been washed clean by the hours in the ocean. Now the bullet hole was exactly that, a hole — an empty space.

In the past two weeks, they had all come to know death. Captain Cascadden of the *Phoenix* had been swept overboard. Their shipmates Lyssa and J.J. had been lost at sea. They had all seen Will descend into unconsciousness, and then a fevered amnesia that could cost him his life. But this was the first time any of the castaways had ever been face-to-face with a real dead body.

It was stunning, gut-wrenching, horrifying, yet oddly mesmerizing. None of them could take their eyes away. But it also presented an awkward problem.

Charla was the first to bring it up. "Uh — what are we going to do with him?"

"We can't just leave him there," Ian put in. "His body will decompose. And birds and animals will . . ." His voice trailed off. When would he ever learn to shut up? No one wanted to hear it!

"We'll give him a decent burial," Luke said suddenly. "I know people who never got funerals no matter how much they deserved them. We've got the chance to bury one guy. Let's take it."

As soon as the words were out of Luke's mouth, Ian knew it was the right choice.

He was full of admiration. *That's what it takes*, he guessed, *to be a leader*.

In his own mind, Luke wasn't so sure. Burying a fully grown man was going to be a huge job — especially without shovels or any kind of digging equipment. They were probably still weak from the raft. They had eaten nothing but fruit in over a week; they were getting water, but not much. Yes, this was the right thing to do. But did it make sense?

SURVIVAL

No one wanted to touch the body any more than absolutely necessary. They rolled the dead man over onto the blackened cabin top and carried it like a stretcher into the jungle.

"Let's take it far in," Charla suggested.

Luke understood instantly and agreed. This man could not hurt them now. But a grave was a reminder of death. If they buried him in the nearby woods where they foraged for food and firewood, they would be inviting death into their daily lives.

The body was heavy, the going rough. Some groves of trees were so dense that the raft wouldn't fit between the trunks, so they were forced to change direction. On they trudged. They kept going mostly because they didn't know where to stop. They were kids on a boat trip. How could they have been ready for all that had happened? Shipwrecked. Adrift at sea. Marooned. And now this.

Crazy, Luke thought. The guy was dead. He wasn't exactly going to be enjoying the view. What difference did it make where they buried him?

He stopped. "Right here," he decided.

Then came the digging. They had no tools, so they used their bare hands. A crisscrossing lattice of thick vines had to be torn away. It was filthy work. The three were soon covered in dirt, which mixed with dripping sweat to form a layer of slimy mud. Was this how Will was living in the middle of the jungle? Bugs everywhere. Worms the size of garter snakes, huge winged cockroaches, giant slugs, strange fat caterpillars — bagworms, Ian called them.

Was it crazy to think that Will was alive somewhere in this never-ending wilderness? They hadn't seen so much as a trace of him in three whole days. Maybe his memory had come back and he was trying to find them, but he was lost in the vast sameness of the jungle. There were so many ways to get hurt out here. An unseen vine, a bad fall or broken ankle — he'd be at the mercy of the snakes; no way to get food or water . . .

Don't think. Dig.

The hole took over an hour. Finally, they lifted the body off the raft, dropped it inside the grave, and filled in the dirt. For Luke, even the burning and sinking of the *Phoenix* had been easier to stomach than this terrible task.

The others felt it too, an overpowering desire to put this gruesome experience behind them.

"Let's get out of here," Ian panted when the last handful of dirt was in place.

"No," Luke said simply.

SURVIVAL

"Come on," urged Charla. "This is creepy. We buried the guy; let's beat it."

"Not yet," Luke insisted. "Somebody should say something."

"We don't even know his name," she complained.

"He's probably got a driver's license or passport or something like that," Ian put in. "We never checked."

Charla was impatient. "You want to go digging for it?"

"Let's just get it over with," said Luke. He had only been to one funeral in his life — his great-uncle's. His parents had gotten him all decked out in his best suit. He looked around. He and his fellow castaways were clothed in ragged shorts and T-shirts, ripped, faded, salt-encrusted, and filthy with mud. Their sneakers were battered and full of holes. They weren't exactly dressed to deliver a eulogy.

Not knowing what to do, Luke stood at attention, as if they were playing the national anthem at a ball game. Ian put a hand on his heart.

"For all we know, you were a bad guy and you got exactly what you deserved," Luke began. "But maybe somebody somewhere is going to miss you the way our families miss us. They won't know where you are, or why you don't come home, or what's happened to you. And that's got to feel pretty sad."

A muffled sob escaped Ian. Charla put an arm around his shoulders.

"Or maybe that person misses you the way we miss Lyssa and J.J., who never got any funeral, not even a lame one like this. Or maybe it's more like Will — we know he's out here, but — "

His voice broke. All three of them were crying now. Even at the times of greatest desperation on the raft, they had never wept like this. The sun was high in the sky — more than half the day, wasted. . . .

Suddenly, Luke's sorrow transformed itself into a flare of anger. Anger at the judge for sentencing him. Anger at Mr. Radford, the mate of the *Phoenix*, for deserting them. Anger at himself for letting Will get away. Anger even at the man in the ground, for dying and putting them through this.

The moment passed. He drew a deep breath. "Anyway, what do you care?" he finished to the mound of earth at their feet. "You're already dead."

"Amen," Ian barely whispered.

"Rest in peace," added Charla.

The ocean, thought Luke. That was the only

SURVIVAL

way to cleanse them of this horror. A good long
swim. He bent down to pick up the raft.

"Wait!" Ian exclaimed suddenly.

The younger boy was pointing at a small gap
in the underbrush not ten feet from the grave site.
Right there in the soft ground — footprints.

Will.

CHAPTER NINE
Day 4, 2:40 P.M.

"He's alive!" Luke exclaimed with relief. He cupped his hands to his mouth. "Will! *Will!*"

Charla grabbed his arm. "Not so loud," she warned. "There are killers on this island!"

"That's another reason we have to find him," Luke retorted. "Before *they* do!"

They listened breathlessly. Birdsong. Chirping of insects.

"Come on, Will," called Luke, a little lower this time. "We know you're out here."

Nothing.

And then, barely audible amid the sounds of the jungle . . . a far-off human voice.

"It's coming from over there!" chorused the three castaways.

They regarded one another in dismay. They were pointing in three different directions.

Luke checked the sneaker print. It was heading to their left. "This way!"

He started off, leading the others. It was pure guesswork, Luke thought. Any other footprints were covered by heavy underbrush. In his mind, he kept an image of the direction of Will's sneaker tread and tried to follow it like a compass needle. Not that it was possible to stay on course in this tangle of greenery.

But when you have only one clue, you follow it.

"Please, Will!" Charla tried to make her quiet voice carry.

They trudged on, searching for any sign of human life — a broken branch, a trampled fern, a torn vine. But nothing stood out.

And then Ian found another footprint.

"You're right!" exclaimed Charla. "Two of them!" She stared. "Uh-oh."

"What's wrong?" asked Luke.

"If this is Will," she said slowly, "he's got two different-sized feet."

Ian knelt. "And two different shoes." He looked up at Luke. "This is two people."

Luke drew in his breath sharply. "Are you sure?"

Charla began to tremble. "The men from the plane!" she breathed. "It's not Will, it's them!"

Ian frowned. "But what are they doing all the way over here?"

"I don't care if they're on an Easter egg hunt," put in Luke. "We've got to get out of here before they come back!"

And then . . . just the tiniest *crack*.

They froze and listened. It was the swishing and snapping of people walking through the jungle.

Luke mouthed the words, *Get down*, and the three dropped, trying to disappear into the dense underbrush.

The swishing was louder now. The men were close! Luke tried to catch a glimpse of them, but he didn't dare move for fear of being spotted. Where were they? Since there was no trail, it was impossible to predict what path someone might take.

Suddenly . . . a flash of red shirt! Luke's breath caught in his throat. Just a few feet away! *The killers were walking straight at them!*

It was too late to run. Luke rolled to his right in a desperate attempt to avoid the stepping foot. Horrified, he felt the sneaker catch him on the shoulder.

"Hey!" came a voice above him.

A split second later, the figure was tumbling into the underbrush behind him. The jig was up. They were caught.

Luke didn't think; he just reacted. In a single motion, he grabbed a rock and jumped upright, aiming at the back of the intruder's blond head. "One move and you're dead!" he hissed.

Ian picked up the sunglasses that had fallen off the prisoner as he tripped. They were strangely familiar — sleek and silver, designer frames. He flashed Luke the earpiece. On it was engraved: JONATHAN LANE, THE TOAST OF LONDON — P.S.

Luke's eyes bulged. These glasses belonged to J.J. Lane, their shipmate from the *Phoenix*! There was no mistaking them! They were one-of-a-kind — originally given to J.J.'s father, movie star Jonathan Lane, by Paul Smith, the fashion designer!

Luke dropped his rock. "J.J.?" he barely whispered.

The actor's son rolled over. *"Luke?"*

"You're alive!" cried Charla, throwing herself at J.J. in a joyous embrace. Ian piled on. Luke was slapping backs, shoulders — any surface he could get a hand on.

All at once, he stopped celebrating and grabbed J.J. by the shirt. "Lyssa — ?"

"Relax — "

And then a familiar voice said, "Do you think these are, like, you know, real bananas?" Lyssa Greenfield stepped into view, a bunch of finger bananas in her arms. She gaped at the four of them rolling around the underbrush. Dumbstruck, she grappled for words. "But you're dead!" she gasped finally.

"*You're* dead," Luke shot back, laughing with relief.

"Man, what happened to you guys?" asked J.J. "You look like coal miners."

It took Lyssa a few seconds to do a head count and realize who was missing. "Where's my brother?"

"Don't panic," Charla said quickly. "He's not dead — at least he wasn't three days ago."

"Why isn't he with you?" she demanded, her voice shrill.

"He ran away from us," Luke explained. "He doesn't remember us; he doesn't remember the trip — he thinks he's lost on Guam and it's all our fault."

She was shocked. "He's gone crazy?"

"Amnesia," Ian supplied.

"He's lost his memory?"

"Just the last couple of weeks of it," Luke replied. "He remembers *you* — he kept asking us, 'What have you done with my sister?' Almost like we kidnapped you or something. He thinks the *Phoenix* is moored at a marina around here, and he has to get you and report for Charting a New Course."

"I saw a show about it once," added Ian. "It's called paranoid delusion."

"We've got to find him," Lyssa said urgently. "I can make him remember."

Charla put a reassuring arm on her shoulder. "We'll keep looking. But it's hard to find someone who doesn't want to be found."

Lyssa blinked back tears. "But you haven't seen him for three days! He could be dead!"

"Or he could be just avoiding us," Luke pointed out. "That would be good news — it means he's alive and alert."

"Can he really survive all by himself on this island?" she asked dubiously.

Luke spread his arms wide. "Can we? He has what we have — which is pretty much nothing."

"Except the supplies on the lifeboat," put in J.J.

"Lifeboat?" Charla repeated.

"The inflatable raft," J.J. explained. "That's how we got away when the boat sank. It's still in the little cove where we washed ashore. We've been living in it."

"How did you guys get here?" asked Lyssa.

"On a piece of cabin top the size of a postage stamp," Charla explained. "One of us had to hang over the side or we'd capsize. You were lucky."

"Hey," the actor's son interrupted sharply, "I could be in L.A. right now, surrounded by fast cars, hot tubs, and chicks, chicks, chicks. Don't lecture me on how I haven't suffered enough."

"No fighting," ordered Luke. "We're all in this together, right? We're scared, we're worried about Will — and we're all sick of coconuts and bananas."

J.J. and Lyssa looked completely blank.

"Maybe you've been eating durians," put in Ian.

"They're hungry, not crazy," Charla mumbled distastefully.

"We've been eating what's in the boat," said Lyssa. "You know, the freeze-dried survival meals. Chicken and mashed potatoes. Beef stew. Chili."

Luke looked so genuinely ravenous that even Lyssa had to laugh. "Put your tongue back in your head. We've only got one left — mac and cheese. That's why we're out in the jungle — looking for food."

"I love mac and cheese," piped up Ian. His face fell. "But I guess we should save it for a special occasion."

J.J. stared at him. "Special occasion? We're in the middle of nowhere! Remember how nowhere we were on the boat? Well, that was the Sunset Strip compared to here! What special occasions are we going to have? National Cockroach-the-Size-of-a-Volkswagen Day?"

Luke was thoughtful. "How about Raft Moving Day? The lifeboat is too easy to spot out on a beach. We should move it to the cover of the trees."

"But being spotted is the whole point," argued Lyssa. "How are we going to get rescued if nobody can see us?"

Solemnly, Luke filled in the newcomers about the murder they'd witnessed and the body that had washed up on the beach.

"It's a real jam," he finished. "If rescuers don't find us, we'll die here. But if we make ourselves visible enough to get rescued, these guys will spot us first, and *they'll* kill us."

"Will," Lyssa said nervously. "They'd kill him too. And he probably doesn't even know they're out there."

J.J. spoke up. "Doesn't anybody else think this is kind of fishy? The boat sinks; we're stranded; murderers on the island — I mean, whose luck is this bad?"

"It even happens to rich people," Charla told him resentfully.

"It's fake," J.J. scoffed. "I say we're still on Charting a New Course, and all this has happened to us on purpose. The boat sank because it was *supposed* to sink — you know, a trick boat. The special effects guys who work on my dad's movies, they could rig something like that in a heartbeat."

Everybody groaned. This had been J.J.'s theory from the beginning.

"The whole point of the trip is to make us forget what a bunch of losers we are and force us to work as a team," he went on. "Well, it's happening. These so-called criminals, they could be actors hired by CNC. They're just another test for us. And we're falling for it — man, we're performing like a bunch of trained seals!"

"You're disgusting, J.J. Lane!" Lyssa snapped at him. "My poor brother could be dying this minute — "

"That's even more evidence that I'm right," J.J. interrupted. "Will got a little too messed up so they stepped in and scooped him out of the game. He's probably watching us on hidden camera right now, eating a steak and laughing his butt off."

"That was a real murder we saw," Luke said darkly. "And it was *definitely* a real dead body."

J.J. shrugged. "When my dad was doing this horror flick, he once brought home a fake disembodied hand from the prop room. It looked so real that my stepmom — number three — she practically had a heart attack."

"You know, it almost doesn't matter," Ian said thoughtfully. "Whether it's a setup or not, we're still shipwrecked and we have to survive."

"Except CNC won't let us die," J.J. reminded him.

"There are exactly two reasons why we're not dead," said Luke grimly. "Dumb luck and coconuts. And the luck ran out when that plane landed. It doesn't get any scarier than this."

CHAPTER TEN
Day 4, 5:25 P.M.

Voices.

Will reacted immediately. He snatched up his bow and a handful of arrows.

He could hear the swish and crackle of legs making their way through heavy underbrush.

They were coming to get him.

And they were close.

He made a move to put out the campfire and froze. That fire was the only thing that kept the bugs away at night. His mosquito-bite bodysuit was finally starting to recede; the churning itch had become almost bearable. He could even open his eyes all the way now, although the silvery mist was still there, and the headaches were worse than ever. How could he willingly feed himself to squadrons of hungry insects?

There must be some way . . .

He jammed the arrows in his back pocket and slung the bow over his shoulder. Then he picked up a sturdy twig and held it to the fire.

The voices were getting louder. From the babble, he made out a single word: *Phoenix*.

They were talking about the boat!

SURVIVAL

His new torch blazing in his hand, he stomped out the fire and kicked a mass of vines and dead leaves to cover the evidence. Then he squeezed himself into a dense stand of ferns and peered out.

It was the little kid — the one who called himself Ian. His companion was a tall blond boy Will hadn't seen before. The newcomer was laughing.

"I swim to the life raft and climb inside, and then it hits me: I forgot to untie the line! The boat's sinking, and *I'm still attached to it.* So I'm hanging over the side trying to chew through that rope with my teeth — which isn't easy because *it's on fire.*"

Will frowned. More lies about the shipwreck. But why tell them to each other?

He froze. Did they suspect he was listening? That made no sense. They'd come get him if they knew where he was. Why were they talking about a disaster that never happened?

"Wasn't there a knife in the survival kit?" Ian was asking.

"Yeah, but who's got time to look for it?" the older boy exclaimed. "I'm chewing for my life here! Then, the *Phoenix* starts down, and I'm thinking, 'That's it. I'm dead,' " and, poof, the rope burns through, and I'm free! These CNC guys — when they scare you, they don't mess around."

"It seems pretty far-fetched that they could be behind all this," said Ian.

"You'll see. We're wasting our time. Will's not on the island anymore. He's probably in some hotel room, living large."

Hotel room? What was he talking about?

As Will watched the blond boy, in a flash he knew with absolute certainty something he couldn't possibly have known. It was a message engraved on one of the earpieces of the kid's sunglasses: THE TOAST OF LONDON.

The toast of London?

He was taken aback. Where would he get a crazy idea like that? This was a total stranger! And yet the feeling was so vivid Will could almost see the words imprinted in the fancy metal.

Impossible. And yet it wouldn't be the weirdest thing that had happened to him in the last few days.

Was he losing his mind?

And then he heard a word that had been very much in his thoughts lately: Lyssa.

"Yeah, she was already in the water when I found her," the blonde was saying. "I'm not sure how she got there. We'll ask her."

Ask her! Will stiffened like a pointer. They knew where she was!

He struggled to force his sluggish mind to reason it out. He couldn't let them get away. He had to attack! There were two of them, but he had his bow and arrow. He would squeeze his sister's whereabouts out of them if it was the last thing he did. If they wouldn't talk, he'd . . .

What? Shoot them? He'd never have the guts.

He thrummed the bowstring with his free hand. *Yes, I would. This is life and death. I shot that boar and I'll shoot them.*

The two boys were no more than twenty feet away. Will prepared himself to spring. They would never get any closer than this. . . .

The moment passed. Will squinted at their receding backs. He took no action.

There was a better way.

CHAPTER ELEVEN
Day 4, 9:45 P.M.

Luke shone the beam of the flashlight at the survival pack.

Just that simple act seemed like a miracle. Only yesterday, the setting of the sun had signified the end of all activity on the island. Darkness was final, total. Now they had artificial light, courtesy of the inflatable raft.

While J.J. and Ian had searched for Will, Luke and the girls had moved the covered lifeboat from the small cove where it was beached to a spot just inside the trees at the castaways' camp. It wasn't easy to maneuver such a bulky object through heavy jungle — it had to be rolled, carried, squeezed, and sometimes tossed. But it was all worth it when Luke took the cover off the survival pack.

"We're rich," he breathed.

No, this was much better than money.

Conveniences.

Small aluminum pots, pans, plates. Plastic cups and cutlery. Compass. Knife. Lighter and waterproof matches. First aid kit. Fishing line and hooks . . .

SURVIVAL

There it was. Macaroni and cheese. A hole opened up in his stomach. Fruit could keep them from starving, but this was *real* food. Big too. The label read: SERVES TEN.

He had an insane desire to bite into the package — straight through the shrink-wrap. Ha! The others would kill him, and they'd be right. He set it back in the survival kit. This was their last meal, their safety net. They had to preserve it for when they were really desperate.

He hefted the raft's water keg. It was almost empty, but it would still come in handy. In the coconut shells, the rainwater was always mostly evaporated by the time they got around to drinking it. Now they had a reservoir they could close. That was a big help.

To keep us alive so we can die here, he thought suddenly. *Or be murdered.*

That was an ongoing battle — Luke's brain versus his morale. He got through the days by setting realistic goals for himself: Find food. Find water. Keep looking for Will.

Two shipmates you'd written off as dead showed up today, he reminded himself. *If that won't keep your spirits up, nothing will.*

He sighed. These days, survival included winning these arguments with himself.

With the keg under his arm, he ducked out of

the raft's sun canopy that loosely covered the lifeboat like a tent. The other four sat around the fire. The dancing light of the flames played across their faces. It felt unreal, like a movie scene. Luke guessed that he had interrupted a conversation.

He picked up a coconut shell, careful not to spill a drop. "From now on, let's use this keg to store our water."

"Good idea," said Lyssa. "Hey, Luke, what do you think happened to Radford?"

Luke clenched the shell harder. Out of six crew members who hadn't been too fond of the *Phoenix*'s mate, Luke had the strongest feelings. "Personally, I don't think about him at all," he replied sourly. "But now that you mention it, I hope the biggest shark in the ocean swam up and bit his ugly head off."

Radford had proved to be much more than just a seagoing bully. With the boat crippled and slowly sinking, he had slipped off during the night in the schooner's twelve-foot dinghy, taking most of their food with him. In effect, he had left them to die. It had been that predicament — and their efforts to restart the engine — that had led to the explosion and fire that had scuttled the ship.

"But do you think he could have made it back to Guam?" asked Charla.

"Rat-face is an experienced sailor," Luke mused, emptying another shell, "but he was in the open Pacific in a tiny boat. One good wave could have flipped him."

"He's fine," scoffed J.J. "It's all part of the game."

"In your fantasy world," Charla added unkindly.

"Well, he never could have survived for real on that pile of Popsicle sticks." The actor's son shrugged. "His own B.O. would have killed him."

"Big joke," snorted Luke. "That guy's as bad as the men from the plane. Worse, because he was getting paid to look after us." His wrist shook, and he brought his lips to the coconut shell to suck up the spilled water. "Just hearing his name again makes me nuts."

The five had decided to bed down in the inflatable lifeboat. The sand of the beach was soft and comfortable, but four nights of ant bites had convinced them it was time for a new home. As the others retired to divvy up sleeping space, Lyssa remained outside to trim down their fire — a sensible precaution to avoid being noticed by the men on the other side of the island.

It was an eerie feeling: killers out there, somewhere in the blackness. Almost too much to accept. After everything else that had happened — murderers on the very same tiny cay where both groups of castaways had washed ashore.

She saw a flicker of light coming from the woods. Her first reaction was panic. It was them!

She squinted into the gloom. Nothing. Were her eyes playing tricks on her?

Suddenly, a hand reached out from behind and clamped down hard over her mouth. Her scream was smothered by the powerful grip. She struggled, but her attacker had too firm a hold.

And then — a whisper in her ear:

"Cut it out, Lyss! It's me!"

Will? If he hadn't been clutching her so tightly, she would have dropped like a stone from relief.

You're alive! What happened to you? Don't you remember the shipwreck? The thoughts darted around in her head. There was so much to say. But when she opened her mouth she couldn't speak. Mute, she wheeled and embraced her brother. He resisted for an instant and then wrapped his arms around her. They held each other with an intensity that momentarily canceled out the danger, the horror, the fear. A small part of Lyssa, standing strangely distant from herself, noted that this was the first time she could ever remember hugging Will.

She found her voice at last. "I can't believe it's you."

"Shhh!" He stiffened, pulled back. "They'll hear us. We've got to get out of here right now!"

"Will, they're our friends."

"Don't listen to them, Lyss," Will warned. "Everything they say is a lie. They told me you were dead."

"They thought I was," Lyssa reasoned. "I thought the same thing about them after the boat sank. About you too."

Clutching his torch, Will backed up a step, wide-eyed with shock. "They've got you brainwashed!"

"No — "

She stopped herself from arguing, because, for the first time, she had gotten a really good look at her brother. He had lost weight — they all had, but it was much more noticeable on the sturdy Will. His hair was matted, his eyes wild, and he had more bug bites than skin. A crude bow was slung over one bony shoulder. He smelled terrible. He was like a savage, she thought in agony. She had no hope of reasoning with him. In fact, she could think of only one way to save him.

"Luke!" she cried. "Everybody! Come quick!"

Shocked by the betrayal, Will turned to run. She lunged at him, wrapping her arms around his thin frame. He shook her off roughly. Her foot hooked on a low vine, and she fell heavily to the ground.

He turned to face her. "I'll be back, Lyss — I promise! I won't let them do this to you!"

By the time Luke and the others burst out of the lifeboat, he had fled into the jungle, the flicker of his torch disappearing in the density of the trees.

CHAPTER TWELVE
Day 4, 11:10 P.M.

The jungle was becoming familiar to Will. Who would have dreamed that he would ever know one clump of ferns from another?

But he did. No, that wasn't exactly true. The individual plants all looked alike, especially by torchlight. It was the progression that he was beginning to recognize: coconut palms on the right, broad-leaf whatchamacallits on the left, big step over the fallen log, those weird crisscrossing ferns dead ahead — he was almost home.

He felt a twinge of pride. He used to be the kind of kid who fell apart when the cable went down, or when the family ran out of microwave popcorn. An eight-minute power failure threw him into a panic. But now he was making his way through dense jungle on his own, in the near-blackness of night.

If only Lyssa could see him.

She *had* seen him, he reminded himself. Barely ten minutes ago. And she had refused to come with him. How was he ever going to rescue her?

ISLAND

To rescue Lyssa, he thought, *first you have to rescue yourself.*

But how would he accomplish that? Where should he go? What should he do?

For a moment, the silvery fog swirled around him once more. He closed his eyes and fought through it. And when he opened them again, he was at the twin palms of his camp.

He brushed a few handfuls of dried leaves onto the remains of his fire and reached down with his torch.

The kindling caught quickly, and in the glow of the sudden flare, he saw that he was not alone.

At first, the creature looked like a small haystack. Then the massive head swung around and whimpered.

Will jumped. It was the wild boar.

Run for it!

He stood poised, waiting for the attack. It didn't come.

The animal whimpered again.

Will squinted in the firelight. Blood stained the bristly snout where the arrow still protruded.

His hand tightened on the bow over his shoulder and he pulled an arrow from his pocket. He could kill this thing. Kill it and eat it.

Yeah, right. You're too squeamish to dig out a splinter.

He took a step forward.

Careful. Nothing's more dangerous than a wounded animal.

But this one was dying.

Well, duh! That's why you shot it, right?

Cautiously, Will approached the boar and squatted down beside it. The red piggy eyes seemed almost colorless now, sunken into the head/snout/body. He leaned over until he was close enough to feel the hot wind of the boar's tortured breathing. The animal regarded him suspiciously, but made no attempt to move. He reached out a hand, and the boar shrank from him, but it lacked the strength to get up.

When he closed his hand on the shaft of the arrow, the boar squealed in pain, shaking its snout. Luckily, the arrow pulled out smoothly and easily — there was no barbed head, just a sharpened point at the end. Fresh blood trickled from the hole.

Why was he doing this? This animal was protein, and easy hunting too. Protein meant energy, and energy was what he needed to rescue Lyssa and figure a way out of this mess.

Will fitted an arrow into the bow and pulled back, straining to aim for the creature's neck.

What neck? It's all neck! Its butt is practically an extension of its neck!

He circled the boar, aiming behind its ears. It regarded him through distant, colorless eyes.

Will was sweating now. This Guam humidity always made him perspire, but now it was pouring off him like Niagara Falls. Why couldn't he do this? It was so stupid. He ate bacon cheeseburgers all the time. This was no different.

Except, Will thought, *when you go to McDonald's, you can't feel your dinner's hot breath on your leg before you eat it.*

He set down the bow. "Tell you what," he said out loud to the boar. "I'm going to find some more wood for the fire. You've got till I get back to beat it."

But when he returned with an armload of twigs, the boar hadn't moved an inch.

"I'm going to take a little nap. If you're not gone by the time I wake up, you're dinner."

Sleep would not come. He kept peeking through half-closed eyelids at the boar, which was still in its spot by the fire.

"Will you get lost?!" raged Will. "Don't you realize your *life* is on the line?"

But somewhere, deep down, he had a sneaking suspicion that the boar was smarter than he was.

Will glared at the animal. "You don't think I've got the guts to do it! Well, you're wrong! You've got the rest of the night to scram. If you're still here at sunup, I'm having boar cutlets for lunch."

In the morning, he awoke to find his legs numb and tingling. He looked down the length of his body. The boar was fast asleep, curled up on his feet.

"Aw, come on, boar, get off!" He kicked himself free, struggled upright, and limped around, trying to restore his circulation. The boar followed him like an adoring puppy.

"You're supposed to be *gone*." Will was half disgusted and half pleased.

The boar rubbed against Will's legs, knocking him over with its sheer size and weight.

"Hey, cut it out, boar! Boar?" Down he went, landing flat on his behind. "I guess I'd better give you a name," he laughed. "I can't just call you boar."

But what did you call a hairy, squinty-eyed slob with no neck and a bad attitude?

"I know." He grinned. "Pig-face."

A frown. Pig-face fit to a T, but another name came to mind — Rat-face.

That made no sense. The face was piggy, not ratty.

Why did the name sound so right? And so familiar?

"Rat-face," he said out loud.

The boar spit out a mouthful of chewed leaves and delivered a resounding belch.

And Rat-face it remained.

SURVIVAL

CHAPTER THIRTEEN

Day 5, 8:05 A.M.

In addition to much-needed shelter and supplies, the inflatable lifeboat provided an unexpected bonus with its sun canopy: darkness. For
the first time since they had landed on the island,
the tropical sun didn't wake up Luke at dawn.

He would have slept hours longer — they all
might have — if it hadn't been for the noise. It
was distant at first, but it grew louder and louder.
The castaways listened intently. It was the buzz of
an airplane engine. Could that mean — ?

"Are they leaving?" Ian asked excitedly.

"Please, God," breathed Charla.

They scrambled out of the raft and looked up
for the twin-engine seaplane. But the dense
canopy of branches and palm fronds blocked out
the sky except for tiny glimpses of bright blue
here and there.

"The beach!" exclaimed J.J., breaking into a
run.

Luke grabbed his wrist and held on. "It's too
dangerous! They might see you."

They waited for the slow fade in the engine
sounds that would indicate the aircraft was far

away. Instead, the buzz remained at full volume, almost as if it were coming from directly over- head. And then, all at once, the noise died out.

Luke frowned. "That's weird."

"You think they're still here?" asked Lyssa.

Charla was confused. "But why would they use their plane if they weren't leaving?"

Ian shrugged. "Maybe they're gone. Sound over water can do some funny things."

"We've got to go over there and find out," Luke decided.

"That lagoon is on the other side of the is- land," Charla reminded him. "It takes half the day to get there."

"Maybe not," Ian put in. "We've got a com- pass now. We can estimate the direction and take a shortcut through the jungle. That should save a lot of time."

They retrieved the compass, and Ian lined up the needle with north. "I'd say just about due east," he guessed. "Maybe a few degrees to the south." He rummaged through the survival pack, coming up with the knife.

J.J. was highly amused. "They've got guns, kid. What are you going to do with that? Floss?"

Ian took the blade and made a small cut in the bark of a coconut palm. "I saw a documen- tary on Lewis and Clark on the History Channel," he explained. "Always mark your trail so you can find your way back."

It was much easier going through the jungle, although they were constantly sidestepping dense thickets, some of them thirty or forty feet wide. In less than an hour, they had reached a low bluff overlooking the shore. There they made a left turn and headed south.

"Hey!"

All at once, Lyssa pitched forward, landing flat on her face in the underbrush.

"Must have been those big island joker ants," snickered J.J., helping her up. "Watch out, they also give wedgies."

"Very fun — " She fell silent in midword, staring at the ground. "I know this sounds crazy, but was there ever a *sidewalk* here, do you think?"

"Oh, sure," J.J. said sarcastically. "They laid it down back when they built the mini-mall — "

"Look!" she interrupted.

Half buried in the damp earth was a familiar gray shape. It was broken and crumbling, with weeds and brush coming up through the cracks. But the edge that stuck out of the ground was perfectly straight.

There was no question about it. This was a slab of poured concrete.

"Here's another," called Charla, kicking at the mud a few feet ahead of them.

They spread out, digging with their hands and feet. They found slabs extending all the way from the bluff, hundreds of yards into the deepest jungle.

"Maybe it's the Walk of Fame," suggested J.J., "where all the celebrity lizards make impressions of their tails in the cement."

"It proves one thing," said Luke. "The island wasn't always deserted. People lived here."

"And later than the invention of paved roads," Ian pointed out.

Charla nodded. "But who builds a road in the middle of the jungle?"

They all turned to Ian, but for once he had no answer.

The castaways continued south. It wasn't long before they spotted the sheltered lagoon where they had witnessed the murder just two days before. To Luke it seemed as if a hundred years had passed since then.

"Get down," he ordered.

The five dropped to a crouch, peering out through the trees.

Lyssa hovered over Luke's shoulder. "Can you see anything? Are they gone?"

There, beached side by side, were *two* seaplanes.

CHAPTER FOURTEEN
Day 5, 9:50 A.M.

Charla was bewildered. "*Another* plane?"

Luke stared in disbelief, but the truth was undeniable. The sound they'd heard hadn't been the departure of the first aircraft, but the arrival of a second.

"They've got company," he commented.

J.J. frowned. "Yeah, but why meet *here*? This island is less than boring. There's nothing but bugs and bananas."

"Privacy," Luke told him. "These guys are criminals. They're probably up to something illegal."

Ian pointed out a place where the jungle advanced down a coral ramp. There was excellent cover in the dense underbrush, plus it was in spying range of the shore, and a good twenty feet above sea level. It would be nearly impossible for the men to spot them there.

It took another few minutes to creep down the steep slope. Luke was in the lead, with the others in line behind him, keeping their heads low. They crouched in the vines, peering out over the lagoon.

ISLAND

The second plane was a single-engine job, smaller than the first one, but with a large cargo hold on its underside.

"Look!" hissed Charla.

It was the red-haired man. Instinctively, Luke's eyes traveled to the thin man's waist, where his gun was jammed into his belt.

"That's the killer," he whispered to Lyssa and J.J. "The guy he's talking to must be from the second plane."

Four others came into view — Red Hair's partners and two newcomers. They were carrying the crates that had been unloaded from the first aircraft. Red Hair pried open the first box and rummaged inside.

"Blankets?" mused Charla in perplexity.

There was something wrapped in them. It was long and gleaming white — taller than the men themselves. It took two of them to hold it up, and the one clutching the foot-thick base was struggling. The thing tapered in a slight curve down to a soft point at the other end.

"Let me guess," put in J.J. "It's the world's largest golf tee."

Ian's mouth formed an O of sudden understanding. "Ivory!"

Lyssa stared at him. "It's soap?"

The younger boy shook his head. "The other

kind of ivory. I think that's an elephant tusk. I saw a show about it once. That's why people hunt elephants. For their ivory."

"But that's *wrong*," protested Charla.

"It's also against the law, isn't it?" asked Luke.

"So's murder," J.J. reminded him darkly.

They watched as the men unwrapped three more tusks — one the same size as the first, and a shorter pair about four feet long. They then turned their attention to a second case. It was smaller, but more high-tech, with sealing latches and various knobs and indicator dials. As they opened it, a cloud of vapor rose and dissipated into the tropical humidity.

"I was afraid of that," Ian said seriously.

Inside they could make out dozens of transparent jars.

"What is it?" asked Luke.

"I think those are animal parts," Ian told them, "probably from an endangered species — tiger, most likely."

"Parts?" Lyssa asked weakly.

"Fur, claws," Ian replied, "meat, vital organs, bones — "

"Yuck," was J.J.'s opinion.

Charla looked as if she were about to throw up. "But why? Who wants that stuff?"

"In a lot of Asian cities, tiger parts are a delicacy for the super-rich, or even a miracle cure. It was all in the documentary I saw. A full-grown tiger can be worth close to a quarter of a million dollars on the streets of Taipei or Hong Kong."

"So what you're saying," Luke began, "is that these guys are smugglers?"

Ian nodded. "Dealers in ivory and illegal animal parts. The men from the first plane — they must buy from poachers around Africa and Asia. Then they sell to the second group."

"But why here?" asked Lyssa.

"Isn't it obvious?" replied Luke. "We're totally isolated. In a million years, the police would never catch them making the exchange."

"It's probably a halfway point too," Ian guessed. "They could be coming from Japan, Korea, the Philippines, Hong Kong, anywhere — even Hawaii."

"That could be why they killed that guy," added Charla solemnly. "Maybe he was ripping them off or something."

They watched grimly as the smugglers went over the rest of the shipment. In addition to three more refrigerated containers, there was an entire crate of what appeared to be rhinoceros horns.

"It's possible that no animals were killed for

those," Ian mused. "You can cut a rhino's horn off and it will grow back. It's actually a type of hair. Then it's ground up and sold as medicine."

By this time, Charla was shaking with outrage. "They probably killed those poor rhinos anyway — just for the fun of it!"

Satisfied that the shipment was in order, one of the newcomers went over and stepped inside the single-engine plane. A moment later, he reappeared, helping an enormously fat man dressed in an all-white silk suit that gleamed even brighter than the ivory.

"Mr. Big," snickered J.J.

"Yes," Ian said seriously. "I mean, that's probably not his name. But he seems to be in charge."

Sweat poured in streaks down the man's face and neck, and he mopped himself with a sopping handkerchief, fighting a losing battle to stay dry. In his free hand, he carried a small suitcase. He was accompanied by the biggest Doberman pinscher Luke had ever seen.

"What's up with the suitcase?" asked J.J. "Is he moving in?"

Then Mr. Big opened the luggage. They goggled.

"Money!" exclaimed Charla in a strangled voice.

The bag was filled with neat bundles of bills,

packed side by side, end to end, and on top of one another. It was a fortune.

Suddenly, the big dog stiffened. Then it began to bark, a loud raspy baritone that cut through the jungle like a hot knife through butter.

"It smells us!" rasped Lyssa, terrified.

"Let's go," whispered Luke.

Charla jumped up. "You don't have to ask *me* twice!"

Luke grabbed her by the shorts and pulled her down again. "*Slowly,*" he insisted. "And stay low till we're well into the woods."

The castaways crawled back up the slope. They could still hear the barking when they reached the top and ran into the depths of the jungle. There was a panic to their flight, and they scrambled through the vines, tripping and stumbling as the foliage grew thicker.

"Slow down!" ordered Luke.

"But what if they come after us?" asked Charla, who was thirty feet ahead of everyone else.

"They probably think he was barking at a lizard or something," said Luke. "Come on, somebody's going to break a leg."

"I'm sorry!" Charla was almost hysterical as she stopped to let the others catch up. "It's just so horrible! Those poor animals!"

"Hey! *Hey!*" J.J. cut her off. "We have no proof that any of that stuff is real. Those tusks could be plastic!"

"So how come you ran too?" she shot back.

"The dog probably isn't in on the hoax." J.J. grinned sheepishly. "Every year hundreds of actors wind up with stitches because stunt animals don't know it's just a movie."

"That's no stunt animal." Luke was angry now. "And this is no stunt!"

"Every time it seems like we've hit bottom, something even more awful happens," Lyssa agreed miserably. "Will goes crazy, or *more* smugglers come, or their dog smells us! How could it be worse?"

She got her answer when they followed Ian's trail back to the inflatable raft. The contents of the survival pack were scattered all around the lifeboat and the surrounding jungle. Precious supplies were opened and strewn every which way.

"Look!" Charla pointed down. There, amid the dozens of sneaker prints, were animal tracks.

Ian squatted to examine them. "Boar," he concluded.

"Uh-oh." Lyssa rummaged through their gear. "Whatever it was, it took the mac and cheese."

"That's impossible!" Luke exploded. "It was freeze-dried and vacuum-packed! It didn't smell any different from the first aid kit. There's no way a pig could be smart enough to go through all this stuff and decide *that* was food!"

His fellow castaways stared uneasily back at him.

Their last meal — their safety net — was gone.

"I don't know which one of us is the bigger pig," mumbled Will, crunching uncooked pasta.

Beside him stood the boar, its snout pumping up and down as the two savaged the freeze-dried macaroni and cheese straight out of the package.

"You know, Rat-face, it's a lot better when you boil it," commented Will to his new companion. He picked up a fistful of orange powder and crammed it in after the macaroni. "The cheese is supposed to be hot and gooey. If I ever get out of here, I'll come back and bring you some."

Rat-face obviously thought it was just fine the way it was. The animal never missed a swallow as it tore at the plastic bag with one sharp tusk.

"Hey, stay on your own side!" snapped Will. "After this, it's back to bananas, you know!"

CHAPTER FIFTEEN
Day 6, 5:35 P.M.

The theft of their last meal changed the castaways' approach to food. No longer could they depend on eleventh-hour runs for coconuts and bananas to stand between them and malnutrition. They needed protein. They needed vegetables. They needed well-balanced meals.

The equipment from the survival pack helped. Suddenly, they had pots and pans. They could fish and cook what they caught. Even durian seeds were tasty when roasted over the fire.

Two forked sticks with a crosspiece allowed a pot to be hung over the flame by its half-hoop handle. This enabled them to boil taro, a native root, which resembled a cross between a yam and an overloaded electrical junction box.

"You know," said J.J. in genuine surprise, "this isn't half bad. It's almost like mashed potatoes."

"It gets very soft when boiled," Ian agreed. "But you have to cook it well to kill off a poisonous chemical that could be fatal to humans."

J.J. spit a mouthful halfway across the beach.

"It's fantastic," beamed Luke, digging in. "The only thing that tastes better than food prepared

ISLAND

by your own hands is food prepared by some-body else's."

Taro was plentiful; the fresh water to boil it in was very scarce. While it seemed to be rain-ing constantly, it never rained for very long. No matter how many coconut shells the castaways set out — now over a hundred — the yield was never more than an inch or so.

Ian tried rigging a still — something he had seen on *National Geographic Explorer*. They boiled a pot of seawater under a three-sided plas-tic tent made from a rain poncho. The water va-por rose as steam, recondensing on the sides of the tent. Then the droplets ran down the inside of the plastic and collected in three bowls on the ground. The salt was left behind in the pot. This was fresh water.

"Seems like a lot of work for a dribble," com-mented J.J.

"You got a busy social calendar?" laughed Lyssa.

"I could have," sighed the actor's son. "In Cal-ifornia."

"That's why you got kicked out of California," Luke butted in. "You were having too much fun."

J.J. glared at him, but had to admit Luke wasn't exaggerating much. His reputation as a wild Hollywood brat had grown almost as large

SURVIVAL

as his famous father's movie career. Gossip columnists used to call to ask about Dad. Now they wanted the details of J.J.'s latest escapade. It had been a great source of satisfaction to him. His brow clouded. Until Jonathan Lane had chosen CNC in the hope that it might straighten out his flaky son.

"*How could you do this to me?*" he screamed at his father in tortured dreams every night. But the next morning he always awoke knowing that he'd given Dad a lot of help making the decision.

Their social calendars may have been blank, but the castaways had plenty to keep them busy. Two patrols per day — morning and afternoon — were dispatched to comb the jungle for signs of Will or his camp. They all took turns searching, with Lyssa leading the group every time.

Ian built three more stills, so one person had to maintain the fires and keep adding seawater to the pots. This assignment also included emptying the bowls of freshly distilled water into the lifeboat's keg.

Each fishing trip began with a spirited round of rock-paper-scissors to determine who would perform the disgusting task of baiting the hooks. This was a job nobody wanted, because, as Luke put it, "The worms are bigger than the fish."

Charla didn't use bait at all. She preferred the

challenge of swimming in the ocean and snaring her fish with a lightning-quick hand.

J.J. volunteered for fishing every day, but spent very little time with his hook in the water. He had discovered sea cucumbers, and was fascinated and delighted by their life process.

"Picture a bag of guts with a hole at each end," he explained. "The water goes straight through it. But when some poor sap gets beached, it just sits there, full of water. Watch this."

He picked up the creature, aimed it like a water pistol, and squeezed. Instantly, the sea cucumber emptied itself in a thin stream that hit Charla full in the face.

She pushed J.J. into the surf and held him under.

Lyssa hauled him out of the drink. "I guess Charla isn't interested in marine biology," she sympathized.

Ian was in charge of food gathering because he was the only person who could tell what was edible. The good news was that food was everywhere, even on the walls of their home. They would wake up each morning to find the lifeboat covered in giant snails.

"They're a delicacy, you know," Ian told them, gathering an armload, "and a good source of protein."

SURVIVAL

"In your dreams," said everybody.

But after bananas and coconuts three times a day, most of them were ready to try anything.

When she wasn't in the jungle looking for her brother, Lyssa spent most of her time tinkering with the lifeboat's scorched and broken radio. She was a straight-A student with a real knack for electronics and machinery.

They were surviving, keeping busy, overcoming obstacles. The depression would come suddenly, unexpectedly, without warning. Charla might reach up to smooth her hair, feel the stiff, salt-encrusted tangle, and burst into tears. The crying would sometimes last for hours. Or Ian would grow suddenly silent and sit for half a day, staring morosely out to sea, visualizing who knew what. Any mention of Will could set Lyssa off.

For J.J., it would start innocently enough. He'd be talking about a great pizza place he knew in L.A. But then, forty-five minutes later, he'd be sitting there on the sand, his arms wrapped around himself straitjacket-style, still mumbling about double-cheese and pepperoni.

Charla ate less, exercised more, and blew up at anybody who dared mention it.

"Why don't you just keep on swimming?" J.J.

suggested. "At your pace, you should hit the Oregon Coast in another three years."

"I should hit your ugly face in another three seconds," she retorted.

"Take it easy," soothed Luke.

J.J. turned on him, blue eyes blazing. "Who died and left you God?"

And before Luke knew it, he was shouting, "The captain did, that's who! And if you hadn't decided to run up the sails in a gale, he'd be alive, we'd still have a boat, and none of us would be having this conversation."

Luke watched in angry satisfaction as J.J.'s face drained of all color. It was the one topic J.J. couldn't smirk away. The tears were already on the way when he started running. At the edge of the trees, he turned and spat a single word back at Luke: "Convict!"

And then Luke was chasing him, intent on war. But the low vines tripped him up and he landed hard, raging at the sky. "No!!"

Wasn't this just perfect? Now — now, of all times — everyone was going nuts! Didn't they see that they had to hold it together if they were going to find Will and get off this rock? *Why can't they be more like me?* Luke thought. *I'm calm! Steady! Balanced! Sensible —*

SURVIVAL

At the sudden pain in his hands, he looked down. His knuckles were skinned and bleeding. With each thought, he had been having a boxing match with a tree trunk.

Sensible and steady. Yeah, right.

J.J. didn't reappear until late that night. He stepped into the lifeboat and tapped Luke on the shoulder. "I'm on fishing tomorrow."

"Okay," Luke replied. "I'll work the stills."

For once, he was grateful there were so many chores.

There was one final task that all the castaways kept up day to day. No matter what other job was in progress, five pairs of ears were always listening for the drone of airplane engines that would mean the smugglers were leaving the island. Until those men were gone, the ship-wrecked crew of the *Phoenix* could not light signal fires, or write distress messages in the sand. They would never be rescued if they continued to be forced into hiding.

"When are they going to *scram*?" asked Lyssa in exasperation. "They've got their tusks and their horns. What are they waiting for?"

"That's what we have to find out," Luke said decisively.

So the next morning, Luke and Charla set off for the other side of the island to spy on their unwanted neighbors. Two hours later, they returned, trembling.

"They're searching the jungle!" Charla rasped. "They've got that Doberman sniffing the ground to pick up our scent!"

"You mean they know we're here?" asked Lyssa in horror.

"The dog definitely smells something when it sniffs someplace we've been," Luke told them. "But those guys can't be sure what they're looking for."

"The island's not that big," Ian said nervously. "Sooner or later, I mean, even if it's just by dumb luck — "

He never finished the sentence. He didn't have to. The five castaways stood rooted in the sand as the thought began to sink in.

They were being hunted.

SURVIVAL

CHAPTER SIXTEEN
Day 9, 10:10 A.M.

They called it the two-minute drill.

The signal came from Charla, atop a palm tree — the hooting of an owl, a sound that would never be heard on a tropical island. That set the vanishing process in motion. The fires were extinguished, the stills folded up and buried in the sand. A few sweeps of a giant fern and their footprints were gone too, leaving a deserted beach.

Two quick kicks took care of the supports for the sun canopy, and the lifeboat lay flat. Ready hands drew a leafy blanket of woven vines and palm fronds over it. Suddenly, the black rubber craft was gone, replaced by the green-brown colors of the jungle. Finally, the castaways themselves disappeared, melting into the dense underbrush.

There was the electronic beep of a digital stopwatch. "One-fifty-seven," Ian reported. "Our best time yet."

Subdued cheering and a few backslaps as the heads popped up again.

Luke wasn't happy. "We can make ourselves

ISLAND

disappear, but we can't hide our smell. The dog's nose won't be fooled."

Ian looked thoughtful. "What if we set out a few fish heads and tails and guts on the beach? That would be a strong enough scent to confuse the dog."

"It'll also gas us out of here," Lyssa noted, making a face.

"We can keep it wrapped up in one of the ponchos," Luke decided. "We'll open it only when we hear the signal."

It was agreed that two-person scout teams would be dispatched to keep an eye on the smugglers. Lyssa objected. This would distract them from the search for Will. But the others overruled her. They hadn't seen Will in five days and had no idea where he was. For all they knew, he was on the other side of the island where the float-planes were beached. They were as likely to spot him there as anywhere.

"That's another reason to spy on those guys," Luke argued. "To make sure they haven't found Will."

Luke and Ian had been scouting for over an hour before they spotted the Doberman. They immediately pulled back, ducking behind a dense stand of ferns. Red Hair had the dog on a leash, and two other men were with him. All three were armed.

"You were right," whispered Ian. "They're looking for something."

They followed along for a while, making sure that nothing was moving in the direction of the castaways' camp. When the dog began to run in circles, barking excitedly, they knew they had to retreat.

Ian frowned. "Three of them out here. How many are with the planes?"

Luke shrugged. "One way to find out."

They backtracked. Staying low, they eased themselves down the slope to their spying place overlooking the cove. The two boys counted and delivered their tallies at the same time: three — two men on the beach, and Mr. Big sitting half in and half out of the smaller plane. They couldn't see his face, but his thick legs and white suit identified him.

In all this time, not one of the traffickers had changed clothes. Which meant . . .

"They weren't planning to stay here," Luke whispered. "They're only hanging around to make sure there's no one else on the island."

Ian was confused. "Where do they sleep? There's no campsite. And they can't all fit in the planes — not lying down, anyway."

It was a good question. They eyeballed every inch of the cove. There was the lagoon, the rocky jetty, a narrow beach, and coral bluffs leading up to the edge of the jungle. No camp.

"We're missing something," Luke murmured.

And then he saw the footprints in the sand. They were mostly heading in one direction. They ended where the beach did, of course. But Luke could envision the trail leading up the slope and into the jungle. The entry point was perhaps a quarter mile from where he and Ian lay hidden.

There had to be something there — something that was important to these men.

Carefully, silently, they picked their way around the apron of the cove. The jungle became so dense that they were doing more wading than walking. Their progress slowed to almost nothing. That was why Luke didn't injure himself when he bumped straight into it.

"A wall?" Ian gasped.

Three steps before, it had been invisible, knit into the fabric of the rain forest. But here it was, the curved corrugated metal siding of a Quonset hut. A big one.

Luke and Ian stared at each other in mute wonder. Their island — isolated, deserted, and empty of any hint of civilization — had a *building* on it! It was mind-blowing.

Luke put his finger to his lips. Then the two of them crept down the length of the structure. Cautiously, they turned the corner and found themselves facing a gray metal front with a door and two windows. A rusted sign, faded and barely legible, read: UNITED STATES ARMY AIR CORPS.

"An Air Force base?" Luke breathed. "In the middle of a jungle?"

Ian pointed to the sign. "Army Air Corps. They haven't been called that for fifty years. This area could have been clear back then, and the jungle just grew up around it."

Luke sidled up to the streaked and smeared window and peered in. The jungle was growing in there too, blasted up through rotted floor planking. There was no one inside.

"Let's check it out," he whispered.

They opened the door — someone had recently oiled the hinges — and slipped through. Desks, chalkboards, filing cabinets. Yellowed old papers and file folders were scattered everywhere.

"Look!" exclaimed Ian.

Sleeping bags were spread out on the old benches. A few beer bottles, empty food cans, and dozens of cigarette butts littered two desks that had been pushed together. The place smelled of stale smoke.

This was the traffickers' camp, all right. This
— what was it? Military, definitely. Old and abandoned, for sure. But a base? It was more like an
office.

Ian touched Luke's arm and pointed to a bul-
letin board suspended from one of the curved
walls. Tacked up there was a faded diagram of a
hut exactly like the one they were standing in.
Two other huts, much smaller, stood behind it.
These three buildings seemed to be the extent of
this installation.

"Did they have bases this small?" Luke asked.

The younger boy shrugged and drew Luke's
attention to something else on the board — a
map of the Pacific. Tiny pins representing boats
and planes were stuck all over the chart. Fallen
ones lay on the floor in front of it.

"World War Two," he noted.

There were a couple of private offices and,
farther back, a barracks room with lines of bunks.
Luke wondered why the smugglers were sleeping
on hard benches when real beds were right here.
Then he got a closer look at the mattresses. They
were ripped to shreds and alive with thousands
of bugs. He shuddered and returned to where Ian
was flipping through file folders.

"Find anything?"

Ian shook his head. "Requisitions for toilet paper and shaving cream. They needed a part for their movie projector in 1945 — " He picked up an envelope marked TOP SECRET that had once been closed with an important-looking seal. A dozen or so stapled pages were inside. The first line caught his eye: *Re: Deployment of Junior.*

His eyes widened like saucers. *"Junior!"*

"Junior?" repeated Luke. "Who's Junior?"

The sound they heard next drove every other thought from their minds — the barking of a dog.

They ran for the door. Gruff voices outside. The men were right there! Luke grabbed Ian and spun him around.

The terror was plain in the younger boy's eyes. He mouthed the words, *Back door?*

As they sped to the rear of the building, Luke knew that the answer to that question would mean the difference between life and death.

Heart sinking, he faced the back wall. No door; just two windows. Jammed and warped, the first one wouldn't budge.

The smugglers clattered in the front door, accompanied by their barking dog.

"Shut up, mutt," came an unfriendly growl.

The second window moved only an inch before seizing up against a thick vine.

Ian began to shake.

That was when Luke looked down. The metal

wall of the hut had come away from the decaying floor about eight inches. It was their only chance. Desperately, he shoved Ian into the gap and followed. The two wriggled through to the outside and crawled off into the jungle. There was no running. The foliage was far too thick. But however slow, it felt like escape — desperate movement, propelled by panic. And when the underbrush thinned, they sprinted headlong, tripping and falling, and getting up to run some more.

They were halfway home before Luke managed to get his hands on Ian's shoulders to slow the boy down.

"Ian!" he panted. "What was all that back there? Who's Junior?"

Still clutching the top-secret envelope and papers, Ian struggled to catch his breath.

"A bomb," he wheezed finally. "An atomic bomb."

CHAPTER SEVENTEEN
Day 9, 3:40 P.M.

Luke stared at him. "An atomic bomb?"

Ian nodded fervently. "It was all in this documentary on the Manhattan Project, where they invented the first nuclear weapons back in World War Two. They were supposed to build three bombs, code-named Fat Man, Little Boy, and Junior. But the war ended after Fat Man and Little Boy were dropped. So Junior never had to be built." He waved the envelope in Luke's face. "That installation was going to be used to launch Junior, the third atomic bomb."

Luke looked doubtful. "And the Air Force just forgot this place?"

"It wasn't a real base," Ian reasoned. "There were only bunks for about twenty or thirty people. All they needed were a couple of planes and someplace to land them."

"The concrete!" Luke exclaimed. "That was their runway, right? And it just got busted up and overgrown after fifty years?"

"Probably," Ian agreed. He looked scared. "You don't think they're going to miss this envelope, do you? The smugglers, I mean? That would tip them off that we're here."

"They don't care about paper," Luke assured him. "Not unless there's money printed on it. But, man, was that a close call, or what?"

"I'm still shaking," Ian admitted.

Soon they spotted Charla in the lookout tree. "What took you guys so long?"

"Don't ask," groaned Luke.

The powwow was held on the beach over bananas and coconut milk.

"You know, this is a really fascinating history lesson," yawned J.J., "but who cares about what happened in some ancient war? Come up with a fully charged cell phone, and you've got my attention."

"Unfortunately," Luke said grimly, "that old war affects us more than we think. Tell them, Ian."

"I've been going through those papers," Ian explained tragically. "As near as I can tell, this installation was so top secret that they picked an island that was never on any maps. So I don't think we should depend on anyone coming to rescue us because — technically — we're nowhere."

Luke could almost hear a slurping sound as the very last ounce of hope was sucked out of the castaways.

SURVIVAL

They fell into a gloomy silence that was broken only by the steady lapping of the ocean.

Will's stomach yawned wide open, sore and empty.

It was the mac and cheese, he thought miserably. Before that day, he hadn't known how starved he really was. But the mac and cheese — that beautiful, delicious, *terrible* mac and cheese! Bliss for a few hours. And then the payback.

The meal had served only to awaken the monster of his hunger. That's how it seemed to him — a living creature, loose inside him and impossible to control. It had started as a rumbling in his belly and had grown to a roar that was drowning out everything else around him. He had tried gorging himself on bananas — dozens of them. But the sheer quantity had made him sick. And still his hunger raged. No, it was beyond hunger now. It was desperation.

A numbing terror rose from the tips of his toes as the fact of his helplessness became clear. He was becoming weaker every hour. Soon he wouldn't be able to *act*, to rescue Lyssa, or even to save himself. All alone in the jungle, there was only one place this could lead, one way it could end.

He was going to die.

But I'm not all alone. . . .

His fevered gaze fell on the boar, curled up and snoring between the twin palms.

Rat-face is food. Rat-face . . .

He reached for his bow and pulled an arrow back against the string.

But —

Go close. That'll give you a quick kill.

He stopped short. How could he even think of killing Rat-face? The boar had been his only friend these last few days — maybe the final days of Will's whole life.

Food. That was all that mattered. This wasn't about friendship. It was a matter of survival.

He drew back the arrow.

Harder! he exhorted himself. If the first shot reached the brain, there would be no suffering.

His eyes filled up with tears. "I'm sorry, Rat-face," he whispered.

As soon as the name passed his lips, he had a startling image of a burly, sour-looking sailor standing on the deck of a ship. It was so vivid that Will could actually make out the word painted on the man's life jacket: PHOENIX.

Shocked, he relaxed his grip on the bow-string. The arrow snapped off the stretched vine, its dull end hitting him in the eye.

"Ow!"

SURVIVAL

He staggered a little, but he hardly noticed the pain over what was going on in his head. It all came rushing back with the force of a runaway train — the other kids, the storm, the explosion, the shipwreck! And those terrible days of drifting on the raft, parched and starving, not knowing if his sister, Lyssa, was alive or dead.

He felt a great swell of joy in his chest. She wasn't dead — he had seen her and talked to her. That was real, wasn't it? And the others too. By some miracle, they had all survived the sinking of the *Phoenix* and had drifted to the same place, wherever it was.

The others! He had been hiding from them, calling them liars and kidnappers, stealing their food, vandalizing their camp. And their only purpose had been to help him.

They must think I'm crazy!

He considered this. They were right. He *was* crazy. Or at least he had been.

Not anymore.

"Come on, Rat-face!" he exclaimed excitedly.

The boar awoke and shot him a questioning look.

"Let's go!" He ran off into the jungle, Rat-face trotting along at his heels.

CHAPTER EIGHTEEN
Day 9, 4:05 P.M.

Smell was a problem for those who lived on the island. In this heat and humidity, just the regular chores of day-to-day survival wrung the perspiration out of the five castaways. Someone was always battling jock itch or athlete's foot or a weird tropical fungus. If it hadn't been for their easy access to the ocean, the stink of the whole group would have been unbearable.

It was always harder to notice on yourself. Luke risked a sniff when nobody was looking. Pee-yew! The mud of his and Ian's tunnel out of the hut and the sweat of their desperate escape had mingled with the usual jungle steaminess to create a pretty strong funk.

Bathing was always a tricky tightrope to walk. With the girls around, Luke wanted his privacy. But he didn't want to be like Ian. The kid was so shy that he would go miles up the beach, and a simple bath would end up taking him all day.

He walked along the shore, past the can opener, to where the sand gave way to rocky coral. He kicked off his shoes and dove through the incoming breakers, letting his clothes wash on

SURVIVAL

his body. He was no expert swimmer like Charla, but he enjoyed the ocean. This was the only good thing about being shipwrecked, he reflected. No beach at home had such perfect water, clear as glass, with not the slightest trace of the murkiness of pollution.

He pulled off his shirt and swished it through the waves like a washing machine agitator. Then he wrung it and spread it on the rocks to dry. Next he wriggled out of his shorts and underwear and did the same. Then he went for a long swim. The water felt cool and refreshing, and some of the tension loosened in his neck and shoulders. Even though it was deep here, he could clearly see plants and rocks and starfish on the bottom ten feet below.

Peace. The ocean was the only place he ever found it, where he could free his mind from the terrible danger all around him. He didn't forget his problems here. But he could somehow separate himself from them. There were times where he could even remember the old Luke Haggerty, the one from way back before this avalanche of troubles had started with that lousy locker inspection.

Here he could lose himself in the pounding of the surf, the screeching of gulls, the rustling of the wind through palm fronds, the hooting of an owl. . . .

An owl?

The signal!

Luke must have swum, but he didn't remember a second of it. The next thing he knew, he was scrambling onto the coral, cutting his feet, shins, and knees to ribbons as he leaped into his shorts. Then he was pounding up the beach. He could see his fellow castaways performing their two-minute drill. The wind roared in his ears as he sprinted — that and a different, terrifying sound: the approaching bark of a hunting dog.

He arrived at the scene at the same time as Charla.

"Two men!" she hissed, pushing sand over a dismantled still. "And the Doberman!"

Luke was proud of the group. There was panic in their eyes, but their bodies were pure efficiency. The stills disappeared beneath the beach. Their footprints were wiped clean. Then into the woods, where they flattened the lifeboat and pulled the palm blanket on top of it.

By now, men's voices could be heard along with the barking. The castaways melted into the underbrush.

"What's the deal with this dog? It's going crazy!"

They were no more than a hundred feet away.

Crouched next to Luke, Charla froze in shock

and horror. "The fish!" she breathed. "We forgot to open the stinky fish! The dog smells *us!*"

Too late, thought Luke. What he heard next turned the blood in his veins to ice.

"It's onto something!" the other man said excitedly. "Let go of the leash!"

A split second later, Luke caught sight of the brown-and-black Doberman bounding through the underbrush, fangs bared. It was fifty feet away, then thirty. Beside him, he heard Charla gasp. His mind worked furiously. What could they do? He came up blank. For the first time, the castaways had truly arrived at zero options. Their adventure was ending right here, right now.

At that moment, a guided missile shot out of the bushes and slammed full-force into the dog.

It all happened so fast that, for a second, Luke had no idea what was going on. He only knew that, instead of being savaged by a vicious animal, he was still in hiding, watching a monumental struggle.

Then he heard the squeal.

"The wild boar!" he whispered.

The fight was furious and deadly. The boar's head pumped up and down like a pile driver as it slashed at the dog with its tusks. The Doberman lunged and growled, biting at the enemy's throat with razor-sharp fangs. The boar was bigger and much heavier, but the Doberman was faster and more agile, leaping up to tear at the thick neck. The boar's head weaved back and forth, slashing at the dog's exposed underbelly.

Blood began to spatter, but it was impossible to tell which animal it was coming from.

Terrible howling. And suddenly, the dog was on the bottom, and the boar was in charge.

All at once, the two men came crashing through the underbrush. Red Hair was in the lead. "What the — ?" He raised his pistol and fired a shot into the boar's neck.

With a squeal that was half rage, half surprise, the boar pulled back from the Doberman and raised its massive, blood-streaked head.

The second man pulled his weapon too, and he and Red Hair opened fire. It was a scene straight out of a gangster movie — shot after shot, bullets flying. Luke tried to burrow himself into the soft ground.

The boar advanced one menacing step and then became seemingly boneless, collapsing in a heap among the vines, dead.

The two men ran up to where the lifeless Doberman lay.

"I can't believe it!" Red Hair was furious. "That fat tub of lard is gonna blow its blubber over this dog!"

SURVIVAL

"And all for nothing," his partner agreed in disgust. "It was smelling that ugly hog all along."

"That's the good news," Red Hair commented. "At least now we can leave this godforsaken bug farm." As the two started back through the jungle, he reached out one heavy boot and kicked the dead boar. "Stupid pig!"

Luke's mind was reeling, but he forced himself to remain perfectly still. All would be lost if one of them jumped up too soon before the smugglers were well out of range. It was only ten minutes, but it felt like two lifetimes. There was a rustling of foliage, and Lyssa crept out of hiding and stood over the body of the boar.

"It saved our lives."

One by one, other castaways emerged from the underbrush.

"But why would it fight for us?" asked Charla.

"Maybe he just didn't like Dobermans," Luke suggested. "I know I don't."

J.J. looked into the boar's open, unseeing eyes. "We'll call it even on the mac and cheese, okay?"

Charla clouted him on the shoulder.

"Well, it's just a *pig*," he defended himself.

All at once, they heard a whimper.

Everybody froze. Luke put his finger to his lips.

There it was again. A weak sigh. Barely a breath.

Definitely human.

They looked around. Where could it be coming from? The two men were gone. The castaways were all accounted for.

And then Ian tripped on something. He gawked. "Luke!"

There, beneath a low fern, lay Will Greenfield, white and still. Ian felt for a pulse. It was strong and steady.

"Oh, my God!" Lyssa dropped to one knee beside her brother. The tattered cuff of Will's shorts was soaked red. She pulled the fabric up. Beneath it was a bullet wound, just above the thigh.

"Aw, Will!" she said, voice shaking. "Why is it always you?"

His eyes fluttered open. "Don't yell at me," he said faintly. "I didn't do it on purpose." He waved. "Hi, Luke. Ian. Charla. J.J. Long time no see."

"You *know* us?" blurted Charla.

Will was sheepish. "I do now. Did you guys see Rat-face?"

"Rat-face?" repeated Luke in disbelief.

"Not *that* Rat-face," Will explained. "I've got a pet boar."

Lyssa put a hand on his arm. "No, you don't," she said gently. "Not anymore. But it was a real hero, Will. You can be proud of it."

"Oh." Will looked sad. Suddenly, he winced in pain, grabbing at his wounded leg. "Man, that hurts!" he groaned. "How bad is it?"

Instinctively, they all turned to Ian.

The younger boy backed off. "How should I know?" He added, "But there's no exit wound, so the bullet must be still in there. He needs a doctor."

"They don't make jungle calls," J.J. reminded him. "I'll get the first aid kit."

"Hang in there," Lyssa encouraged her brother. "You're going to be just fine."

She was grateful that he couldn't see how little she believed her own words.

CHAPTER NINETEEN
Day 10, 11:35 A.M.

The stills were up again, their small fires burn-ing, not on the beach, but just inside the trees. In their midst lay Will, stretched out on the small piece of cabin top that had miraculously deliv-ered four of the castaways from a burning, sink-ing ship to the safety of the island.

"Hey, Lyss, I never said thanks for blowing up the boat."

"You were the one who was supposed to be ventilating the engine room," his sister retorted. "Shut up and rest."

It was a pointless argument. But somehow it felt comforting to be bickering again.

She checked the bandage on his wounded leg, not having the slightest idea what she was looking for. "Uh-huh," she said — competently, she hoped.

She joined Ian, who was picking heavy seeds out of a durian and setting them aside for roast-ing. "The ocean has to be out of fish before I eat those things," she commented sourly.

Ian looked grave. "We've got to get your brother off this island."

SURVIVAL

"Will's just a big complainer," she pointed out. "That shows he's getting better. The bleeding has finally stopped."

The boy shook his head seriously. "There's going to be an infection for sure with that bullet in there. It's no big deal if you can get medical attention. But our first aid stuff is going to run out fast."

Lyssa blinked. "He could *die*?"

He shrugged helplessly. "Not tomorrow, not next week. But if we can't get him to a hospital — "

"Lyss," called Will from the raft, "could you get me some water?"

"You've got legs!" she snapped automatically.

It was so instant, so instinctive for her to take a shot at him — the result of twelve years of sibling warfare. Practically every detail of her life existed to be in opposition to something about Will. He struggled in school, so she slaved for straight A's. He was cautious, so she tried to be impulsive.

What would she do without him? In a bizarre way, they were a team. They were even named as a pair, after flowers — Sweet William and Sweet Alyssum. A cheesy move by their parents, she'd always thought. But now it seemed wiser and more telling than Lyssa had ever imagined.

What would she be without Will to fight with, to push off against? Would she just disappear?

"I mean — " She wasn't going to cry. No way. Not in front of Will. "I mean, coming right up." She ran for the water keg. "Anything you want, you just ask."

The twin-engine plane left first, carrying away Red Hair and his two colleagues. Mr. Big left on the second aircraft. By this time, his white suit was a mass of wrinkles and sweaty soil. If he was broken up by the death of his Doberman, he gave no sign.

Luke, J.J., and Charla watched from their usual spying place as the single-engine plane rose from the water, carrying its illegal cargo of tusks and animal parts to who knew where.

"Think they'll be back?" asked Charla.

"Count on it," said Luke. "This is the perfect meeting place for an exchange like that. Why do you think they needed to make sure there wasn't anyone here but them?"

After so many days of hiding, it felt almost unnatural to be able to run down the coral bluffs to the beach without fear of the smugglers. Luke kicked off a shoe and dipped his toe in the warm water of the lagoon. It was hard to believe that only a week had passed since they had witnessed Red Hair executing one of his own men in this very spot.

J.J. skipped a flat rock on the surface of the lagoon. "Well, we've got the run of the place now. We can throw wild parties. Too bad there's nobody to invite but a bunch of snakes."

"We can get rescued," Charla corrected pointedly. "This is our big chance until the smugglers come back. If we blow this . . ." Her voice trailed off.

Once again, Luke used the footprints on the beach as a guide to find the hidden military installation. Even though he'd been there before, the jungle was so dense that the Quonset hut was virtually invisible until the castaways were standing right in front of it.

J.J. stepped inside and looked around with distaste. "What a dump!" he said sourly. "Man, remind me never to join the army."

Charla's eyes were wide. "It's hard to believe that all this was here to kill people."

"There was a war on," Luke reminded her.

"Yeah, but one bomb — wiping out a whole city." She shook her head sadly. "It's scary what we've taught ourselves to do."

Luke noted that the sleeping bags were no longer on the benches. A newspaper lay folded over on one of the seats. He flipped it open. *USA*

Today, from July twenty-fifth — the day the first group of traffickers had arrived on the island.

Luke's jaw dropped. "Guys — "

There, at the top of the front page, was Mr. Radford, the mate of the *Phoenix.* The photograph showed him being pulled out of a battered dinghy by sailors on a Chinese freighter. As the others gathered around, Luke began to read:

HEROIC MATE FOUGHT IN VAIN TO SAVE KIDS ON SINKING BOAT

J.J. Lane, son of actor Jonathan Lane, is one of six youths lost at sea and presumed dead after the sinking of the *Phoenix,* the flagship of Charting a New Course, a renowned sailing program for problem kids. James Cascadden, 61, captain of the sixty-foot schooner, was also lost in the accident, which took place in near-typhoon conditions five hundred miles northeast of Guam.

According to Calvin Radford, 37, the only survivor, the tragedy began to unfold when Lane, 14, inexplicably tried to raise sails at the height of the storm. At that point, wind gusts up to seventy knots and forty-foot waves "tore the boat to splinters," according to Radford.

"He was a crazy kid — maybe Hollywood does it to them. But he didn't deserve to die like that," Radford said emotionally. "None of them did."

Luke Haggerty, 13, of Haverhill, MA; Charla Swann, 12, of Detroit, MI; Ian Sikorsky, 11, of Lake Forest, IL; and Will Greenfield, 13, and his sister, Lyssa, 12, of Huntington, NY, were the other victims.

Radford, the *Phoenix*'s mate, fought desperately to save the six young people after Cascadden was swept overboard by "a freak wave." It was only after the schooner sank out of sight that he climbed aboard the twelve-foot dinghy he would sail for eight days and more than two hundred miles before being rescued by the *Wu Liang*, a freighter out of Shanghai en route to Honolulu.

When called a hero, Radford broke down in tears. "Those kids were my responsibility! I should have found a way to save them."

The Maritime Commission has submitted his name for their highest medal for bravery.

Jonathan Lane could not be reached for comment, but according to spokesman Dan Rapaport . . .

Luke put down the paper, shaking with rage. "I'm speechless!" he seethed. "Rat-face — a hero! After what he did to us — "

"Will's Rat-face had more heroism in his little

finger," Charla agreed emotionally. "You know, if boars have fingers."

J.J. shook his head. "My dad made a comment through a spokesman," he chuckled. "A *spokesman*! It's so totally like him that they almost had me fooled."

Charla stared at him. "What are you talking about?"

"If CNC could sink our boat and strand us on an island," the actor's son explained, "then it's definitely no big deal to print a fake issue of *USA Today*."

Luke waved the paper in his face. "They interviewed my *mother* about me being dead!" he seethed. "Is that real enough for you?"

"She's in on it," J.J. argued. "All our parents are. They're the ones who sent us to this Sleepaway Camp of the Damned."

Charla was furious. "I can't believe you're still talking about this! Poor Will's got a *bullet* in his leg! You think *that's* part of CNC's plan?"

"That must have been a mistake," J.J. said seriously. "It could be our ticket out of here. Sooner or later they're going to have to call the whole thing off to get Will to a doctor. We just have to hang tough."

"Oh, we'll hang tough, all right," Luke vowed. "But it has nothing to do with your idiot theories.

We're going to hang tough so we can live to tell the world what Rat-face did to us, and watch him rot in jail for it!"

Ian had asked them to bring back whatever medical supplies they could find in the hope that there might be something that would help Will. They came up empty in the main building, but one of the smaller huts in back turned out to be a dispensary. Loaded down with bottles, bandages, and sterile pads in yellowed packets, the three started out on the return journey to their camp on the other side of the island.

They had been walking for only a few minutes when, all at once, J.J. disappeared. One minute he was striding at the head of the group; the next, he was just *gone*.

"J.J.?" called Charla, mystified.

"Down here," came a strangely distant voice.

"Quit fooling around," Luke said sharply. "We've got to get this stuff to Will."

"No, really!"

A hand reached up and parted the thick underbrush. They stared. J.J. stood at the bottom of a large square pit, up to his knees in dirt and rotted leaves. Bottles and gauze pads were scattered everywhere.

"Is that supposed to be there?" asked Charla. "Like a trap or something?"

"Sure trapped me." J.J. shrugged, rubbing his head. "I think I fractured my skull."

Luke was impatient. "If the fall didn't break those bottles, I'm sure your thick head's okay too."

"There's something hard down here," J.J. insisted. He began kicking at the dirt of the pit. There was a dull clang, and he jumped back. "Ow!"

Luke frowned. "That sounded like metal." He eased himself into the hole and reached up to help Charla after him.

J.J. was already digging at the earth and leaves of a mound at the center of the pit. A few inches below the surface, he struck black metal with a smooth rounded surface.

The dirt came away easily, and the other three joined him in clearing off the strange object. It was huge — maybe ten feet long and far too heavy to budge. The thing resembled a very tall black garbage can with fins on one end.

"Let me guess," ventured J.J. "It's Chap Stick for giants."

Suddenly, Luke just knew. There was no flash of inspiration, no lightbulb going off in his brain. He simply looked at the object, and in that instant, realized exactly what it was.

Involuntarily, he took a step back.

SURVIVAL

"What's wrong?" asked Charla in concern. "All of a sudden, you're pale as a ghost!"

"I think — " Luke began shakily, "I think we just found Junior."

They goggled. Wide staring eyes moved from Luke, to the object, and then back to Luke again.

Charla was the first to speak. "You're not saying — ?"

Luke nodded weakly. "The Discovery Channel was wrong. They *did* build it. And they left it right here."

This time, everybody stepped backward. J.J. plastered himself against the wall of the pit.

A harsh reality dropped over the castaways like a smothering blanket. A hostile environment and dangerous enemies were only part of the problem. Their friend Will was beginning a fight for his very life. And now, thrown into the mix by some insane quirk of fate — an atomic bomb.

ISLAND

For Nicholas Parcharidis Jr.

SEPTEMBER 3, 1945
0835 hours

The Second World War ended on September 2, 1945, after the United States dropped two atomic bombs on Japanese cities. Most of the planet had suffered six terrible years of fighting and destruction, so there was rejoicing throughout the globe. Millions of soldiers worked around the clock to shut down their military operations and return to their families.

At a small U.S. Army Air Corps installation located on a tiny unnamed island in the Pacific, twenty-six airmen rushed to load equipment onto a transport plane bound for home. Their presence there had been so top secret that not even the Secretary of Defense knew about them. Their mission was to deploy a third atomic weapon — code name: Junior — a backup bomb. It was only to be dropped in the event that the first two failed to end the war.

The day was burning hot like every day on the tropical island. But today the sweat on the faces and bodies smelled distinctly of champagne. The celebration that marked the end of the war had set corks popping long into the

ESCAPE

night. Most of the men struggled through split-
ting headaches after little or no sleep.

When the heavy crane seized up, Staff
Sergeant Raymond Holliday pounded the con-
trols in frustration. "Blast these hydraulics!" The
lift mechanism had been acting up for months,
but it was impossible to get parts way out here
in the Pacific. The crew had been told to "make
do."

Barely a foot off the ground dangled Junior,
the third bomb. Holliday tried the stick again.
Nothing.

From the pit, Corporal Connerly hoisted himself up by the chain, setting his feet down on the
curved surface of the bomb. He had no fear of
the weapon going off. It would have to be
armed first. "Dead?" he called to the sergeant.

Holliday scratched the fire-ant bites on his
arms and thought longingly of his home in
Michigan. "For good this time."

Both men looked to the landing strip a quarter of a mile away. Junior weighed over nine
thousand pounds. Without the crane, there was
no way to get it into the plane's cargo bay. They
were silent as the sun beat down.

"We're going to be the last guys home from
this war," Connerly said with melancholy convic-
tion. "And for what? To nursemaid a souped-up

firecracker on an island that Rand McNally himself couldn't find with a telescope!"

The corporal was wrong on two counts. First, he was reunited with his family within forty-eight hours. And second, someone did find the tiny secret island.

Fifty-six years later, six young people, survivors of a deadly shipwreck, washed up on the sandy shores.

ESCAPE

CHAPTER ONE
Day 16, 3:35 P.M.

Luke Haggerty peered out between the palm fronds. "Call me crazy," he said in amazement, "but I think that's a *chicken*."

The feathered creature perched on a fallen log was smaller than a farm hen, and a deep rusty brown rather than the usual white, speckled, or Rhode Island red. Otherwise, it was a dead ringer — the same four-toed bird feet, fleshy crest, and gizzard. It bobbed as it moved, pecking absently at the rotted wood, clucking softly.

"It *is* a chicken," confirmed his companion, Ian Sikorsky. "Before they were bred for food thousands of years ago, all chickens were like this — the Pacific jungle fowl, living in the wild."

Luke shot him a cockeyed look. "You're putting me on."

"No, really," Ian insisted. "It was in a show I saw on the Discovery Channel. This is a living fossil."

Luke grinned at the younger boy. He knew from experience that Ian was never wrong about something he'd seen on TV. Pushing up his too-long sleeves, Luke stepped out from behind the

ISLAND

tree. With their own shorts and T-shirts in rags, the castaways had taken to wearing fatigues from the abandoned army installation on the other side of the island. These were in perfect shape, if a little faded. But they were adult size. Slight Ian's new clothes hung on him like a tent.

Ian grabbed the baggy fabric of Luke's shirt. "Where are you going?"

"We've been living on fish and bananas," Luke replied. "If that's a chicken, it's dinner. It'll be our present for Will."

Will Greenfield rested back at their camp with a bullet wound in his thigh. Today was his birthday, or at least as nearly as they could reckon the date it was. There had been so little to celebrate lately — so much danger, so much fear. But real meat — their first in weeks — that would be a worthy present. It would also be the only present. As their fellow castaway J.J. Lane put it, "None of these coconut trees take American Express."

Luke approached the log from behind, stepping softly in the tangle of vines and underbrush. The bird clucked and pecked, seemingly unaware. Then, just as the boy lunged, it took off, flapping furiously. Luke tumbled painfully over the log, landing in a heap on the ground. Ian grabbed at the fowl, but it beat its wings in his face before flying off through the rain forest.

ESCAPE

Yelling, Luke ran after it, Ian hot on his heels. It was an awkward chase. Every ten feet or so, the bird would have to land, its chicken legs pumping like miniature pistons before it could take off again. The castaways were faster, but they had the jungle to contend with. Branches and palm fronds slashed at their bodies and faces, and low vines tripped them up.

Ian pointed. "It's heading for the beach!"

Lyssa Greenfield handed her brother, Will, a small aluminum cup of water and a single pill. "Happy birthday," she said dryly.

Will sat up on his "hospital bed," the wooden raft that had brought four of the castaways to the island more than two weeks earlier. "It's better than what you gave me last year — cracked ribs."

"You melted my computer disks," she reminded him.

Will swallowed the capsule and regarded his sister. She looked too upset to be still angry over a fight they'd had a year ago. "What's the matter, Lyss? Was that the last pill?"

Ever since the shooting, Will had been taking the antibiotics from the first-aid kit. He was pretty certain that this was what had kept infection from setting in. But he had always known that the pills would not last forever.

She nodded. "Great present, huh?"

Will tried to sound upbeat. "It doesn't hurt anymore. It's just kind of numb."

Lyssa tried to hide her wince. The patient always looked away when his bandage was being changed, but Lyssa had seen that wound — swollen black and blue around a tattered, gaping hole. Add infection to that —

Infection. At home or in a hospital, it was a pretty simple thing. But here in this sweltering, insect-laden humidity, with medical attention hundreds of miles away, it was a death sentence.

Her brother struggled up to his knees and tried to shift a little weight to his bad side. He shrugged. "With any luck it's healed already."

With any luck. Luck had abandoned them so long ago that Lyssa couldn't remember what it felt like to be lucky. Not just shipwrecked — *marooned* on an uncharted island. And then there were the smugglers — murderous dealers in ivory and illegal animal parts. They were gone now, flown off in their floatplanes. But they would be back. The old military installation was the perfect place for them to carry on their illicit trade.

Anyway, the damage had already been

done. The bullet in Will's leg had come from one of their guns. Not on purpose — the smugglers had no idea there was anyone else on the island. No, it had been a stray shot. Collateral damage. Yet another piece of the castaways' brand of luck.

She grimaced inwardly. There was also this little matter of an atomic bomb. Of course, it had been there for more than fifty years, so it probably wasn't going to go off in their faces. But if the smugglers ever found it . . .

She tried to smile over at Will, but the corners of her mouth simply refused to turn up. Small wonder. Lyssa honestly felt she might never smile again.

Suddenly, a cry from the jungle:

"Dinner! *Dinner!*"

The Greenfields exchanged a bewildered look. That was Ian. What was he babbling about?

As they watched, Luke and Ian burst out onto the beach. They were running full speed and screaming. What was Luke saying?

"Grab that chicken!"

Chicken?!

But then Lyssa saw it — a scrawny, undersized brown hen, flap-hopping for its life.

"I got it!" Charla Swann ran across the beach, lining up the bird with her keen athlete's eye. She lunged, arms outstretched, hands ready. But the fowl squawked loudly and scrambled just out of her reach. Charla went down, eating sand.

The sixth castaway, J.J. Lane, pulled a four-foot branch out of the woodpile. "There's only one way to hit a knuckleball." He cocked it back over his shoulder and took a home-run swing.

"Strike one!" he cheered, fanning.

"Get out of the way!" panted Luke.

But J.J. lined up the chicken and took another cut. "Strike two!"

Will flattened himself to the raft. "Hey, watch it with that thing!"

But it was hard to stop J.J. once he had decided on a course of action. He raced into position, colliding with Luke, sending the two of them staggering. J.J. recovered, pulled back his "bat," and took his final swing. "Strike — "

Whack!

J.J. himself was the most surprised person on the beach when he made contact. The bird sailed twenty feet through the air and fell to the sand, stone dead. J.J. dropped the branch as if it had suddenly become electrified.

ESCAPE

Charla turned on him. "J.J. Lane, how could you do that to an innocent little bird?"

"And why were *you* chasing it?" J.J. sneered. "To give it a check from Publishers Clearing House?"

"No, this is good!" Ian exclaimed. "It's a Pacific jungle fowl — "

"It's Will's birthday present!" added Luke, glaring at J.J.

Charla was still mad. "You didn't have to bludgeon it!"

J.J.'s father was the movie star Jonathan Lane. Growing up in a rich and powerful family had given him little patience for criticism. "The bird had to die somehow, right?" he argued. "What difference does it make if I Babe-Ruthed it?"

"It makes a difference to the bird," Charla insisted.

"Not anymore," J.J. chuckled.

Luke turned his attention away from his irritation with J.J. "This is *meat*. Less fighting; more eating."

The castaways soon learned that having meat was much more complicated than merely opening a shrink-wrapped package from the supermarket. The fowl's head and feet had to be removed. The carcass had to be sliced open. It was a gruesome job. The smell of warm blood in the tropical humidity was nauseating. Luke fought hard to keep from throwing up as he used the knife from their survival pack to scoop the innards away. Lyssa held her nose with one hand while using the other to bury the mess in the sand.

"I don't think I can eat it now," breathed Charla.

"We've come this far," Luke groaned. Out of the corner of his eye, he caught sight of J.J. strolling away. "What do you think you're doing?"

The actor's son paused. "When the going gets tough, the tough get going. I thought I'd, you know, get going. Maybe take a swim — "

For Luke it was the last straw. J.J. was always goofing off. The spoiled Hollywood brat had probably never done any real work in his life and for sure not any dirty work. Daddy's staff took care of all that.

But the famous Jonathan Lane wasn't here right now.

Luke stood up. "All right, smart guy. You're going to pluck this chicken."

"In your dreams," laughed J.J. "If it wasn't for me, you'd still be chasing that dumb bird around the beach. I'm the hunter; you guys are the kitchen staff."

Luke fixed the actor's son with a murderous

look. "No matter what we do, you're always standing around cracking jokes. Well, today you're going to make yourself useful." He held out the bloody carcass.

"If you don't want that up your nose," J.J. said warningly, "get it out of my face."

"I'm not falling for that!" snarled Luke. "Fighting's just another way for you to goof off!"

"You and me," J.J. said evenly. "Right here, right now."

"*Enough!*"

It was a cry from Will that froze everyone like the subjects in a still picture.

"I don't want any chicken!" Will exclaimed bitterly. "Not if it means a big stink like this! It's my birthday, and I'm lost, and I'm shot up, and I'm probably never going to see another one! So take that dumb chicken and throw it in the ocean for the fish!"

J.J. snatched the carcass out of Luke's hand. "I'll pluck it," he mumbled.

"I can help," Ian volunteered.

"Forget it," said J.J. "Go watch the Discovery Channel."

CHAPTER TWO
Day 16, 5:05 P.M.

Blood and feathers. Ugh . . .

In no time, J.J. was covered in both. He'd never forgive the others for this!

Not fair for them to gang up on him. They were jealous — that was pretty plain. They were nobodies, especially Luke, a kid with a criminal record. He said he was innocent — that someone else had stashed that gun in his locker. But that was probably a lie. The kid was so full of himself. Look at how he pushed everybody around, acting like the leader of the castaways. Who voted him king?

Not me, that's for sure!

One stubborn tail feather wouldn't come out. J.J. yanked with both hands. As it jerked free, a splatter of blood hit him in the eye.

"Ow!"

Hard to believe — no, *impossible* — that barely a month ago, he'd been lounging around the pool with Gwyneth Paltrow and Julia Roberts. Then came the mistake. Okay, a few mistakes. Just a bunch of stuff to get his father's attention: a

ESCAPE

case of champagne at the eighth-grade dance, a couple of CDs at the five-finger discount, a ride on Dad's Harley through the front window of an art gallery on Rodeo Drive —

Yeah, he'd probably gone too far that time. It was what had earned him a ticket on Charting a New Course, a four-week boat trip for troubled youth. They had all done stupid things like that: Luke with the gun in his locker; Charla with her driven obsession to be a star athlete; Ian for being a TV-addicted couch potato; and Will and Lyssa for sibling warfare. Those were the offenses that had gotten them sent halfway around the world on a boat trip. Then — a few lousy breaks, and here they were.

A few lousy breaks. Yeah, right.

It was J.J.'s opinion that there had been no disaster. The wreck of the *Phoenix* and everything that had happened since was, he felt, all carefully planned by Charting a New Course. A trick boat, designed to "sink" — it was probably part submarine. By now it had resurfaced to be fixed up for the next group of suckers. Luke and the others said it was impossible. But they'd never lived in Hollywood, where special-effects wizards created the impossible every day.

So gullible! Wasn't it too much of a coincidence that two separate rafts had drifted to exactly the same tiny island? One that happened to be a rendezvous point for dangerous smugglers? It was a setup. The whole theme of CNC was learning teamwork and building character through adventure. J.J. was convinced the "smugglers" had been professional actors. The old military installation was fake too. Like the army would just *forget* an atomic bomb!

No one was in any danger. At the first sign of trouble, CNC would stop the simulation and send them all home. But the others insisted on playing Robinson Crusoe — living off the land, scrambling for coconuts and bananas. And now — gag! — a chicken.

J.J. could picture Captain Cascadden — who *supposedly* drowned — and Mr. Radford — who *supposedly* jumped ship and left them to die. For sure, the two men were watching the castaways on hidden cameras, high-fiving and laughing about how everything had unfolded exactly according to plan.

Well, *almost* according to plan. Will getting shot — that must have been a mistake. It was good news, really. At some point, Will needed to have that bullet removed from his leg. Which meant that any day now, CNC would stop this game and take the poor kid to a doctor. All the castaways had to do was wait it out.

ESCAPE

Blood spattered on J.J.'s shirt. He wheeled to face the jungle. That was where the hidden cameras probably were. "Hey, look!" he bellowed. "Jonathan Lane's only son is plucking a chicken! He's turning into a better person with every feather!"

The others were staring over at him, but nobody said a word. They thought he was nuts. J.J. knew better. Somewhere — in an office, or a plane, or a special surveillance boat — CNC was observing all this and making notes. He refused to give them the satisfaction of thinking that he couldn't see through their charade!

He stood up. "Hey, Haggerty."

When Luke looked over, J.J. tossed the plucked bird right to him in a chest pass.

"How do we cook it?" asked Lyssa.

Instantly, all eyes turned to Ian.

The younger boy backed up a step. "I don't know anything about cooking!"

"You spent your whole life in front of the TV," said J.J. "Didn't you ever catch Chef Emeril?"

Luke dismantled one of the three stills the castaways used to boil the salt out of seawater to make it drinkable. Using two sticks, he held the fowl over the fire, turning it like a rotating spit on a barbecue.

"Nothing's happening," Charla observed after a few breathless minutes.

So they tried cooking over the bonfire. This was a huge blaze — it was intended to alert passing planes and ships to their presence on the island. The sizzling sound was instant, along with a delicious smell of cooking meat. A split second later, half the bird was ablaze.

Lyssa beat at the fire with a plastic rain poncho, but that only fanned the flames, which spread to the sticks in Luke's hands.

Luke looked around in alarm. "Quick! Grab the chicken!"

"Are you crazy?" exclaimed Charla. "It's on fire!"

Lyssa held up the pot of freshwater from the dismantled still. Luke deposited the bird inside and dropped the burning sticks to the sand. A plop and a hiss, and Will's birthday dinner was extinguished.

Luke blew on his hands. "Thanks," he told Lyssa.

"Hey, why don't we just boil it?" suggested Charla. "You can boil anything, right?"

Lyssa hung the pot by its half-hoop handle over the fire. Since the water had just been boiling, it began to churn and bubble almost right away.

"How long do we cook it for?" asked Will.

"Better make it a while," put in Charla. "Nothing is grosser than raw chicken."

Leaving the birthday dinner to boil, they went about their business. Ian's mission: find taro, a potatolike root vegetable that would make a good side dish. Luke went into the jungle with him, to collect firewood. Since large logs were rare, and smaller twigs and branches burned quickly, keeping the voracious bonfire going was a full-time job. Charla went along to help.

J.J. opted for a swim to wash away the blood, sweat, and feathers of his plucking experience. Only Lyssa stuck around to keep Will company. But there was work to do there too. She had to tend the bonfire and also the smaller fires on the two working stills. From these, she collected the bowls of freshwater and poured them into their keg. It, like most of their conveniences, came from the *Phoenix*'s rubber lifeboat. Lyssa and J.J. had drifted to the island on this inflatable craft. Seven days lost at sea. The memory of it still brought her chills. But it had been a luxury cruise compared with what the other four had suffered — bobbing around on a tiny piece of the destroyed *Phoenix*, big enough only for three, while the fourth hung over the side. It was amazing any of them had survived — especially her brother, who was a suburban kid and kind of soft.

Sharply, she reminded herself that Will wasn't out of the woods yet. None of them were if they couldn't find a way off this island.

Now the covered lifeboat sat just inside the trees, where it served as the castaways' sleeping quarters.

Lyssa recorked the water keg and plucked three large snails from the sun canopy. These would go into the boiling pot as soon as the chicken was done.

The chicken. The position of the sun told her that more than an hour had passed. Surely the birthday dinner was ready by now.

She ran over and checked the pot. "Oh, no!" she gasped.

Will sat bolt upright on the raft. "Don't tell me you've burned my chicken!"

"No," she managed. "Not burned." How would you describe it? Pieces of meat and skin floated everywhere. Down in the bottom of the pot rested a small pile of bare bones. They had cooked the living daylights out of that poor little hen.

Painstakingly, she began spooning pieces of meat onto a plate. "They're going to kill me," she told Will.

"*I'm* going to kill you," Will retorted. "Is it ruined?"

"Not exactly. But it's not good either."

She was about to pour out the water when Will suddenly sniffed the air. "Lyss, I may be delirious, but — I think I smell Grandma's matzoh ball soup!"

Lyssa took a whiff, and then a taste of the water she had been about to dump. "It *is* soup!" she exclaimed in amazement. "We made chicken soup!"

Bouncing on his bottom, Will managed to "sit" his way over to the fire. He accepted a taste from his sister.

"Unbelievable!" he exclaimed. "We don't even have toilet paper, but we managed to cook homemade chicken soup! The others are going to drop dead!"

As Lyssa took another taste, she caught sight of her reflection in the aluminum pot.

The girl who thought she would never smile again was already smiling.

CHAPTER THREE
Day 17, 2:15 P.M.

Will ran a fever the very next day.

J.J. was the first to notice the flush in his face. "Dude, it looks like you're wearing old-lady makeup. Your cheeks are bright red."

For most of the afternoon, Will had been asking if the weather was getting colder. This close to the equator, the weather never got any colder, and the humidity stayed permanently at sweatbath level.

"Chills," was Ian's diagnosis.

The thermometer in the first-aid kit confirmed that, yes, the patient was running a temperature of 99.8 degrees.

Will tried to treat it lightly. "Impossible," he wisecracked. "A person can't get sick after eating Grandma's chicken soup."

Lyssa took Luke and Ian aside. "That's not a high fever. It's okay, right?"

If she was looking to them for reassurance, she didn't get it.

"He's only been off the antibiotic for a day," Ian said nervously. "If there's an infection already, it could spread very fast."

ESCAPE

Lyssa swore them both to secrecy. "I don't want Will worrying about this. He's such a wimp that he could make himself even sicker."

Luke looked thoughtful. "Maybe he was like that in his old life. But your brother's been through a lot in these last few weeks. He's not a pushover anymore."

But she was adamant. "Let's not play with his head — at least not until we know we've got trouble."

If they were fooling Will, they certainly weren't fooling Charla. "We should go back to the army base," she urged quietly. "They had alcohol and bandages. Maybe they've got some pills or something."

It was decided that Luke and Charla would go over to the other side of the island and raid the dispensary.

This was a trip the castaways didn't make very often, although it was less than two miles. The foliage was so dense, the vines and underbrush so tangled, the insects so relentless, that it wasn't a very pleasant walk. Even under the best of circumstances it took an hour and a half, but it could easily be double that. Since there was no trail, every journey was different, climbing over new-fallen logs, squeezing through new stands of ferns, ducking under new low-growing branches.

Luke hated these island crossings, and it wasn't just because of the mosquito bites. If the smugglers returned to their meeting place at the old base, there couldn't be any clue that there were others on the island. The slightest sign — a misplaced footprint, a fallen button — could alert these dangerous criminals to the castaways' presence. Luke had already seen them execute one of their own men without mercy. They would not hesitate to kill six kids to protect their illegal operation.

There was such a sameness to the rain forest that Luke and Charla clung to the few landmarks they knew. First came the crumbling concrete. It had once been the air base's runway, but now it was overgrown with jungle. From there, they became more careful because they knew the bomb pit was near. Luke had always assumed that nuclear devices were stored in high-tech containers. But back in World War Two, the atomic bombs had been kept right out in the open, in shallow pits just like this one. They had it on the authority of Ian and the Discovery Channel that this was true of Fat Man and Little Boy, the weapons that had actually been used. Junior, the third bomb, had been so top secret that the history books said it had never been built. But it made perfect sense that Junior would be housed the same way.

ESCAPE

Luke and Charla grew quiet as they drew close. Of course, you couldn't set off an atomic bomb by talking too loud. But they still felt a certain fearful respect for the awesome power of the device and the terrible destruction and death that had been brought about by its two brothers.

They exchanged a knowing glance as they passed a little notch on the trunk of a palm tree. Luke himself had made that mark. It told them that the pit was here, hidden in what looked like an unbroken expanse of jungle floor. He'd been unwilling to risk more obvious marking. There could be no greater disaster than having the smugglers find Junior. These men made money from the blood of endangered animals. They would not think twice about selling an atomic bomb to the highest bidder.

Charla put it on a more basic level. "This place gives me the creeps."

"Amen," Luke agreed.

At this point, the jungle was so dense that progress came closer to wading than walking. They pushed through ferns and twining vines. It still amazed Luke that the building remained invisible until he was practically close enough to touch it. The foliage was so thick and overgrown that there was a leaf here, a frond there, to obscure every inch of a hundred-foot Quonset hut.

Feeling their way along the corrugated metal, they headed for the rear, where two smaller huts were located. One of these showed a faded sign: DISPENSARY.

The door was off its hinges. Luke shoved it open and they stepped inside.

ESCAPE

CHAPTER FOUR
Day 17, 4:35 P.M.

Mangosteens.

Will Greenfield sat up on his raft, working with a knife to cut open a mountain of the plum-sized fruit.

Mangosteens! In the world of naming foods, who had come up with that one? It sounded like a partner in his father's law firm: Berkowitz, Greenfield, and Mangosteen.

They were good, though. Actually, they were delicious. But that was beside the point. Six lives were in danger. Important work had to be done for their very survival. And what was Will's job? A mangosteen fruit salad.

Just because he'd had the bad luck to get shot. And now this fever. 99.8 degrees, and everyone was treating him like he was on his deathbed.

He'd run higher fevers from a bad cold.

For an instant, a sense of foreboding replaced his irritation. His thigh didn't hurt exactly, and the numbness was gone now, so that was a good sign, wasn't it? But still it felt somehow — *wrong*. There was a strange rhythmic throbbing, almost like a second heartbeat down there. One minute

ISLAND

the leg would seem strong enough for him to get up and dance. The next, it would be so weak he wasn't sure it would even support him.

No way! It was all in his imagination. And no wonder, with Lyssa moping around, looking at him like he was dying. He was perfectly okay. He could be helping — *contributing!* Not cutting up some fruit with a name that sounded more like a pediatrician.

Dr. Mangosteen will see you now. . . .

He looked around the beach. Everyone was busy. Even J.J. was fishing. Lyssa was fiddling with the lifeboat's broken radio. If they got off this island, Lyssa was probably going to end up the hero somehow. It was just the way things went for her — Lyssa, the beautiful, talented, straight-A student. And her older brother, the awkward, freckled slug.

He could picture his sister on the front page of every newspaper. Even on TV:

"Lyssa, how did it feel when you fixed the radio and made a long-distance antenna out of a banana to call in the marines to save you?"

After a long interview, the cameras would turn to Will. "Weren't you shipwrecked too? What was your job on the island?"

What would he tell them? *Oh, I sat around and cut up mangosteens.*

ESCAPE

And the reporter's face would go suddenly blank. "Cut up *what?*"

That was the story of his life with Lyssa. Will never had a chance to succeed. What kind of contribution could you make by sitting on a beach staring off into space?

And then he saw the black speck move. It was just over the horizon and getting larger every second.

Forgetting his wound, he leaped to his feet and immediately crumpled back to the raft.

"Plane!" he bellowed. "*Plane!*"

On the surface, it looked like pandemonium. But in reality, it was a carefully planned and well-practiced drill. Lyssa and J.J. dropped everything and raced to fill pots with seawater. Ian ran for the tarpaulin in the jungle. It was made of four rain ponchos sewn together and filled with dead leaves. He grabbed it and hauled it over to the bonfire.

If those leaves were thrown on the blaze and then the water dumped on top, the result would be a column of thick gray smoke that would extend hundreds of yards into the sky — an SOS that would be seen for miles around.

It was a moment the castaways had played over in their minds dozens of times — their chance at rescue.

Will had never felt more helpless. This could mean his life — all their lives! And he couldn't even walk. He got on his hands and knees and crawled across the sand to the bonfire.

Don't blow it! he tried to will the others. *Do everything exactly right!*

Still, they hesitated. They did not dare signal until they knew for sure whom they were signaling to. If they sent up the smoke, and the plane turned out to be carrying the smugglers, they'd be giving away their presence on the island. And that would be fatal.

Lyssa peered through the binoculars that had come with the survival kit.

Will tugged at the legs of her fatigues. "Can you see it? It's rescuers, right?"

She shook her head. "They're still too far off."

"Let's just go for it," urged J.J. "Get this over with one way or the other."

"Don't you dare!" snapped Lyssa. "Maybe you've got a death wish, but the rest of us want to live to grow up."

"This is awful," said Ian. "I wish we could just *know.*"

"Wait a minute." Lyssa squinted into the binoculars. "It's banking to the side . . . it's definitely a floatplane . . . oh, my God!"

"What?" squeaked Ian.

ESCAPE

"It's them! The smugglers!"

"Are you sure?" Will asked breathlessly. "All planes look alike!"

His sister shook her head. "Single engine, with a fat cargo hold underneath. It's them, all right."

Her words triggered more frantic action. But if the last drill had been fueled by hopeful anticipation, this one was driven by disappointment and dread. The castaways, even Will, began throwing sand on the bonfire. Soon the flames were smothered to nothing, and not a trace, not so much as a whiff of smoke, remained.

Will held on to his sister's shoulders and began to hop toward the lifeboat under cover of the trees. J.J. was hot on their heels. Ian brought up the rear, brushing their footprints from the sand with a leafy branch.

All four looked up. Through the canopy of the rain forest, they watched the floatplane descend over the island. As it swept overhead, suddenly one of the doors burst open. A dark object fell out and plummeted to the jungle below.

The castaways ducked, even though the thing was nowhere near them. They stayed down, bracing for — what? An explosion?

"Was that a *bomb*?" hissed Will.

"How could it be?" scoffed Lyssa. "They don't even know we're here!"

J.J. was the first to get up. "We're such saps. The guy was probably having a Big Mac and he tossed the bag so he wouldn't have to mess up the air base."

All at once, Lyssa froze. "The air base!" she exclaimed. "That's where Luke and Charla are!"

Will frowned. "What are they doing way over there?"

"Looking for medicine," she replied. "For you."

ESCAPE

CHAPTER FIVE
Day 17, 5:35 P.M.

Whack! Whack! Whack!

Luke hacked at the rusty padlock with a sharp rock. With every blow that fell, a cloud of dust and cobwebs swirled up around him, making him cough.

The dispensary was set up like a doctor's office, with a single desk and chair, cabinet, and examining table. Nothing else had been needed. This small installation had never been home to more than thirty people. These had been the crew, pilots, technicians, and officers required to do a single job — to deliver an atomic bomb to its target.

Whack!

In a shower of rust flakes, the lock smashed and fell to the floor, disappearing in the weeds and rotted planking.

Luke opened the cabinet. "Jackpot." On the shelves stood dozens of medicine bottles.

Charla grabbed a couple and examined the labels. She looked up, her face blank. "How do we know which of this stuff could help Will?"

Luke grabbed the pillow from the examining

table, dumped out the stuffing, and began tossing bottles into the case. "We'll take it all," he decided. "With any luck, the Discovery Channel did a show on medicines."

"Right." Charla joined him. "Let's hurry up and get out of here. We don't want to be stuck in the middle of the jungle in the dark."

Luke tossed in a box of tongue depressors. It was dumb, he knew. Will had a bullet in his leg; no one was going to ask him to say "ah." He paused over a tray of surgical instruments.

Charla read his mind. "God forbid!"

But they took the tray anyway. They took everything, even the medic's journal, yellowed and tattered around the edges.

"You never know what might come in handy," Luke explained.

Charla nodded grimly. She no longer argued with any statement that began, "You never know . . ."

They were halfway out the door when the shouting began — loud, furious, and too close for comfort. It was so unexpected that, for a second or two, they froze, right in the open.

Charla snapped out of it first. She dragged Luke back inside the dispensary and pulled the broken door shut. They dropped to their knees and peered through the mud-streaked window.

ESCAPE

It was the smugglers! While Luke and Charla had been working in the Quonset hut, they had missed the sound of the floatplane landing. And now they were trapped. . . .

The leader was a hugely fat man in a pale green silk suit and matching fedora. His nickname had come from J.J.: Mr. Big. He was fatter than ever and in a towering rage about something.

"I don't care if he had *five* aces up his sleeve! You don't start a fistfight in a moving plane!"

"I'll find it! I'll find it!" promised a gravelly voice with a British accent.

In an amazingly graceful move for such a huge man, Mr. Big wheeled. As he turned, he pulled a large handgun from his pocket and pistol-whipped his unfortunate associate.

The sound of the blow, metal against human flesh, was a sickening thud. Huddled inside the dispensary, both Luke and Charla flinched.

The victim went down, and a third man quickly stepped between him and his boss.

Mr. Big wasn't finished yet. "You'll find it," he agreed, "or the next thing you'll find will be a bullet in your head!"

"It's too late now, boss," reasoned the third man. "It'll be dark soon. We'll have to look for it in the morning. What can happen to it? There's nobody here but us."

In the gloom of the dispensary, Luke and Charla exchanged an agonized look. Neither of them dared speak until the voices of the three men faded.

"Where are they?" asked Charla in something much less than a whisper.

"Probably in the main building," breathed Luke. "Or maybe down by the beach, getting stuff from the plane. Either way, we can't risk leaving now."

She nodded. "But when?"

In the diminishing light, she felt rather than saw Luke's shrug.

Night fell quickly in the tropics. With the thick rain forest blocking even starlight, the darkness in the dispensary became total and suffocating. There was an isolation to it, Luke thought. He knew Charla was only a few inches away, but he could not see her at all. They wouldn't make it ten feet in the jungle in this blackness.

They were stuck here until morning — stuck here together, yet separated by a complete absence of light.

He felt her hand steal into his. Her fingers were cold as ice.

ESCAPE

CHAPTER SIX
Day 18, 5:50 A.M.

Fear.

Charla couldn't believe some of things she used to consider fear. Like the butterflies as she crouched in the blocks, waiting for the starter's gun in an important race.

Tension, sure. Doubts, always. But fear?

These last few weeks had taught her the true meaning of fear: losing the captain at sea, dangling like shark bait from a tiny raft, facing a lifetime marooned.

And now cowering in the pitch-black of the dispensary, hiding from certain death.

That was fear.

All through the terrible night, she revisited her old anxieties: that moment, still in midair after the dismount from the balance beam, not yet knowing if she could stick the landing.

Nerve-wracking? Of course. Gut-wrenching? Maybe. Fear? Not even close.

Even her ultimate old fear — the disappointment on her father's face as he held up the stopwatch: "Now that wasn't exactly a personal best,

ISLAND

was it?" — made her smile in the darkness. In this place, this situation, who cared about a few hundredths of a second?

Her whole life so far had consisted of training and striving for athletic perfection. And right now that seemed about as important as ice cubes in the Arctic. . . .

"Charla — wake up."

Luke knelt before her, one hand over her mouth, the other shaking her by the shoulder.

She looked out the smeared, cracked glass. It was still dark, with just the first few tendrils of dawn creeping across the sky.

"Let's get out into the trees," Luke whispered. "Then we can wait for the light and take off."

They invested precious seconds closing the rickety door, determined that the dispensary should look as if no one had been there for decades. Then they were crawling through tightly woven underbrush, praying that the screeching of the awakening birds was covering the rustle of their movements.

They were well away from the Quonset huts by sunup. They found the broken concrete of the old runway with a minimum of wandering. From there, they were able to point themselves in the direction of their own side of the island.

ESCAPE

Charla let out a mournful sigh. "Can you believe that they're back so soon? We almost walked out of the hut right in their faces!"

"I thought we'd have more time," Luke agreed, hefting the pillowcase over his shoulder. "Man, was our signal fire a bust or what? We didn't even see a plane or boat, much less get rescued!"

"Nobody's looking for us," Charla reminded him. "We're dead, remember?"

It was true. Mr. Radford, the *Phoenix*'s mate who had abandoned them, was safely back on dry land. The smugglers had left behind a *USA Today* with the whole story — Radford telling the world that the six kids in his charge had all died in the shipwreck.

"Great guy, that Rat-face," said Luke bitterly. "He has the same warm, fuzzy personality as the Green Blimp back there."

Charla shuddered visibly. "That was awful! I can still hear the sound it made when he hit that man! I wonder what they lost."

"It must have been something important," Luke said grimly. "Mr. Big wouldn't threaten to kill somebody just to scare him. He's really ready to shoot that guy."

They walked in silence for a few moments, listening to the rustling of the palms as a slight wind blew. Luke reached up to brush a bug from his cheek. But instead of an insect, he felt his hand close on a small piece of paper.

Litter? In the jungle?

He looked down and saw Benjamin Franklin staring back at him. This was a *hundred-dollar bill*! Wordlessly, he showed it to Charla.

"Money!" she breathed.

Then they saw it, lying in the underbrush, its lock sprung — a black suitcase. It gaped open, and out of it poured neat bundles of bills, all hundreds.

"Oh, wow!" Luke groaned. "Now we know what they lost, and why they're so upset about it."

Mesmerized, Charla dropped to her knees and ran her hands over the pile of money. "In my neighborhood," she whispered, "this could buy — my neighborhood!"

"There's got to be a couple of million at least." Luke nodded. "They're going to come after it, no question."

Charla looked stricken. "Yeah, but it's like finding a needle in a haystack! It was a total accident that we found it! They'll have to search the island fern by fern. They'll stumble on our camp twenty times before they ever track down this suitcase!"

ESCAPE

Luke crouched beside her and began stuffing bundles of bills back into the luggage. "That's exactly why we have to help them."

"Help them?" Her voice was shrill. "We're dead if they even find out we're here! How can we help them?"

"By making the suitcase easier to find," Luke explained. "We just have to put it somewhere they're bound to notice."

"We can't lean it up against the door of the Quonset hut," she pointed out. "They'll know something's fishy."

"I'm not that stupid," said Luke. "We'll just take it closer to their camp and leave it out in the open. The sooner they find it, the sooner they stop looking."

At the castaways' camp, the gloom had begun the previous nightfall and had settled into despair with every passing hour.

Two facts: One, the smugglers were back; and two, Luke and Charla had gone over to the military installation and had not returned.

Ian mulled over the information every which way, but a single word kept bubbling to the surface: *caught*. The smugglers had them, and that meant they were probably dead.

He choked on a lump in his throat. Or maybe they were alive, being interrogated about who they were and who was with them.

He felt a surge of pride. Luke was strong; he would never talk! But the feeling evaporated in a second as he recalled a TV documentary on interrogation methods. Luke would talk. Everybody talked. Which meant the smugglers could be coming for them right now.

The night had been terrible. Ian was pretty sure no one had slept, except maybe Will, whose temperature had gone over 101, and who mumbled through fevered dreams. Everybody was sure they should be doing something, but no one could decide what that might be. Though the castaways had no official leader, without Luke they would never agree on a course of action. Luke was the mortar that held them together. And it was beginning to look as if he would never be back.

"Haggerty can't be dead," J.J. assured everyone. "He's too mean to die. And Charla — who could catch her?"

But even he looked worried. And he hid right along with the rest of them when they heard a rustling in the foliage.

Crouched in the underbrush, Ian let his mind

ESCAPE

run riot. Would the castaways be discovered? How long could they stay hidden? Could Will keep up?

And then a surprised voice asked, "Where'd everybody go?"

"Luke!" cried Will.

It was interesting, Ian reflected during the celebration that followed. Things were not good and getting worse. Yet the glory of little triumphs like this — welcoming two friends back from the brink of death — would surely rank among his greatest memories. You know — if he lived long enough to have memories.

As the castaways shared accounts of the last day and night, they were able to piece together what had happened. During a fistfight over a poker game, the door of the smugglers' plane had been accidentally knocked open, and a suitcase full of money had dropped out over the jungle. Soon a second group of smugglers would arrive, carrying a shipment of elephant tusks, rhino horns, and other illegal animal parts. They were the sellers; Mr. Big was the customer. He needed the lost money to pay for his goods.

"So we left it where they're bound to find it," Charla concluded. "It's in plain sight in just about the only clear spot over by the air base."

Lyssa was horrified. "You *helped* them?"

"We helped ourselves," Luke amended. "The last thing we need is those guys combing the island."

Charla shook her head in wonder. "You should have seen it. Millions of dollars just lying there. I swear I was tempted to roll in it."

"It's fake," scoffed J.J.

Charla shot him a resentful look. "Even poor people know what money looks like."

J.J. was disgusted. "CNC can't print up a batch of phony bills that look real?"

Luke groaned. "We all know what you think. Let us think what we think."

Later, Luke, Lyssa, and Ian went through the pillowcase and tried to take stock of the supplies from the dispensary.

Lyssa was dubious. "Is any of this stuff even good after all that time?"

"There's no way of knowing," Ian replied. "I don't see penicillin, which is what we really need. The rest — " He shook his head. "I have no idea what most of it is for."

"This might help." Luke fished in the case and came up with the medic's journal. "Maybe it says something about bullet wounds."

All day and half the night, Ian pored over the fifty-six-year-old diary of Captain Hap Skelly, M.D. He devoured the details of Sergeant Holli-

ESCAPE

day's fire-ant bites, Colonel Dupont's gout, and Lieutenant Bosco's stomach flu, searching for the tiniest hint of anything that might help Will. He skipped lunch and dinner too, reading by flashlight when it got dark. He owed it to Will, sure. But there was another reason.

For weeks, Ian had watched no television, surfed no Internet, and read not a single word. In the anxiety and fear of these terrible weeks, it had never crossed his mind how much he missed *information*.

On the beach of a tiny island in the vast Pacific, Ian felt like Ian again.

CHAPTER SEVEN
Day 19, 9:45 A.M.

Feb. 17, 1945. Having trouble keeping supplies. Who to order from? As far as the army's concerned, we don't exist on this tiny island. Can't even send letters home. Mission is too top secret. Our families must think we've vanished off the face of the earth.

Penicillin ran out weeks ago. Have been using an infusion of bitter melon — a local plant that resembles a small cucumber with acne. Seems to control Holliday's infection. But am I turning into a witch doctor?

Will hated the idea from the start. "What's an infusion?"

"It's sort of like making tea out of something," Ian replied, handing him a steaming cup.

The patient was appalled. "You guys have been plotting against me! I've been minding my own business here, and you've been picking weird jungle plants so you can poison me!"

"Most medicines come from tropical vegeta-

ESCAPE

tion," Ian explained. "I saw it in a show about saving the rain forest."

"That World War Two doctor said it was safe," added Luke.

"Forget it. I won't drink it."

But he did drink it, largely due to his sister's threat to have it poured down his throat. The complaining was a filibuster. Will never seemed to run out of new ways to describe the taste of bittermelon tea — skunk juice, crankcase oil, toxic waste, boiled sweat, and Sasquatch drool, to name a few.

It became so entertaining to listen to his graphic descriptions as the day wore on that they almost lost sight of a very serious reality: Will's fever was still rising.

"It's not working," Lyssa whispered nervously. "Isn't there anything else we can give him? How about that stuff from the dispensary?"

"Well, there is one thing," Ian ventured reluctantly. "Novocain."

"Novocain?" laughed J.J. "What are you going to do — drill his teeth?"

Ian flushed. "Today Novocain is mostly used by dentists. But it can actually freeze any part of the body for surgery."

"You mean surgery on *Will?*" Lyssa was shaken by the sudden realization of what the younger boy was leading up to. "Shoot his leg full of painkiller and try to cut the bullet out?" She turned blazing eyes on him. "Are you crazy? It's only a little fever! He's not that sick!"

"I agree," said Ian. "But if he *gets* that sick, the bullet has to come out."

"In a nice clean hospital!" Lyssa added, a shrill edge to her voice. "With a doctor who didn't learn his job by watching the Surgery Channel!"

"Nobody's cutting up anybody," soothed Luke. "Ian's just laying out our options."

"This isn't an option," insisted Lyssa. "Never, never, never!"

Ian's expression plainly told her that *never* might come sooner than she thought.

The second group of smugglers arrived the very next afternoon. Will choked on a mouthful of bitter-melon tea when he spotted the aircraft.

Lyssa put her hands on her hips. "Oh, come on. Don't be such a baby."

Will kept on gagging and pointing.

"Plane!" shouted J.J.

Luke peered through the binoculars. "Twin-engine floatplane," he reported in a subdued tone. "It's them, all right."

Lyssa's hope popped before her like a soap

bubble. For a few seconds, this plane had carried rescuers and not a fresh set of problems. Oh, God, what if help *never* came? What would happen to Will?

Watching her brother was like observing somebody with a bad flu. But while flu built, peaked, and then went away, this was growing worse with every passing moment.

That evening, Will's fever went well over 102 degrees. His face was flushed, his eyes were sunken, and he seemed languid and hazy.

In the middle of the night, he woke up the castaways with loud shouting. When Lyssa finally managed to shake him out of his nightmare, he was annoyed with her.

"Come on, Lyss, I'm trying to get some sleep. I'm not feeling so great, you know."

The next night, he kept everyone up with hours of high-pitched giggling.

"Hey," muttered J.J., "lose the laugh track."

But the snickers and guffaws continued until almost dawn. At that point, Will fell silent, dozing on and off all day. At four o'clock, his fever topped 103.

"That's bad, right?" he asked feebly. "That can't be good."

"You're burning up," Ian admitted. "We're going to take you down to the water and cool you off."

Luke and Ian helped Will into the surf. He was really weak, but once in the ocean he seemed better, with a natural buoyancy that made him comfortable in the water.

Will winced from the pain in his thigh. "Man, that stings!"

"Salt water's good for the infection," Ian reminded him. They had been applying compresses to the wound at every bandage change.

With a chest-pounding Tarzan yell, J.J. leaped off the high rocks at the edge of the cove and hit the waves with a drenching splash.

What a flake, Luke thought in disgust. *We're trying to keep Will from boiling over, and all it means to J.J. is a beach party.* Not to mention that it was just plain nuts to make unnecessary noise when the smugglers were on the island. Okay, J.J. made it pretty plain that he believed the whole thing was a CNC hoax. But surely, somewhere in the back of his mind there had to be a sliver of doubt. . . .

It had become the castaways' habit to enter the ocean fully clothed, letting their fatigues wash on their bodies. Then they would undress in the water, throw everything on the rocks, and go for

ESCAPE

a swim. The tropical sun was so hot that even the thick GI clothes dried almost instantly.

Luke had just pulled off his shirt when Will disappeared. One second he was bobbing like a cork; the next he had sunk out of sight, leaving barely a ripple.

CHAPTER EIGHT

Day 22, 4:40 P.M.

J.J. got there first, slapping at the waves, hollering, "*Will!*"

Luke grabbed his arms. "Cut it out! I can't see anything!" He stuck his face under and forced his eyes open, ignoring the stinging of the salt.

There was Will, curled up peacefully as if he had suddenly decided to go to sleep on the ocean floor.

Luke grabbed him under the arms and yanked his head up to the air. J.J. and Ian were right there, and they hustled Will, coughing and spitting, onto the beach.

The girls were already pounding across the sand, Charla out front with Lyssa hot on her heels.

"I'm okay!" Will tried to call, only to come up choking again.

"What happened?" gasped Lyssa.

"I don't know," Will wheezed. "I was swimming, and then — " He shrugged. "Then I was here."

"You blacked out," Luke informed him.

"But I feel better," Will insisted weakly. "In the

ESCAPE

water, it was like I was waking up for the first time all day."

Lyssa squeezed his hand.

"I'm losing it, Lyss," he confessed fearfully. "Even I can tell, and I'm the one who's losing it."

Lyssa swallowed a lump in her throat. "Ian had an idea — "

J.J. stared at her. "*That* idea? The operation? A few days ago you almost strangled the kid for mentioning it!"

There were tears in her eyes. "Things weren't so bad then."

"I'm always the last to know everything," Will complained. "What are you talking about? What operation?"

Luke filled him in on Ian's idea of using Novocain and surgical instruments to remove the bullet.

Will was round-eyed. "And I'd get better?"

Ian shuffled uncomfortably. "It's very risky."

Will spoke once more. "Riskier than doing nothing?"

His voice was quiet, but the logic of his words resounded like a cannon shot. Yes, if they botched this operation, Will would probably die. But if they just left him . . .

"Wait a minute." J.J. looked from face to face.

"You're *serious*? You say *I'm* crazy, and you want to cut someone open?"

"But if there's no other choice — " Will began.

"There's the choice of *not doing it*!" the actor's son exclaimed hotly.

"We have to help Will," Charla insisted.

"Don't let them!" J.J. pleaded with Will. "They'll mess you up real bad, and by the time CNC gets here to rescue us, it'll be too late!"

"I don't want to hear it," Lyssa said scornfully. "Who does less around here than you, J.J. Lane? We break our backs, and you treat this like some kind of tropical vacation! And now, suddenly, you're so concerned about Will? What a crock!"

J.J. took a step back, shocked and hurt. All at once, he wheeled and ran up the beach. "Hey, you!" he shouted at the trees. "Whoever's out there! It's over! You've got to come get us!"

"Whoa!" Luke exclaimed angrily. "We're not alone on this rock, remember?"

But J.J. was pleading with the hidden cameras and microphones he was sure were all over the jungle. "Hurry! They're gonna cut him! They're gonna *cut* him!"

Charla started after him. "Stop it, J.J.! There are *killers* on this island!"

ESCAPE

With a furious look back at her, J.J. ran into the trees. Charla moved to pursue.

"Let him go," ordered Luke.

"But the smugglers — " she protested.

"They're too far away. They won't hear anything."

The group straggled back to their camp. Lyssa helped her brother resettle himself on the raft.

"Captain!" J.J.'s voice carried from the jungle. "Mr. Radford! Whoever you are!"

Lyssa was nervous. "He'll come back, right?"

Luke nodded absently. "He always does. Listen, we need to talk. I've got an idea. And to be honest, it's scaring the daylights out of me." He took a deep breath. "But if it works out, nobody's going to have to operate on anyone."

Silence fell. Luke had everybody's attention. Ian leaned forward eagerly.

Even as Luke spoke the words, a part of him hung back, detached, amazed that it had come to this. Five months ago he had trusted a "friend" with his locker combination. A random inspection, a thirty-two-caliber pistol in Luke's rolled-up backpack . . .

But it isn't mine!

If the principal, the police, or the judge had believed those four simple words, everything

would have been different. Luke Haggerty
wouldn't be standing here, about to suggest the
unthinkable. A plan that was little better than suicide.

"The smugglers leave their cargo in the float-
planes," he explained, laboring to keep his voice
steady. "There's no way they'd ever see me if I
stowed away in one of the crates. The next morning they'd fly me off the island without even
knowing I was there. Then all I'd have to do is
slip away from them at the other end and go to
the police."

"*All you have to do?*" Charla was horrified.
"Luke, you're one kid. They're three adults with
guns. Plus who knows how many guys waiting at
the place where the plane lands."

"Yeah, but they'll be looking for the shipment,
not me," Luke argued. "I'll climb out of the crate
while we're in the air. Maybe I can stay hidden
until there's a chance to make a run for it."

"That's a big maybe," said Ian. "You're dead
if they catch you."

"Don't you think I know that? But look, we've
been on this island almost a month and we
haven't seen so much as a lousy canoe paddling
by. Face it, the air force picked this place because it's totally nowhere. It took more than fifty

ESCAPE

years for somebody else to show up here — the smugglers and us. How'd you like to wait that long to be rescued?"

A gloomy silence descended on the group. Luke knew he had them. "Yeah, it's dangerous. But if we're ready to operate on Will, we should try this first. It's exactly the same risk — one life. And if it pays off, we get *rescued*. Once I'm back in the world, I can contact the police or the coast guard or somebody."

"How will they find us?" asked Lyssa. "I mean, you know the island, but you can't pick it out of a whole ocean."

Ian spoke up. "I've got some papers from the base that give our latitude and longitude."

Charla frowned. "When would you stow away? We have no way of knowing when the smugglers plan to leave."

"That's our biggest problem," Luke agreed. "Actually, I can't figure out why they didn't fly off a couple of days ago. How long could it take to trade the cargo for the money and scram? Why would they stick around?"

Ian looked puzzled. "You don't think — "

Charla read his mind. "The suitcase! They still haven't found the money! And they won't leave without it!"

"That's impossible!" Luke protested. "We left it

right out in the open near their camp! We did everything but put up a neon sign!"

"The jungle's a funny place," said Ian. "Your eyes play tricks on you in there."

Will looked even paler than usual. "If they don't have their money, that means they're probably out looking for it. We're lucky they didn't stumble into our camp by mistake."

"We can't let that happen," said Lyssa with gritted teeth. "First thing in the morning, we'll move the suitcase somewhere so obvious a blind man couldn't miss it."

"In the jungle there's no such place," Luke said thoughtfully. "We've got to do it *right* this time — even if we have to shove that suitcase down Fatso's throat!"

ESCAPE

CHAPTER NINE
Day 22, 11:55 P.M.

Luke dozed in and out of uneasy dreams to the raspy metronome of Will's tortured breathing. He had never been much of a sleeper at times of stress.

This isn't stress, he reminded himself. *This is being scared out of your mind.*

He lay awake, staring at the sun canopy that covered them. Outside, their small fire cast a dim glow through the rubberized material.

The others were asleep, and all was quiet except — the snap of a twig seemed as loud as a gunshot. He sat bolt upright, instantly alert. He could make out a silhouette against the canopy. Someone was out there!

The smugglers! His mind raced as he wracked his brain for a way to wake his fellow castaways without alerting the intruder.

And then the head turned. In profile, Luke caught a glimpse of the outline of sleek sunglasses.

He relaxed. It was J.J., back at last.

Only a true Hollywood idiot would wear shades at night on a deserted island. J.J. adored those dumb glasses. He hardly ever took them off. They were one-of-a-kind frames, custom-made for J.J.'s father by Paul Smith, the fashion designer. Luke had an image of the boy blundering through the rain forest in the pitch-black, walking into trees because he refused to remove those ridiculous shades.

Luke picked his way around his sleeping companions. He noted that Will's face glistened with perspiration. Night sweats again. And getting worse.

He stepped through the flap. "Hey," he greeted.

J.J. stared into the fire, his arms hugging his knees. He didn't look up.

Luke tried again. "You okay?"

"Fine," came the hoarse reply.

Luke could tell that the actor's son had not been far away. Anyone who spent nighttime hours in the heavy rain forest would come out eaten alive by mosquitoes. J.J. had only a few bug bites. Most likely he had retreated to the edge of the jungle at the first sign of darkness. There he had remained hidden, too embarrassed or too stubborn to rejoin the group.

J.J. flipped up his shades, and in the glow of the fire Luke could see he had been crying. "Did you do it? Did you cut him?"

ESCAPE

Luke shook his head and explained his stow-away plan. "We just have to get that suitcase into the smugglers' hands," he finished. "We could use your help tomorrow."

"Forget it," said J.J. "Somebody has to stay here to meet CNC."

For the first time, Luke felt no jealousy toward the actor's son. When he looked at J.J. now, all he saw was a scared boy clinging to a half-baked theory because the alternative was just too awful. Because bad things like that didn't happen to a movie star's kid.

"You know, CNC isn't coming," Luke said almost kindly.

J.J. flipped the shades back down, shutting Luke out.

They had all messed up to get sent on the trip, Luke reflected. But in a strange way, J.J. was the grand champion mess of the group. For the rest of them, the very problems that had brought them to CNC had yielded strengths that had helped them survive. Yes, Ian was a TV addict. But his Discovery Channel knowledge had saved their lives time and time again. The same was true of Charla's obsessed athleticism. Will and Lyssa had been shipped out because of an inability to get along. Yet hidden somewhere inside the fighting had been a loyalty to each other that grew stronger even as Will's health failed. And as for Luke, it was misplaced trust that had started him on this roller coaster. But that trusting way had made him the only one who could bring this ragtag band of castaways together and keep them from losing hope.

That left just J.J. What was his special talent?

Spoiled brat, flake, impulsive hothead. Not exactly an impressive résumé.

How would *that* help the castaways through the most terrifying experience of their lives?

CHAPTER TEN
Day 23, 1:25 P.M.

Charla shinnied quickly up the narrow palm tree. Twenty feet below, Luke, Lyssa, and Ian craned their necks, regarding her nervously.

"Quit staring!" she called down in annoyance.

But they continued to follow her effortless progress up the trunk. Did they expect her to fall and kill herself? When were they ever going to figure out that this was easy for her? Compared with a back giant, long-hang kip dismount from the uneven bars, this was nothing!

She continued her climb up the smooth trunk. The tree was tall — fifty feet, she guessed. But she wasn't going all the way to the top. There she'd be lost in the canopy of the rain forest, out of touch with the ground. When she was about thirty feet up, she stopped and signaled the others.

It wasn't exactly a panoramic view — in heavy jungle there was far too much foliage in the way. But this was the closest thing to a lookout spot they were going to find on this side of the island. She couldn't see the Quonset hut, of

ISLAND

course. The plant life around it was too dense. But she'd see the smugglers when they came to continue their search for the money. At least she hoped she would. Charla's signal would tell the others where to drop the suitcase. She had to pay careful attention. Their lives depended on it.

An hour earlier they had found the suitcase exactly where Luke and Charla had left it — on the edge of the small clearing.

"How could they miss it?" Luke had asked in disbelief.

From the clearing, it was the most obvious thing in the world. But Charla could see how, just a few short yards into the jungle, it disappeared in the thick weave of foliage.

The waiting began. Now *that* was every bit as hard as being a star athlete. Hanging in a tree was easy, but hanging there for *hours*, knowing that if you let your guard down . . .

No, don't think about that.

Hours. It felt more like months. Thirty feet below, she could see the others talking among themselves. The image made her feel alone and resentful. Stupid, she realized. Who else could do this?

It was amazing that, even after all these weeks, she was still so suspicious of the others. Were they talking about her behind her back?

ESCAPE

About how she was the poor girl whose father worked three jobs to support her training, and who went into debt to pay for CNC?

She shook her head to clear it. Yeah, they knew. But why should they care? They had their own problems to worry about. If there was a bright side to their terrible predicament, this was it: Being shipwrecked was a great equalizer. According to J.J., his father made thirteen million dollars a movie — twenty working lifetimes for her dad. But here they were both castaways. And neither was better, richer, safer, or more comfortable than the other.

When she saw the movement, it took a moment to identify it. Tiny gaps in the leaves and tall grasses gave glimpses of colored shirts, almost like staccato pulses of light.

Deep shock. She wasn't surprised that the smugglers were coming, but by how *close* they were before she spotted them. She tried to give the signal — the hooting of an owl. But she was breathing too hard and couldn't seem to manufacture the sound. Thinking fast, she kicked off a tattered sneaker and watched it drop.

Coming from thirty feet up, when it hit Luke in the shoulder, the impact knocked him to his knees. By this time Charla was already scrambling down the trunk. She leaped the last five feet, stepping into her shoe.

"They're coming?" Luke whispered.

"They're *here*!" Charla hissed back.

Lyssa and Ian looked around desperately.

And then they heard the swishing sound of legs plodding through the vines and bush.

Luke mouthed the word: *Freeze*, but the command was unnecessary. Fear had turned the castaways to statues. There wasn't even time to duck down into the underbrush. The men were nearly upon them.

Charla's mind worked furiously. What should they do? Fight? Run? She looked to Luke but his face was all horror and indecision.

A blue-jean-clad leg burst out from a fern not four feet away. She felt a scream forming in her throat. She shut her eyes tightly and grimaced it down. When she opened them again, his face was right there. Through the gridlike leaves of the fern, she recognized his red hair. This man was a murderer. The castaways had seen him kill one of his own people in cold blood.

And now he had found them.

Or had he? Looking straight ahead, Red Hair stepped right past them and disappeared into the jungle. Charla let out a low whimper and nearly

ESCAPE

choked on it. The other man was only half a step behind him.

She watched his beady eyes dart around. Had he seen them?

No, he was looking down — for the suitcase. She held her breath as he passed by.

The castaways stood frozen, breathing silent relief into one another's faces.

Lyssa was the first to speak, her voice barely a whisper. "We are so lucky."

"I don't feel lucky," Luke grumbled. "Now that those guys are past us, we'll be chasing them around all day."

"Wait here!" Charla snatched up the suitcase and ran off after the smugglers.

It was impossible to sprint in the jungle; a high-stepping jog was the best she could do. A low vine tripped her up, but she was able to use the suitcase as a shield when she collided with a tree. *Careful*, she admonished, speeding up again. If she knocked herself unconscious out here, only the snakes would find her.

As she ran, she formulated her plan. It was a classic outflanking move — used by track stars to get the inside lane. Setting herself on a course parallel to the smugglers, she raced ahead until she was sure she had passed them. Then she made a right turn, stopping where she estimated their path would take them. Hidden in the underbrush, she waited, the suitcase in her trembling arms.

Good-bye, megabucks. I'll never see this much of you again.

A thin smile came to her lips. Her whole life, money had been a worry. Now she had her mitts on a boatload of the stuff — in the one place where money meant absolutely nothing!

I wouldn't take it anyway, she thought. *It's dirty money, earned with the blood of endangered elephants and tigers.*

Crackling in the underbrush. The smugglers were here already! Only — where were they? Frantically, she looked around for the warning signs — swaying fronds, snapping twigs, hints of color behind the foliage. Nothing, except —

There, fifteen feet to her left, a stand of ferns was rocking. She had guessed wrong. And now she'd have to start all over again.

I can't do this. A whole day of shadowing these killers, trying to predict where they'll be —

Acting on instinct, she picked up the suitcase and hurled it with all her might into the smugglers' path. While it was still in midair, she realized the mistake she had made. If the men saw it

ESCAPE

land, they would know someone had thrown it.

A body pushed through the fern. Oh, no! She was caught!

But wait! Red Hair was turned away, talking to his partner behind him.

The suitcase landed with a soft thud. Money spilled out.

See it! See it! See it!

But he didn't. Charla was thunderstruck. She wanted to scream: *There, you idiot! Right in front of your nose!*

The jungle hit you with such a vast array of *details*. With that overload of input, it was possible to miss anything.

Red Hair was walking again. In a second he'd be past it. Charla was in agony. They'd never get the suitcase any closer than this.

And then . . .

"Ow!"

He stubbed his toe on it, looked down, and found himself gazing into two million dollars.

"I got it! *I got it!*"

Charla held her own silent celebration alongside the smugglers' raucous one.

"Now we can get out of here!" Red Hair exclaimed.

Music to her ears. She followed the smugglers at a safe distance, keeping an eye out for any landmark that might point her in the direction of the lookout tree, where Luke, Lyssa, and Ian should be waiting.

Suddenly, there was a yelp, followed by the crashing sound of someone tumbling through the underbrush. Her stomach tightened. Her friends!

But then she heard Red Hair's voice. "Chelton! You okay?"

"I fell in a hole!" came the muffled reply. "A *big* one. And — hey, there's something down here!"

Charla came up a few yards behind Red Hair, who was on his hands and knees searching the jungle floor for the other man. A familiar notch was carved into a palm trunk close to where he knelt. A feeling of deep dread took hold in her gut.

The smugglers had found the bomb.

SEPTEMBER 3, 1945
1240 hours

Colonel Dupont stared at Junior, which had been dangling at the end of the defective crane for more than four hours.

"And that's the only way to move it?"

"Ninety-five hundred pounds, Colonel," replied Holliday.

Lieutenant Bosco, communications officer, ran up. "HQ says the nearest hydraulic is in Tinian. They can get it to us in three days."

"Three days!" The colonel regarded the flurry of activity on the runway. There was almost a carnival atmosphere as the men loaded up the plane, looking forward to reunions with wives and families.

If he gave the order to wait three more days, he'd have a revolution on his hands. . . .

ISLAND

CHAPTER ELEVEN
Day 23, 5:50 P.M.

The day had started out hopeful for J.J. Lane. It didn't stay that way.

His one-of-a-kind sunglasses remained focused on the cloudless sky, now dimming, awaiting the arrival of the plane that would not appear — Charting a New Course, come for Will and, with any luck, the rest of them.

That had been one flaw in his reasoning — that CNC might try to rescue Will, the sickest, but leave the others to serve out their "sentence" of maturing and learning teamwork and building character —

And whatever else those professional torturers think we have to do.

For that reason, he was sticking to Will like glue. It wasn't exactly hard to do. Will had barely moved all day. He was burning with fever, and J.J. had the feeling the kid wasn't all there. Oh, he knew when he was hungry, or when he had to set out into the jungle to go to the bathroom. But one time when J.J. was helping Will into the trees, the boy said, "Get out of here, Lyss! I'm going to the can!"

ESCAPE

J.J. was taken aback. "It's not Lyssa, it's J.J."

Will seemed indignant. "My leg hurts, but I'm not blind," he muttered.

"They're coming to get us today," J.J. reassured him. "Just hang in there and you'll be okay."

And what was the bleary reply? "I hope Dad takes the tunnel. There's traffic on the bridge."

Two months ago J.J. Lane had been riding down Sunset Boulevard in the passenger seat of Leonardo DiCaprio's Porsche. Now he was the bathroom monitor on Gilligan's Island.

Instantly, he felt guilty for the thought. None of this was Will's fault.

J.J. scanned the horizon. Where was CNC? What was taking so long?

The waiting was hard, but he passed the time by imagining the looks on the others' faces when they returned to the campsite to see a rescue plane. Especially Haggerty. Luke always acted like he had some special confirmation from God that whatever he did was exactly the right thing.

A juvenile delinquent from some rusty old mill town who thinks he's better than me! If CNC comes, I'm going to rub it in Haggerty's face all the way home.

If? No, he meant *when*. CNC was definitely coming. They'd be here soon. Only —

He checked Ian's *National Geographic Explorer* watch — how this cheap piece of junk still worked when J.J.'s Rolex had dropped dead was one of the great mysteries of the planet.

6:15. Soon it would be too dark to land.

Maybe they were coming tomorrow.

But Will's sick now! For all they know, we're getting ready to cut him open!

CNC were jerks, but they wouldn't let a bunch of kids operate on a real person. It wasn't just crazy — it was illegal. They could all go to jail for that, couldn't they?

It didn't make sense. The struggle to reason it out felt almost physical — like a wrestling match in J.J.'s head.

If they knew, then they'd come. Why aren't they here?

And finally — the answer . . .

Because they don't know.

J.J. squeezed his eyes shut as if he could stop his weeping by sealing it inside. But his tears were a flood he couldn't control any more than he could reverse the explosion of truth in his brain.

"Quit sniveling, Lyss," mumbled Will, half asleep on the raft.

The others had been right all along. Charting a New Course was over. It had gone up in a fireball and sunk to the bottom of the Pacific along with the *Phoenix* and its unfortunate captain. All this — the island, the smugglers, the bomb — was *real!*

No one was watching them. No one was protecting them. They were on their own.

"No," he breathed. Weeks of desperation and fear crystallized into a single moment of perfect horror. "No!"

"Shut up, Lyss. I didn't hit you that hard," murmured Will.

J.J.'s heart was pounding like a pile driver in his chest. He had to go somewhere, do something — to move, to act. Otherwise this terrible feeling would destroy him.

Voices! He jumped at the unexpected sounds. The others!

Lyssa took in the stricken look on J.J.'s face. "Is my brother okay?"

"He's fine," J.J. said absently. "You know — for him. How did it go with the suitcase?"

"Good news and bad news," groaned Luke. "We got the suitcase delivered. But in the process, the smugglers found the bomb."

"You're kidding!" J.J. exclaimed. "So — what does that mean?"

"It's impossible to tell," Ian reasoned. "We can't even be sure they know what it is."

"They'll figure it out," Charla said grimly. "We did."

Lyssa looked scared. "Men like that — they'll do anything for money. Can you imagine what an atomic bomb is worth?"

"We're not going to give those guys the chance to find out," Luke said definitely. "They've got their money. They'll be leaving tomorrow. Tonight's the night I stow away with the cargo."

There was a chilling moment that mingled sheer fright with the acceptance that this was their only path.

Charla spoke first. "I wish there was some other way."

"There isn't," said Luke bleakly. "We've had almost a month to think about getting off this rock. This is the best we can do."

"And we have to do it now if we're going to help Will," added Lyssa.

Ian nodded slowly. All eyes turned to J.J.

"I agree," said the actor's son.

Luke was surprised. "Really?" They had been expecting him to give them a hard time.

"But with one change of plan," J.J. went on. "Haggerty doesn't go. It should be me."

"You?" Luke laughed bitterly. "I thought you wanted to be here on the beach to meet the CNC rescue party."

"I was wrong about that," J.J. said seriously. "I'm not wrong about this."

Luke glared at him. "You idiot! This isn't like extreme snowboarding, where you brag to your Hollywood friends about all your bumps and bruises! It could be a suicide mission!"

"That's exactly why I have to go," J.J. argued. "Look — no offense — you're nobody. If they catch you in the cargo hold, they'll blow you away without thinking twice about it."

Luke was disgusted. "And they won't shoot you because your dad's famous?"

"Not famous," said J.J. "Rich! They won't kill me. They'll try to ransom me off to my old man." He flashed a crooked grin. "He might even pay too. He's got to be feeling pretty guilty about sending me on this trip."

"Listen to yourself!" Lyssa exclaimed. "Everything's a joke to you. How can we trust you to take it seriously?"

Luke was shocked. "Wait a minute — you're *considering* this?"

"J.J.'s right, you know," came Ian's thoughtful voice. "That *USA Today* the smugglers had — the article wasn't about us; it was mostly about Jonathan Lane's son."

"J.J.'s picture was in that paper," added

Charla. "If the smugglers catch him, there's a chance they might recognize him."

"What good is that if he doesn't get the job done?" Luke exploded. "This isn't about who's in better shape if he gets caught! This is about sneaking away and getting us rescued! This guy'll be on Space Mountain at Disneyland when he'll suddenly remember, 'Oops, I forgot to tell the rescuers about Luke, Charla, Lyssa, Will, and Ian.' "

J.J. bit back an angry retort. "Listen, I don't blame you if maybe you think I'm a bit of a flake — "

"A *bit* of a flake?" raved Luke. "If you look up 'flake' in the dictionary, there's a picture of your ugly face! Don't forget whose fault it was that the captain got killed!"

"And who was right there with me when it happened?" J.J. shot back.

"Someone had to stop you!" Luke raged.

"And you sure did a great job of it!"

There was a rustling sound and Will turned over on the raft. "We're not fighting, Mom," he mumbled. "Honest."

Luke folded his arms across his chest. "I'm not putting my life in your hands," he said in a lower tone.

ESCAPE

J.J. looked him squarely in the eye. "You think I like it that it has to be me? I've spent fourteen years doing things the easy way. That's my style — coasting. Nothing would thrill me more than hanging out here while you risk your neck. But this has to work, and I'm our best shot."

CHAPTER TWELVE
Day 24, 1:25 A.M.

The flashlight beam cast a dim glow over the lagoon where the two floatplanes were beached. The rear of the twin-engine craft bobbed in the shallow water. The other — with a single engine — sat heavy in the sand, fully loaded.

"That's the one," whispered J.J. "Fatso's plane."

Luke grimaced. Now that they were faced with it, the plan seemed totally insane.

The good-byes back at the camp had been shattering. Charla, Lyssa, and Ian had cried openly. Even Will, drifting in and out of delirium, had picked up on the mood of distress. It was clear that the castaways thought they were sending a friend to his death.

If it wasn't so awful, it would be interesting, Luke thought. Had the six gone to the same school, they probably wouldn't even have noticed one another. Will and Lyssa, the only two who had known each other before CNC, had been lifelong enemies. Yet the terrible and tragic events of the past weeks had bonded the group into a unit so close that to tear one away — even J.J. — left a painful, gaping wound.

ESCAPE

Luke and J.J. crept out of the brush and made their way furtively down the coral slope to the beach.

The cargo hold was in the underbelly of the single-engine plane. Luke lowered the hatch cover, and they shone the beam inside. There were three large wooden crates that the smugglers used to transport elephant tusks. Smaller squarer boxes contained rhino horns. There were also two refrigerated units whose humming batteries confirmed they were in operation. These held vital organs and other body parts harvested from endangered species.

J.J. opened one of the ivory crates. Inside, wrapped in soft blankets, were two tusks, each about six feet long.

"No room," Luke whispered.

They moved on to the second crate. The tusks were shorter but fatter, so it was also full. They turned to the third box. Inside were two four-foot tusks, one of them broken.

"It'll be tight," said Luke.

J.J. shrugged. "Good thing I've been on the banana diet for the past month." He swung a leg into the crate.

Luke put a hand on J.J.'s shoulder. "It's not too late, you know. I can still do this."

J.J. clambered inside and lay down flat. From

the pocket of his fatigues, he pulled out his sunglasses and popped them onto his nose. "How do I look?"

Any reply stuck fast in Luke's throat. The truth was that J.J. looked exactly like a dead body in a coffin. Finally, he managed, "You remember the location of the island, right? Our latitude and longitude?"

"Oh, sure," J.J. said, grinning. "First you go to Hawaii, then you hang a left — "

"J.J. — " Could this kid ever be serious, even in a moment like this?

"I remember," the actor's son insisted. "I'll be back soon, okay? Don't operate on Will."

Luke felt himself starting to lose it. "For God's sake, be careful. *Think* before you act. There are no do-overs now!"

J.J. nodded. "You'd better get going." He helped Luke maneuver the lid into place.

Luke secured the box. It was the hardest thing he'd ever done. "You can breathe, right?"

J.J.'s voice was muffled. "If you make it home and I don't, tell my dad I'm sorry I never grew up."

As Luke headed back into the jungle on shaky legs, he noted that the kid had it wrong. J.J. *had* grown up — more in the last few hours than in fourteen years.

ESCAPE

* * *

Both planes took off at six-thirty that morning. The twin-engine, carrying Red Hair and the money, turned east into the rising sun. The single engine, with Mr. Big, the cargo, and J.J., banked southwest toward Asia.

Crouched in a finger of jungle that extended out over the beach, a bleary-eyed Luke followed the progress of J.J.'s plane until it had disappeared into the distant haze.

"Good luck, J.J.," he whispered aloud.

At the castaways' camp, all activity ceased at the first sound of the propellers' buzz. The fire was smothered, the stills were kicked down and buried in sand, and the raft where Will lay was pushed under cover of the trees. All watched in silence as the aircraft carried their friend and their hopes far away.

"Lousy lawnmower," muttered Will. "Can't ever get any sleep around here."

Remarkably, J.J. slept away the hours before takeoff — concluding that he was either very cool or very tired. He was not cool, however, when the motor roared to life. He practically jumped out of his skin, smashing his head on the lid of the crate. The noise was unbelievable, and the vibration was making his bones come unglued. It was like front-row seats at a Metallica concert (courtesy of Dad) times a thousand.

He was aware of the bobbing of the craft as it moved out from the beach. Then a brief but powerful acceleration, and they were airborne.

It's really happening, he thought. The train had left the station, and it was too late to get off. He couldn't escape the impression that his life had changed so completely that he was now somebody he barely knew. It was terrifying, no doubt about it. But he also felt very alive and excited. Whatever happened, he was sure that it was better than rotting away on that island.

He eased open the lid of the crate and looked around. There were no windows, but some light was sneaking in through the door seal, making it possible to examine his surroundings. He squeezed himself out of the box, keeping low to avoid hitting his head. It was even louder out here, and he could see why. The front of the cargo hold opened into the engine housing. He tried to climb into it, but the heat of the roaring motor drove him back.

When they came to unload the cargo, he'd better not be here. . . .

ESCAPE

CHAPTER THIRTEEN
Day 24, 3:20 P.M.

J.J. had never been good with boredom. In his world, a whole lot of people and money had always been devoted to the entertainment of J.J. Lane. But even a week adrift on the lifeboat and almost a month stranded on the island hadn't prepared him for this plane trip.

It was long — hour after hour, cooped up in a cargo hold where he couldn't even stand. Not a window to look out of. And through it all, a teeth-rattling, never-ending roar that drowned out all thought.

Where were they going? Mars?

Wherever it is, let's just get there.

Then he felt it — the beginnings of descent. A wild panic knifed through him. They'd be on the ground soon. And then what?

The turmoil in his head threatened to tear him in two, a wrestling match between a craving for excitement and a dark voice repeating, *You could be dead soon.*

It was a smooth landing, but to J.J. it was jarring and unexpected. As they taxied, jouncing along a bumpy runway, he silently went over the

ISLAND

details of his plan. It would work. It had to. His life depended on it — his and the lives of Will and the others.

The plane came to a halt, and the engine shut down. The sudden absence of all that noise was like falling off the edge of the earth.

There were voices outside and the slamming of a door. The time was now.

Taking a deep breath, J.J. rolled over to the engine opening, clamped his hands on a metal bar, and hoisted himself inside. It was still painfully hot, but bearable now that the motor was off. His elbow brushed against the engine block, and a searing pain caused him to snatch his arm back. There, on the sleeve of his fatigues, was a small brown scorch mark.

The curse was halfway out of his mouth when he heard someone fumbling with the catch of the cargo bay. Scrambling with his heels, he backed into a corner and tried to be very, very small.

Light flooded the hold. One by one, the crates were hauled out by men speaking a language that could have been almost anything. Then a voice with an English accent: "Yeah, we had a spot of misery on that ruddy island. Don't even ask why. Got a mosquito bite for every minute I spent there."

J.J. huddled in the shadows, hardly daring to

ESCAPE

breathe. And then it was over. The plane was un-loaded; the voices grew more distant.

He felt a great surge of relief and triumph. He'd pulled it off! Now all he had to do was lie low until the men went home. Then he could sneak out and find the nearest policeman.

Suddenly, without warning, the engine roared to life again. A blast of heat hit J.J. in the face, and he lost his grip on the bar. He dropped like a stone to the floor of the empty cargo bay.

Frantically, he looked out the open hatch. The plane was swinging around to park inside a large aircraft hangar. It was like being on display on a rotating dessert rack at a diner. There was no place to hide.

The element of surprise was his only weapon. He had to make a break for it.

Crawling on all fours, he scrambled to the edge of the hold and prepared to jump.

Do it! he urged himself. *Don't wait till they see you!*

When he hit the floor of the hangar, he was already running. First he made for the cover of a pile of tires. But excited shouts told him he'd been spotted. He shifted direction for the hangar doors, yelling, "Cop! Cop!"

Heart sinking, he took in his surroundings. Dense jungle flanked the single runway. This was not a busy airport, but a private landing strip. Which meant there were no police around — only enemies. He was alone and badly outnumbered.

J.J. was fast, and the electricity of the moment made him even faster. He gave no thought to where he was or where he might go. All his concentration was on escape.

The jeep came out of nowhere, slicing across the doorway to cut off his exit. J.J. tried to put on the brakes, but he was running too hard. His knees hit metal, and he bounced back, looking around desperately for a clear field.

There! To the left!

But just as he sidestepped the jeep, a beefy arm grabbed him around the neck.

The race was over.

On the same day that J.J. left on the smugglers' plane, Will Greenfield failed to wake up.

Lyssa was frantic. She had spent the entire day trying to snap her brother out of his stupor. She used everything from bitter-melon tea dribbled between his lips to pots of seawater splashed in his face. She slapped, pinched, and shook him, but with no result.

"Is he in a coma?" she asked fearfully.

Ian just looked bewildered. He loosened the

bandage on Will's leg and lifted it. The wound was an angry red, with threatening lines of lighter red emanating from the center like a sunburst. The skin around it was hot to the touch.

"He needs a doctor," said Ian, stating a fact that everyone had known for some time.

There was almost a click as the castaways made the same connection: a doctor — rescue — J.J.

"J.J.'s got to be where he's going by now," decided Luke. "If Will's going to get his doctor, we'll know in the next couple of days."

"What if no one comes?" put in Charla.

Luke took a deep breath. "Well, then we'll know that J.J.'s — that he didn't make it."

"If that happens, we'll have to operate," said Ian. "It'll be Will's only chance."

Luke went gray in the face. "Before he left, J.J. made me promise we wouldn't do it."

"Let's pick a deadline," Lyssa said bravely. "If we don't hear anything by that time, we've got to figure that J.J.'s — not coming. And we do our best to get the bullet out."

"I wouldn't wait too long," Ian advised nervously.

Luke thought it over. "Let's give J.J. a few hours to escape and find help. Then they have to put together a rescue team and come back here to find us." He did a rapid calculation. "Not to-morrow, but the morning after that."

He looked around the circle of faces. Every-body nodded in agreement.

On his broken piece of raft, Will slumbered on.

ESCAPE

CHAPTER FOURTEEN
Day 24, 5:50 P.M.

On the island of Taiwan, off mainland China, a small private airstrip was the final destination for the smugglers' cargo of illegal animal parts.

In an empty storeroom in back of the hangar, J.J. found himself in a rickety bridge chair, opposite none other than Mr. Big himself.

The fat man had neither the time nor the desire to be pleasant. "What were you doing on that island?"

"My boat sank," J.J. replied earnestly.

Mr. Big reached out and delivered an open-handed slap right across J.J.'s mouth. "The truth, right now."

"Honest!" exclaimed J.J., tasting blood from a cut lip. "I was shipwrecked! I only stowed away with you guys to get out of there."

English Accent stepped forward. "Boss, you don't think he could be off that kids' boat trip that went down?"

"That was a month ago," said the fat man in the soiled green suit. "There's no way any of those kids could have survived for so long."

ISLAND

"It's amazing what you can pick up from the Discovery Channel," said J.J.

Another slap. This one hurt.

"How can I make you believe me?" J.J. exclaimed. "We left Guam on the *Phoenix* on July eleventh! Captain Cascadden was the skipper, and the mate was a guy named Radford. The *Phoenix* sank. I was in the lifeboat for a week, and I've been eating bananas and fending off lizards ever since."

Mr. Big considered this. His piggy eyes got even smaller. "And your fellow survivors?"

J.J. shook his head. "I was the only one who made it. All the others went down with the ship."

The fat man nodded to English Accent. "Naslund."

Naslund grabbed J.J.'s arm, forced it behind his back, and yanked it high.

J.J. gasped. The pain was unbearable. He had taken his share of cuts and bruises in his life, but this was different. This pain was being applied by a professional, who knew exactly what to twist and how hard to twist it. It was cold and calculated, like a chess move.

"Come on, boy," Naslund urged. "I don't want to snap your arm. Just tell us who else is on the island."

J.J. fought to reason through the pain. It was something the castaways had never considered

ESCAPE

in coming up with this plan. They had always known J.J. would be at risk if he got caught, but this scenario had not occurred to them — that he might betray the others, and the smugglers would go back to the island and kill them all.

"I was alone!" J.J. grunted.

A quick twist, and the agony was double.

"You're breaking my arm!"

"Who was with you on the island?" insisted Mr. Big.

J.J. thought of the others. In that instant, he knew that his friends were worth a broken arm. "Nobody!" he gasped.

Another yank. The jolt cranked up the level of pain higher than he could have imagined. Black inkblots began to stain the edge of his vision. He was going to pass out.

And then it was over. Naslund released him and he dropped to the floor, sucking air.

He heard the squeak of a chair as Mr. Big stood up. "Clean up afterward," he instructed his employee.

"After *what*?" From the corner of his eye, J.J. saw Naslund pull a small handgun out of his belt. It was like living a scene straight out of one of his father's movies. It didn't seem real. But it was happening *right now*! This stupid boat trip was costing him his life! He was going to *die*!

Die. The word echoed in his head like the tolling of a bell. It was unthinkable! Bad things happened — bad luck — lousy days. But not *this!*

He was so shocked and panic-stricken that he almost forgot his trump card.

"Wait!" he screamed into the gun barrel. "You can't kill me! I'm worth money! *Big* money! My father is Jonathan Lane!"

The two smugglers exchanged a look.

"It could be true, boss," said Naslund. "The news said Lane's kid was on that boat."

The gun disappeared from J.J.'s line of vision. He allowed himself to breathe again.

That storeroom became J.J.'s prison cell, where he was held under constant watch. His guards were two Asian men who stayed with him in four-hour shifts. They didn't speak English, or perhaps they just had nothing to say to him, because he never got a word out of either of them. Privately, he nicknamed them "Mean" and "Meaner."

Mean was the thief. He patted J.J. down for valuables and seemed really annoyed when all he got was the designer sunglasses. Meaner was the music lover. He brought along a tinny portable radio, and spent his shifts leaning against the door, listening to a country-and-

ESCAPE

western station. In between songs by George Strait and Shania Twain, an excited DJ emitted a flood of what sounded like Chinese, addressing his listeners as "pardner."

His meals were fast-food packs of odd-tasting instant noodles that came with plastic chopsticks. He had thrown up from his first helping. After the island diet — mostly fruit and taro — the food seemed so rich and heavy that it lay in his stomach like a shotput.

Mean and Meaner found nothing more hilarious than watching him trying to shovel and slurp his dinner. Finally, Naslund took pity on him and conducted a crash course on eating with chopsticks.

J.J. was absurdly glad to see the Englishman. The hours and hours of not knowing what was going on were even harder than the number Naslund had done on J.J.'s arm.

"Did you talk to my dad?" he asked anxiously. "He's going to pay, right?"

"Don't get your knickers in a twist," was the reply. "We've got to prove you're alive first." He slapped a copy of *USA Today* into J.J.'s hands. "Hold this up. And watch the birdie." He raised a Polaroid camera.

"What's the newspaper for?" asked J.J.

"Don't block the headline," ordered the smuggler. "You have to be able to tell it's today."

Click. A whirring noise produced the picture, which began to develop.

"You're going to *mail* it? I'll be stuck here forever!"

Naslund shook his head. "We've got a friend who's a whiz with computers. The way he e-mails, it's like it just pops out of thin air, totally untraceable."

"Dad'll pay up," J.J. mumbled, mostly to himself. "He has to. He won't let me die."

Naslund chuckled. "You're a valuable little piece of merchandise, you know that? You might even fetch a better price than that atom bomb."

"You'll never sell that bomb," J.J. blurted without thinking. "You couldn't get it off the island. It weighs a million tons!"

Naslund raised both bushy eyebrows. "So you know about that, do you? Not as sweet and innocent as you'd like us to believe."

J.J. reddened and said nothing.

"Funny thing about that bomb," the Englishman went on cheerfully. "It's not the shell that's valuable; it's what's inside. I don't know how to take that stuff out — but I'll bet we can find somebody who does."

By the time he strolled out of the storeroom, J.J. was almost happy to be left with the country music stylings of Meaner.

ESCAPE

CHAPTER FIFTEEN
Day 26, 6:40 A.M.

Luke stood at the water's edge watching the sky lighten as dawn broke. No plane, no boat, no helicopter — no J.J. Time had run out on the boy from California.

He felt a twinge of guilt for all the times he and J.J. had locked horns. True, the kid was a flake. But a lot of Luke's resentment had been envy. With Jonathan Lane's money and connections, Luke would have been acquitted with an apology, not shipped off on Charting a New Course.

He studied the sand at his feet. There was no reason to be jealous of J.J. now. The poor guy was probably dead.

A light touch on his elbow. Luke jumped.

Charla stood beside him, her eyes huge. "Ian's getting the stuff together."

Luke didn't move. "I can't shake the feeling that if I stand here longer, I'll think of something we missed — something that means we don't have to do this."

Soon the instruments were boiling in a pot,

and the bandages were rolled and ready.

Ian presented himself, paper-white. Lyssa was already crying silently. She sat cross-legged beside her unconscious brother, cradling his limp hand in both of hers. The beach was their operating theater; the sun provided their work light.

First came a shot of fifty-six-year-old Novocain. Even though Will was unconscious, Ian had heard that the trauma of the operation could jolt him awake. That was unthinkable.

They waited. Five minutes passed to allow the freezing to take effect.

"Will that stuff even work after so long?" asked Lyssa in a whisper.

Ian could not answer. It was just more evidence of how little they knew about what they were doing. In any other situation, they would be arrested and locked up for trying this on a living creature. How had things ever gotten to the point where this butchery was the only choice?

And then it was time.

Charla held out the tray of sterilized instruments. Ian reached for the scalpel, but couldn't make his fingers work. His hand started to shake, and when Luke looked at him, he realized that it was the younger boy's whole body that was trembling.

Gently, he moved Ian aside. "I'll do it."

When the sharp blade pierced the skin, Luke was amazed at how easy it was. It reminded him of slicing into an orange with an Exacto knife from art class. He looked anxiously at Will, expecting him to jump up screaming. But the patient slumbered on. He cut a neat slit about one inch long right through the center of the bullet hole. For a second he could see the thin red line. Then the blood oozed and spilled over.

He fought through a moment of light-headedness and scolded himself inwardly. What did he expect — chocolate milk? Of course there was blood.

Charla did her best to clean off the incision with a sterilized cloth ripped from fifty-six-year-old toweling.

Luke put the scalpel back on the tray and picked up a pair of surgical tweezers. Grimacing in deep concentration, he inserted the instrument into the slit and began to probe around for the bullet. More blood. And resistance too. Since the tweezers couldn't cut, moving it around was difficult.

Panic bubbled up inside Luke. This was crazy! He couldn't do this! They were nuts even to consider it! He pulled out the probe and dropped it onto the tray.

"It's no good," he managed to rasp. "I don't feel anything!"

"We can't stop now!" sobbed Lyssa.

"I'm hurting him!" Luke insisted hoarsely. "I don't know what I'm doing in there! I might as well be using a pickax!"

Ian spoke up in a shaky voice. "I saw a show once where the doctors made a second cut across the first one. Like an X."

And because Ian's TV knowledge had never failed them, Luke picked up the scalpel and tried again. There was a lot more blood this time, enough to scent the humid air. Charla gagged, but kept on mopping.

Luke felt the difference immediately. The second incision had opened the wound further, and the tweezers moved easily through the torn flesh. Then suddenly he felt it — something small and hard.

"It's here!" he breathed. He began to probe more delicately, attempting to maneuver the tweezers around the bullet. Sweat poured off his forehead, stinging his eyes. Time and time again he felt the tines close over the slug only to slide off its awkward shape. A terrible frustration

ESCAPE

gripped his gut, magnified by the knowledge that every minute this went on could be damaging Will even more.

He was wallowing in blood now. There was far too much for Charla to sponge away. But Luke didn't need to see. He had that bullet, knew exactly where it was.

A wave of nausea washed over him. *Don't stop,* he exhorted himself. *You just have to find the right angle! A little luck and a little wrist action and —*

"Gotcha!" The tweezers held the slug fast. Without even daring to breathe, he drew the bullet straight up and straight out. It was maddeningly slow, but he couldn't risk losing his grip. At long last, the tweezers came free. And there was the slug — ugly, misshapen, gory, but out.

Ian opened one of the old bottles from the dispensary and poured alcohol into the wound. Then another fifty-plus-year-old antiseptic — iodine — painted a bright orange spot on Will's thigh.

Luke's hands, surprisingly steady now, fit together the edges of the incisions and applied pressure. Last came a piece of modern medicine — an adhesive steri-patch from the first-aid kit off the lifeboat. It stuck like a second skin, holding the cut flesh together.

At last, Luke leaned back. They had done all they could do. The rest was up to Will.

It was only when Luke got to his feet that he noticed his jaw ached from clenching his teeth. His head was pounding. He took three shaky steps and passed out cold, face-first in the sand.

ESCAPE

CHAPTER SIXTEEN
Day 27, 2:40 P.M.

J.J. sat on the floor of the storeroom, leaning on one knee. His thoughts were hundreds of miles away, back on the island. It was a dumb thing to do, but he found himself trying to conjure up a vision of the other five castaways, almost as if thinking hard would patch him into their frequency and give him an update. What were they doing? Was Will all right? What did they figure had happened to J.J.?

Well, that was an easy one, he reminded himself. He hadn't sent help, so they assumed he was dead. He and Haggerty had talked about that — rescue would come quickly or not at all.

Hang in there, he tried to urge the others over all that distance. *As soon as Dad coughs up the ransom, I'll send the cavalry for you.*

What a disaster this mission had turned out to be. In his mind he'd always pictured himself either free or dead. Not locked in a bare room for days, with worry and boredom intermingling in him to form a lethal cocktail of — what? He didn't know, but it was driving him crazy.

ISLAND

Especially with that never-ending sound track of twangy music!

He regarded Meaner, who was draped against the door, chain-smoking. "Could you please change the station?" he asked as politely as he could.

The guard looked back at him. His expression was so blank that J.J. couldn't tell if he'd even heard, let alone understood.

J.J. stood up. "The *radio*. How about some *different music*?" He pointed to the small portable and covered his ears.

He had Meaner's attention, but the guy still didn't get it.

"Here — I'll do it." J.J. took a step forward. It was a big mistake.

Meaner jumped up, pulled out his gun, and pointed it at J.J., screaming in Chinese.

J.J. raised his hands. "Hold on! Don't get excited! It's just the music, okay? The *music*!"

The door was flung open, and in burst Naslund. The Englishman yelled back in two languages until finally he began to laugh. He turned to J.J.

"Don't like the concert, eh? Can't say I blame you."

"I just wanted to change the station," J.J. mumbled resentfully.

ESCAPE

"No time for that now," said Naslund briskly. He grabbed J.J. by the arm. "Let's have a little chat with your father."

J.J. brightened. "He's here? He paid?"

"On the phone," the smuggler amended. "He wants to hear his little boy's voice before he ponies up the cash."

J.J.'s face fell the distance between speaking to home and actually going there. "Okay, where's the phone?"

Naslund hustled him out into the hangar where a Mercedes stood waiting. "Your daddy's probably got half the FBI tracing this call. We're going to take a ride to a special phone."

They tied a burlap sack over J.J.'s head and pushed him to the floor in the back of the car.

J.J. guessed that it was mostly highway driving at first, but then the Mercedes entered what must have been a city. There were frequent stops, and he could make out horns and motorcycle engines all around.

He heard Mr. Big's voice: "There's a cop on horseback. Sit the kid up."

So the sack was ripped off his head, and he was plucked from the floor and squeezed onto the backseat between Naslund and Meaner. They were in the middle of a bustling Asian city — Hong Kong? Shanghai? Neon billboards with

Chinese characters flashed everywhere. Hundreds of motor scooters threaded through the crush of vehicles. Just ahead, a mounted policeman was directing traffic. No sooner had J.J.'s eyes locked on the cop than he felt the muzzle of a gun pressed against his side.

"Don't even think about it," whispered Naslund.

J.J. stared straight ahead, his blood chilled to freezing. They passed the officer close enough to reach out a hand and touch his boot.

As soon as the policeman was out of sight, on went the hood, and J.J. was back on the floor.

There were a lot of stairs — forty-two, J.J. counted. Every landing seemed to have a different cooking smell. Weeks on the island had gotten him used to the heat, but this was stifling.

When the burlap sack was finally pulled off, he was in a small seedy apartment crammed full of computer equipment and piles of books and manuals.

J.J. looked around for the phone, but Naslund sat him down in front of a computer that ran some kind of Internet long-distance calling program.

A young Chinese man with shoulder-length hair was expertly pounding the keyboard. He

ESCAPE

turned to Mr. Big. "It will be untraceable for two minutes."

They heard a single ring and a quick pickup. "Jonathan Lane."

It was all J.J. could do to keep from bursting into tears like a two-year-old. Since he'd last spoken to his father six weeks ago, the whole world had gone crazy. He'd been shipwrecked, marooned, and held at gunpoint. And here was this voice that came from a life before all that. It was a comfort and a torment at the same time.

"Hi, Dad."

"J.J., you're okay, right? They haven't hurt you?"

"I'm fine," he said shakily. "No, I'm not! You've got to get me out of this, Dad!"

"It's being taken care of," promised his father. "Just sit tight and stay calm."

"*Fast!*" J.J. insisted, agonized that he couldn't tell his father about the castaways still on the island. "You have to come quick! That's the most important thing!"

His father's voice was choked with emotion. "I know you're scared, J.J. But for me this is *happy*! Three days ago I thought you were dead! To talk to you, hear your voice — you can't know what it means to me — "

J.J. was struck dumb. His father was *crying*!

Jonathan Lane never cried, not even in the movies. He had instructed his agent never to consider a role that involved "blubbering."

Mr. Big grabbed the microphone. "This is all very touching, but we have business. I assume you've got the money?"

"It's ready."

"Good. You get your plane fueled and sitting on the tarmac, and when the time comes, we'll tell you where to fly." He made a cutting motion across his throat. The longhaired man broke the connection.

Naslund let J.J. sit up in the car and look around on the drive back to the hangar. He even provided a bit of a guided tour. This was Taipei; there was downtown; the Grand Palace was on that hill; the haze was air pollution.

Air pollution. Smog. J.J. never thought he'd miss it. But after six long weeks, this was his first faint echo of his beloved L.A. In spite of himself, he couldn't help but enjoy the action and feel of a busy, crowded city.

Idly, he wondered about the change of attitude among his captors. *They're in a good mood. They know they've got a big payday coming.*

It made sense. On the way over, they couldn't let him see his surroundings for fear that he might let slip something to his father. But now that the phone call was over . . .

He frowned. What was to stop him from giving up the smugglers once he was safe at home in California? He knew their location, their airstrip, and their secret island. He knew their faces and could testify against them and probably put them away for a thousand years.

How could they take that risk?

When the answer came to him, he realized that a part of him had always known it: He was never going to see California or his father again. When the smugglers had the ransom money in their hands, he was going to be killed.

CHAPTER SEVENTEEN
Day 28, 11:15 A.M.

Will Greenfield came awake into a world of pain and confusion. His leg was on fire.

What happened? Yeah, it hurt before, but not like this!

He sat up and practically passed out from the effort. Trickling moisture on his cheeks. He was *crying!* Sure, they'd all cried in the past few weeks — from terror, anger, hopelessness. Only a baby cried from pain. *But it hurts so much!*

He looked down. One entire leg of his fatigues was cut off, laying bare a thigh that looked like it had taken a direct hit from a cannonball. A square patch, crusty with dried blood, sat over the bullet wound at the center of a bright orange circle of iodine. Around that was an area of black-and-blue bruising that extended from knee to hip.

"Lyssa?" His voice was barely a rasp.

No answer.

"*Lyssa!*" He tried to drag himself to the flap of the sun canopy. Every inch of movement made his leg erupt with a searing agony. He had to bite on his sleeve to keep from screaming. *Come on,*

ESCAPE

you can do this. With a muffled moan, he crawled forward and peered outside. An amazing sight met his eyes. The beach was a beehive of activity. Nine stills worked side by side, boiling the salt out of seawater. Enormous stacks of fruit stood everywhere — coconuts, bananas, mangosteens, jackfruit, and durians, all waiting for — for what? The castaways could never eat that much stuff.

Speaking of eating, was he hungry? He thought so, but he could hardly feel his stomach over the explosion in his thigh.

Ian and Luke passed his line of vision, carrying something odd. It looked like a sort of blanket made out of army fatigues sewn together. And it was stretched between the two oars that came with the lifeboat.

How long have I been sleeping? What did I miss?

And then it hit him. That looked like — a *sail!* "Lyssa! Lyss!"

This time the others came running. And when they found him awake and alert, the celebration was boisterous. He couldn't get a word in edgewise. When he opened his mouth to ask what was going on, Lyssa stuck a thermometer in it. That was when Luke explained that Will had been out for the better part of a week, and during that time, the bullet in his leg had been surgically removed.

"Without asking me?" blurted Will, spitting the thermometer clear out of the lifeboat.

Lyssa retrieved it and brushed the sand off. "And it worked, Will! Your temperature is almost down to normal! We thought we'd killed you for sure!"

"It feels like you did," Will gasped. "My leg, anyway. Why'd you have to do it?"

"This is better," Ian insisted. "I know it hurts, but that infection could have been fatal."

Will nodded slowly, struggling to think through the firestorm of pain.

"What's with the" — he strained to point at the beach — "the fruit market? And that thing between the oars?"

Luke took a deep breath. "J.J. stowed away on the smugglers' plane," he said gravely. "We haven't heard from him since."

It was the one thought that could have drawn Will's mind off his leg. "Oh, my God, they killed him!"

Luke nodded grimly. "We think so. And we also think they probably interrogated him before they did it."

"Which means they're going to come after us," Lyssa went on. "And this time there's no

ESCAPE

place to hide. We've got to get away from here."

"But not on the ocean!" Will protested, panting with the effort of his words. "Don't you remember? We almost died out there!"

"But this time we'll be prepared," Charla insisted. "We've got the lifeboat, and we're stocking up on food and water."

"Come on," groaned Will. "We'll never carry enough water to get us across the whole ocean!"

"No," agreed Ian. "But maybe the wind will take us into the shipping lanes or someplace where planes fly over, and we can be spotted. It's a long shot, but it could be our only chance."

"We can't just wait here to be slaughtered," added Lyssa.

Will lay back in torment and despair, staring up at the sun canopy. No, they shouldn't sit around waiting for their own murders. But was the only alternative to go out and quite probably kill themselves?

CHAPTER EIGHTEEN
Day 28, 11:45 A.M.

The country music was louder than ever, and Meaner was in an especially foul mood. That morning his fellow guard, Mean, had failed to show up for work, leaving Meaner with a triple shift as J.J.'s jailer.

The actor's son lay on his stomach on the hard concrete floor, his chin resting on folded arms. He had not set foot outside the storeroom since his guided tour of Taipei a day and a half before. He couldn't remember the last time he'd slept.

They're going to kill you. The thought was a heavy-duty wake-up call, a piercing alarm broadcast directly into his brain whenever drowsiness was about to get the better of him. If Dad paid up, the smugglers would shoot him the minute they had the money. But even if Dad held out, they'd eventually get wise and whack him anyway.

Better to stay awake, he told himself. *Don't sleep through any of the little time you've got left.*

Even after the shipwreck and all those terrible weeks on the island, this was the first time J.J.

ESCAPE

had thought seriously about what death would feel like. Blackness. Nothingness. But just for him. That part was especially hard to accept. The rest of the world would go about its business. In California, there would be traffic and surfing and all-night Hollywood parties. On the island, his fellow castaways would continue to think about rescue. Even this lousy music would probably go on.

"Howdy, pardners!" enthused the DJ. A string of lightning-quick Chinese was followed by the word *hoedown.*

My last memory is going to be Boxcar Willy.

He stood up. "I'm changing the station."

Meaner regarded him, a bored expression on his face.

J.J. headed for the radio. "I'm serious. There's got to be some decent music around here."

The guard barked something at him. His hand hovered over the gun in his belt.

J.J. swallowed hard and kept walking. A plan was taking shape in his mind.

He didn't shoot me last time. . . .

Now the gun was out. The man yelled a steady stream of agitated Chinese that mingled with the DJ's harangue to sound like a heated argument.

So long as he thinks I'm just a country music hater.

"Changing the station, got it? I'm changing the station." J.J. reached for the dial.

Shouting, Meaner took a menacing step forward, and J.J. picked up the radio and swung it with all his might.

Smack! The portable made contact with Meaner's hand. With a cry of pain, the guard dropped the gun, which skittered across the cement floor.

J.J. lunged for it. He knew speed was his only advantage in a fight with an adult. If Meaner ever got him in a wrestling match, he was doomed. His eyes were locked on the gun — only a few inches away! He reached for it, but Meaner hurled himself bodily into the way.

Wham! He hit the floor between J.J. and the weapon. There was a sick-sounding *crack* as the guard's head struck the concrete.

J.J. sprang to his feet, but Meaner was unmoving. A trickle of blood trailed out of his ear to the floor.

J.J. picked up the weapon and stuck it in the waistband of his fatigues. He was free. But how was he ever going to get out of the hangar?

He eased the door open about an inch and peered through the gap. The building was deserted.

I couldn't get this lucky.

ESCAPE

He looked from every angle. The plane was parked, and the big hangar door was closed. But there was no sign of his captors, and he could hear no voices. All was quiet.

He took three tentative steps and then broke into a run. Where was the control that opened the hangar door? It was probably pretty obvious, but in his excited state he couldn't locate it. Then he spotted a small emergency exit in the corner of the building. He sprinted for it.

Locked!

He fought with the knob, shaking with all his might. Cold panic. Anger too. He was so close! How could fate do this to him?

The gun. It came to him in a series of flashes from at least a dozen of his father's movies. The cop/detective/secret agent shoots the lock to make his escape. But that was the movies. Would it work in real life?

There's only one way to find out!

Hand shaking, he held the pistol about six inches from the doorknob and took careful aim. He had never fired a gun in his life. He was amazed at how hard it was to budge the trigger. But once it began to move, it was like a toboggan — accelerating, inevitable.

Three sounds came in such rapid succession

that J.J. heard them all at once: the crack of the gun, a violent screech of splintering metal, and a yowl of pain. The recoil took the pistol clear out of J.J.'s hand. It clattered to the floor five feet behind him. The ruined exit door swung slowly open to reveal Naslund and Mr. Big. The Englishman was doubled over, clutching his side where the bullet had struck him. His shirt was stained with blood.

"You!" exclaimed Mr. Big.

Naslund reached out menacingly, but J.J. exploded through the doorway past him, convinced to the core of his being that the prize of this footrace would be his very life. The Englishman pursued until the pain in his side became too great and he pulled up short.

"Get the car!" he croaked.

His words sent ice water coursing through J.J.'s veins. J.J. pounded down the runway, footfalls resounding in his head like the beating of his heart. *Fly!* he exhorted himself. It was a moment of such crystal-clear purpose it was almost exhilarating: Speed equals escape — that simple law governed his entire universe. If it weren't for the terror that held him in its grip, he might have been cheering himself on.

He wheeled off the runway onto a dirt road.

ESCAPE

All at once, his field of vision was filled with the front grille and headlights of a car — coming up fast!

There was no time to get out of the way. J.J. vaulted onto the hood and rolled. A split second before the windshield hurtled into him, he tumbled off the car, landing in a heap in light underbrush.

The squeal of tires. "Freeze! Hands on your head!"

J.J. didn't respond to the command. There were no moves left in him. Instead, he steeled himself for the impact of the bullets that would end this crazy ride.

"Geez, don't shoot!" shouted another voice. "It's him! It's Lane's kid!"

That was when J.J. took note of the vehicle that had almost obliterated him. It was a police cruiser.

CHAPTER NINETEEN
Day 28, 8:50 A.M.

"*Row!*" bellowed Luke.

He and Charla splashed through the waist-deep surf, pushing the loaded lifeboat out to sea. On board, Ian and Lyssa heaved at the oars, propelling the covered raft into the oncoming breakers.

The tide was going out, but the seas were rougher than usual. Every time they made any progress, a powerful wave would take hold of the craft and send it careening back toward the island.

Will's cries of pain resounded from the raft. With the wild pitching of the sea, it was impossible to keep his injured leg immobilized.

"We're hurting him!" shouted Lyssa, her voice barely audible over the pounding of the surf. "Let's try again when the ocean calms down!"

"No!" exclaimed Ian. "We make our move when we've got the tide!"

A breaker hit Luke in the face. He came up sputtering. He would have been overjoyed to postpone their departure until conditions were better. But the smugglers could already be on their way back to the island. Waiting an extra day might well be fatal.

"I hate this place!" raged Charla. "Getting here almost killed us and getting away is going to finish the job!"

Suddenly, the raft was in the grasp of a monster swell. For a breathless few seconds, it teetered on the crest, looming over Luke, threatening to come down and crush him. He was frozen, powerless to move, staring up at the terrified face of Will, who stared back at him through the flap of the sun canopy.

After all I've survived, Luke thought ruefully, *I'm going to be drowned by my own lifeboat!*

His eyes searched out the telltale foam that meant the wave was about to break. It never came. Instead, the raft bobbed up to the top of the swell and disappeared down the other side. The moving mountain of water rolled over Luke and Charla, driving them under.

Luke floundered, kicking for the light. When he surfaced, choking and spitting, he looked desperately around for the lifeboat.

Charla pointed. "Out there!"

Luke stared. In only a handful of seconds, the raft was forty feet away. Now free of the incoming surf, it was being pulled out to sea by a relentless undertow.

The rowers, Lyssa and Ian, were paddling like mad to slow things down. Their efforts had no effect at all on the drag of the ocean.

"Swim for it!" called Luke, launching himself through the waves.

Charla took off, cutting the water like a cabin cruiser. Her powerful arms churning, she passed Luke and bore down on the raft.

Still swimming, he saw her heave herself up over the side. It was only then that he realized how very far the boat still was, and how tired and heavy his arms and legs felt. An overwhelming isolation gripped him. If he couldn't reach the raft, he'd have to swim back to shore. Then he'd be marooned *alone*.

Never! he vowed to himself. *I won't go back there! If I can't reach the others, I'll drown right here and now!*

The thought was a booster rocket. His arms windmilled wildly; his legs manufactured the strength to kick on. He could barely hear the shouts of the others over the pounding of his own heart in his ears. He closed his eyes and swam blindly. If he looked and saw the lifeboat pulling away, it would mean there was no hope.

Splash!

Something hit the water inches from his face. He pulled up, and his arms smacked right into it

ESCAPE

— the raft's life preserver. He barely had the energy to clamp himself onto it.

Charla and Lyssa hauled on the rope, pulling him alongside the raft. Even hanging on to the edge of the sun canopy, he was too exhausted to climb onto the lifeboat. Instead, he allowed himself to be towed for twenty minutes before working up the strength to accept his friends' help and clamber aboard.

What came next had been carefully scripted. The paddles were tied into the oarlocks, pointing straight up. Between them was stretched the makeshift sail. Next, the flat wooden raft that had served as Will's hospital bed was maneuvered out the flap of the sun canopy and dropped over the side. It contained forty-six shelled coconuts, tied tightly in place under a blanket taken from the military base. It bobbed in tow behind the lifeboat.

Totally spent, Luke found an empty space and slumped back. Even with the coconut stash trailing behind, there was more food than people on the lifeboat. Wedged between the bunches of finger bananas and the sacks of roasted durian seeds, he fell into a deep sleep.

Six hours.

For the first time, the island was completely

out of sight. Once again the castaways found themselves at the mercy of the sea.

"Why didn't I remember how much I hate bobbing around the ocean?" mumbled Charla. "Maybe I would have had the brains to stay back on dry land and take my chances with the smugglers."

Luke regarded Lyssa. The girl had suffered from terrible seasickness while on the *Phoenix*. Now her face was a telltale shade of oatmeal.

"Hey," he said kindly. "No one's going to get on your case if you have to hang your head over the side."

"Just don't barf on the coconuts," Will added weakly.

She cast him a withering glare. "Big talk from the guy who bled on everybody here."

"Lyss — "

But his sister's queasiness bubbled up inside her. With a strangled gurgle, she headed for the flap. She threw the canopy wide, then dropped back among them with a scream of shock.

Luke grabbed her by the shoulders. "What? What?"

The raft lurched and dipped to one side. A moment later, the head and shoulders of a man in a short-sleeved hooded wet suit were thrust through the opening.

ESCAPE

The effect was so stupefying that the cast-aways were turned to stone.

Luke's gaping disbelief changed abruptly to terror as his mind made the jump from bewilderment to explanation. The smugglers had tracked them down! This frogman was here to kill them!

He grabbed wildly for a weapon and came up with a heavy bunch of finger bananas. He reared back to take a murderous swing.

"U.S. Marines!" barked a commanding voice from behind the goggles. "Drop those bananas!" He rumbled a laugh into the stunned silence. "I never thought I'd get a chance to say *that*."

He spoke into a tiny mouthpiece that stuck out of his rubberized helmet: "Swimmer to base. Got 'em."

From his belt he pulled a razor-sharp eight-inch hunting knife. With a powerful sweep, he slashed through the sun canopy from one side to the other. Blinding light streamed in as the cover fell away, exposing the lifeboat to brilliant blue sky.

A roar from above drew five sets of dazzled eyes. A massive helicopter was moving into position over them.

Charla was the first to speak. Her voice was so shrill and full of disbelief that it was almost unrecognizable: "We're — rescued?"

The instant the word was out of her mouth, she began to cry. Each in turn, Lyssa, Ian, Will, and Luke gave in to the juggernaut of emotion. Twenty-eight days marooned. A week adrift before that. Suffocated with danger and fear. Surrounded by death.

And now — just like that — it was all over. It seemed almost unreal.

The chopper lowered a cable to the swimmer.

"Take my brother first!" begged Lyssa. "And watch out for his bad leg!"

The marine fastened the straps around Will. The boy turned his tear-streaked face to his fellow castaways. "You did it, guys. You got me out."

Then he was gone, winched up to the helicopter, where waiting hands pulled him aboard.

Luke's mind was in a fog as he watched the others drawn up to safety. *I'm going home.* Tentatively, he turned the idea over. It had been so long that he didn't really think of home very much anymore. It was even hard to picture his room or his parents' faces.

"Okay, kid," said the swimmer. "Last customer."

Luke allowed himself to be strapped into the harness. It was almost too easy. A kind of cheating. Five weeks of terror and struggle, and then a helicopter comes along — a Get Out of Jail Free

ESCAPE

card. He felt a pang of grief. If only all of them could have been here to play it.

His ascent to the chopper was faster than he expected. Two marines dragged him aboard and ripped the harness from him. He looked around for the others, but saw only one face — a million-dollar smile behind custom-made designer sunglasses.

"I came back for you, Haggerty," said J.J. in an injured voice. "You weren't there."

Luke grabbed him by the collar. "The smugglers?"

"In jail," beamed the actor's son. "And they're already looking for Radford."

Luke shook his head in amazement. "I can't believe you did it."

"Well — I had a little help."

Luke frowned. "From who?"

In answer, J.J. pulled off his shades and waved them in Luke's face. The inscription on the earpiece flashed in the sun: JONATHAN LANE, THE TOAST OF LONDON — PS.

Luke was impatient. "Yeah, yeah. You've got great sunglasses. Come on, how did you get away from the smugglers?"

"The guy they had guarding me tried to sell my shades," J.J. explained, "and the pawnshop owner wanted proof that the inscription was legit.

He got in touch with my dad's office, and they called the FBI."

"But how did they know where to find you?"

"The cops squeezed it out of my guard." J.J. grinned. "It was the glasses, Haggerty. I told you they were special."

Luke stared at the one-of-a-kind shades. He had always hated them; they were the ultimate symbol of J.J.'s cocky, Hollywood attitude. Never could he have imagined that they would save all their lives.

The chopper crew hauled the swimmer in through the door and sealed the sliding hatch. The helicopter banked southwest, heading back to its base.

"Guam in forty minutes," the pilot called to the castaways.

"You mean we're not going to the island?" Luke asked anxiously.

The swimmer put a hand on his arm. "Whatever you left there, I'm sure your folks'll get you a new one."

"It's not what we left," insisted Luke. "It's what you left."

"Us?" The pilot turned around to regard him. "We weren't even there."

"Not now," Luke informed him. "In 1945 — you forgot your atomic bomb!"

ESCAPE

SEPTEMBER 3, 1945
1805 hours

The tropical sun set on an island of impatience. The transport plane was loaded. Airmen jammed their hands in their pockets and tried not to fidget. The war was over. They should have left hours ago. What was the holdup?

Still hanging from the broken crane, Junior, the third atomic bomb, had been opened like a five-ton cookie jar.

Sergeant Holliday and Corporal Connerly watched as the technician removed two pieces of radioactive uranium that provided Junior's nuclear fuel.

For the most destructive weapon humankind had ever devised, the trigger was astonishingly simple. At detonation, the smaller uranium slug would be fired into the larger bowl-shaped piece to set off a nuclear blast strong enough to destroy an entire city. It seemed scarcely more technical than starting a fire by rubbing two sticks together.

The uranium pieces were packed in separate lead-lined containers. Next, the detonator was removed — an ordinary gun barrel hooked up

ISLAND

to an altimeter. The components were put in the back of a truck to be driven to the airstrip and loaded onto the plane.

Holliday stared as the technician stepped onto the flatbed of the truck to accompany the nuclear material.

"Wait a minute! Where are you going? What about the bomb?"

The man patted the lead-lined containers. "The real bomb's in here, Sarge. That" — he pointed to the shell of Junior — "is a very expensive paperweight." And the truck drove off.

Holliday was annoyed. "Well, what are we supposed to do with it?"

Connerly surveyed the small crowd of airmen that had gathered around the bomb pit. "Anybody got a piece of paper?"

ESCAPE

EPILOGUE

When the six young people entered the lab, they were dressed in identical air force coveralls. This seemed completely appropriate, because the military doctors had never before seen such a close-knit group.

They demanded adjoining hospital rooms, ate every single meal together, and stayed up until all hours of the night watching the Discovery Channel in the lounge. They could not seem to get enough of one another's company and conversation.

Later in the afternoon, they were scheduled to fly to Hawaii, where their parents would be waiting to welcome them back from the dead. But that morning, they were guests of the highest-ranking general on Guam. He had declared that these six, of all people, had the right to be present for this procedure.

The six took their front-row VIP seats. They seemed fit enough, although they were thin and very sunburned. One of them was on crutches. Their eyes were focused on the concrete floor where the atomic bomb lay, its long body extending three-quarters of the way across the lab.

ISLAND

The operation began. Physicists and technicians cut their way through black metal and removed a large piece of the rounded side. The chief scientist beckoned the six forward. They approached gingerly. This was, after all, an atomic bomb, the most awesome man-made force of all time. It had scared them when they'd first stumbled across it on their island; it scared them now.

The compartment was empty, except for one small item. It was a yellowed sheet of paper that had been torn from a loose-leaf notebook. On it, in faded ink, someone had written a single word:

KA-BOOM!

The flash of the reporter's camera captured the moment — six castaways seized by the kind of laughter that could only come from those who had not truly laughed for a very long time.

That picture made it to the front page of every newspaper in the world.

On September 12, 2001, Calvin Radford, former mate of the *Phoenix*, was arrested in a waterfront bar in Macao. He was charged with six counts of attempted murder.

* * *

ESCAPE

On October 23, 2001, the International Geographical Commission made an addition to their map of the Pacific, a tiny cay at latitude 17'31" North, longitude 157'42" East. They called it Junior Island.

On December 28, 2001, the six castaways held their first reunion at the Los Angeles home of movie star Jonathan Lane.

They did not go to the beach.

ABOUT THE AUTHOR

GORDON KORMAN is the author of more than thirty-five books for children and young adults, including most recently *The Chicken Doesn't Skate*, the Slapshots series, and *Liar, Liar, Pants on Fire*. He lives in Long Island with his wife and son. Although he has never been stranded on a desert island, he did a lot of research to write this adventure series.